W9-ACB-483
WITHDRAWN
L. R. COLLEGE LIBRARY

THE QUEEN BEE

For HAPPY AND LIND AND MIKE

AND LITTLE MARTHA

The Queen Bee

by

EDNA LEE

APPLETON-CENTURY-CROFTS, INC.

NEW YORK

All names, characters, and events in this book are fictional, and any resemblance which may seem to exist to real persons is purely coincidental.

The lines quoted on page 129, reproduced by permission of the publishers, are from the following books:

Beekeeping for Profit and Pleasure by Addison Webb. Copyright 1943 by the Macmillan Company, New York.

The ABC & XYZ of Bee Culture by A. I. & E. R. Root. Published by the A. I. Root Company, Medina, Ohio.

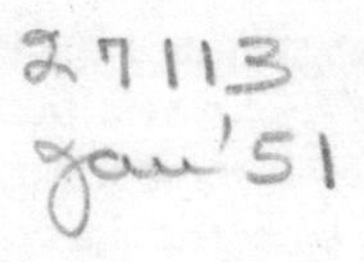

PRINTED IN THE UNITED STATES OF AMERICA

One

YOU awake in the night, I thought, in a place where you've never been before and will never be again and you are as nothing. Nothing, cradled in the vast womb of night and suspended between two points—the place from which you come, the place to which you go. For a moment you lie staring into the dark, your mind as blank as an idiot's. Then memories one after another begin to thrust their way up from the subconscious like sentinels who, having slept, spring to attention again. And suddenly all of the past is with you, all that has happened to you is clear. Only the future looms darkly and unrevealed.

I do not know what woke me. Perhaps the train jerking to a stop, for I heard the crunch of the trainmen's feet outside my window and their voices flat against the November night. For the first sleep-drugged moment I lay staring into the dark. Then the past was in the dark berth with me. The shabby high-ceilinged flat, Mama's hyacinths—pink and purple—blooming in the window, the firelight gleaming on Father's books. Even the little kitchen with the spot before the stove worn by Mama's tireless feet. Small trivialities of living, all of them, hardly noticed then. Now because they were gone forever, transient miracles vested with radiance.

I cried out, soundlessly of course (I must not disturb the other passengers) "What am I doing here? I must go back." But I knew I couldn't go back. There was no place for me back there. There was no place for me anywhere. I was like the little china cream pitcher Mama had carried when the truck hurtled around the corner. Suddenly belonging nowhere.

The policeman on our block had brought it to me. "It was thrown clear," he said, "I found it on a snowdrift just a few feet from the corner where the truck—" he broke off, and cleared his throat. "I thought you might like to have it."

I thanked him, my hands cradling the little pitcher. I knew as well as if I'd seen it how Mama had come to have it. She and Father had walked home in the snow, from their early movie, Mama stopping to peer into the bright windows of little shops. In one she had spied the pitcher. I could hear her delighted exclamations. She was always tender toward small things, and it was tiny. Only four inches tall, beautifully shaped and of a lovely grayed blue. And so fragile I could have crushed it with my fingers. Yet it had been spared. Did it ask itself why? I wondered.

But this wouldn't do, I told myself sharply, this lying in the dark berth and feeling sorry for yourself. You must never feel sorry for yourself. You rubbed color on your mouth and lighted a cigarette, smoked it a little boredly. Then no one knew what went on inside. Or knew only that nothing went on inside except the struggle to endure what was unendurable.

As the train racketed into motion again I groped in my bag for a cigarette and when I had lighted it lay there smoking as you smoke in a pullman, surreptitiously and without pleasure. So after the first few puffs I ground it on the tray at the window. Then I raised the shade.

The night was over. In the east the sky had begun to lighten but the world that slipped by my window still slept, as unalive beneath dawn's death-gray pallor as a flimsy stage set in an empty theater. I saw the weathered houses, the cluttered yards, the sagging fences, soiled fingerprints left by shiftlessness and inertia. Seeing, I was almost unbelieving. I thought, "This is Mama's South."

Mama had been southern born and raised and ever since I could remember I had heard the wonders of the South extolled. Beautiful women! Gallant men! Perfect climate! There was nothing about the South—to hear Mama—which lacked perfection. And I had believed, even when Father laughed.

"Magnolias and mint juleps!" he would jibe; "and Jim Crow laws and illiteracy and hookworm!"

Mama would laugh but her eyes would be intent on far places. "Now I tell you, Mart," she would shake her head, "the South does have something. Next summer," (or next fall or next winter, for she always adapted that mythical visit to a mythical season) "I'm just going down and stay awhile with Eva."

"Better wait until you're invited, hadn't you?" Father would tease.

"Invited! Goodness, Mart. My niece? My own sister's child? That shows how little you know about the South. Kinfolk don't have to wait for invitations."

She never made that trip South. Spring would come and her nebulous planning would yield to summer vacations with Father, who was a professor of literature, freed from the tyranny of classes. If it happened to be fall there were hyacinth bulbs to be started, or the wool dress she meant to make for me, or Father's annual cold. Anyway she never made that trip South. Now it was I who was going South, swept like a stray uprooted growth toward a strange destination, drawn there by nothing except the solitude of the heart.

Propped against my pillows I saw Mama's South for the first time. Watched it slide by my windows as the train rattled between red hills and stretches of pine, panted to stops beside drab little stations, then clattered on again past houses and stores scattered as haphazardly as if flung there by a careless hand. As dawn grew into a day hardly less gray I saw the houses and towns come awake. On a porch a woman in faded gingham threw food to chickens clustered in the yard. Children began to watch the train from doorways, breakfast in their hands, the wonder of far places, I knew, in their eyes. And the first reckless T-Ford which spluttered down the highway was vanguard for a legion of cars which as day advanced scurried along the highways like giant bugs frenziedly bound on futile errands.

It was when men began to amble from rickety gates and up sidewalks toward some job or other that I became aware of time. Looking at my watch I realized that the leaden sky had misled me. It was after eight. And as if time were its master, my body responded to its ordering. Suddenly I wanted cold water on my face, the biting taste of toothpaste in my mouth—most of all I wanted coffee. It was time to get up.

We were in North Carolina, the Negro porter said when, dressed and ready for breakfast, I inquired the way to the diner. The last stop had been Charlotte.

I asked, "And when do we reach Atlanta?"

Grinning he ticked off the states on his sooty fingers. "Nawf C'lina, Souf C'lina"—the grin broadened—"den Jawja." He slid a big silver watch from his vest pocket and consulted it judicially. "We gits to Atlanta at 4 P.M., ma'am. De diner is straight ahead. Fo'cars."

Thanking him I started toward the diner. Made my way along pullman aisles where other porters wrestled with tumbled berths, where men with hair askew lurched toward the washroom and the return of dignity, and women in robes teetered along the aisles. Some with the straight-backed mien which proclaimed virginity; others with the lush swinging grace which proclaimed the lack of it. But at last I came to the diner and none too soon. Already its tables were nearly filled; the small one for two at which the steward put me was the last with vacant places. And as I unfolded my napkin I breathed a little sigh of gratitude because I had apparently been spared the sterile companionship of strangers.

My thankfulness was premature. I had hardly ordered my coffee when the steward was ushering a woman into the chair across from mine; an absurd overdressed little person with her high-flung hat and too-smart dress. But, I learned, a friendly one. As she settled herself in her chair and groped in her bag for cigarettes she popped little staccato sentences across the table like firecrackers. Had I ever seen a nastier day? Going to rain cats and dogs! Better than New York, though, and all that snow! Did I have a match?

Her friendliness won over my instinct for privacy. Almost without volition I found myself responding, unable to rebuff her artless inquisitiveness. Was I going to Atlanta? Did I live there? Oh—just a visit? With relatives? My aunt? Then "Who is your aunt, honey?"

When I told her she stared at me almost unbelieving, her doll-like eyes incredulous beneath the extravagant hat. "You are Mrs. Avery's niece?"

Before the mention of Aunt Eva's name she had, I knew, considered me of no importance. Her bright glance had taken in my cheap little suit, the sweater Mama had knitted, and had ticketed me. But Aunt Eva's name changed this. Her eyes ran over me again, appraising me anew as if the name had transformed me into one who was not to be treated lightly. Wondering why, I asked her if she knew Aunt Eva.

"Know her?" There was a shocked implication in her voice as if not knowing her would constitute a major tragedy. "Oh yes! Why, Mrs. Avery is one of our very best customers!"

This was to me revealing. One Christmas, to earn money for Mama's and Father's presents, I had worked during the holidays in the College Shop, had learned of the adulation bestowed by shops on "best customers." I asked her if she was in a shop.

Her lacquered head assented vigorously. "Wendell's—woman's specialty shop. Smartest in Atlanta too, honey. I'm buyer in the French Salon. Better dresses—you know."

Drinking my coffee I pictured an imaginary Wendell's, a place of mauve and rose, its fitting rooms with mirrored walls. I saw her there, busily efficient, secure, in her suave black dress with each golden hair lacquered to perfection, wearing the supercilious manner which saleswomen in such shops invariably assume. I was envious. To have a job like that seemed splendid. I said as much.

She looked at me skeptically. "Splendid? Honey, are you kidding?"

"But it *is* splendid. Why, you're on your own! You're independent."

"Independent!" With shrugged shoulders and curled mouth she stripped independence of its value. "Honey, that's not what I want out of life."

Now it was I who was incredulous. "But what more does anybody want?"

She surveyed me with a tolerant smile that said I was very young, then with a provocative little laugh, leaned toward me. "I'll tell you something, honey. I'll swap places with your aunt—Mrs. Avery—any day."

"With Aunt Eva?" I was startled. "But why?"

"Listen, honey," her voice was as practical as the toast she buttered. "Your Aunt Eva's beautiful. She wears gorgeous clothes—and wears 'em like nothing in this world. She has that marvelous home. She goes with the best people." Holding a morsel of toast ready for her lips she shrugged. "I ask you!" she said, and ate the toast.

I asked dubiously, "Aunt Eva is like that?"

The glance she sent me was shrewd. "Honey, don't you know what your aunt is like?"

I explained. I hadn't seen her since I was practically a baby. Of course I didn't remember.

Her nod accepted my explanation. "Well, honey," she said flatly, "she's really—" she paused, groped for a word, "really something. She's just got *everything*. I tell you I don't see a woman in New York that can touch her. For looks or style either. And," she added quickly, "I go to some darned smart places too. The Stork Club and Twenty One and once the Colony for lunch." She sipped her coffee, looking at me over the rim of her cup, waiting for me to be impressed. "And to top everything," she took another sip, then rolled her eyes heavenward, "married to Beauty Avery."

"Beauty?" I was startled. "Oh!" I laughed. "We're talking of different Mrs. Averys. My aunt's husband is Ross—Ross Avery."

She put her cup down and lit another cigarette. "Sure, honey. But everybody in Atlanta calls him Beauty. Nickname, you know. Or," she held the match to her cigarette, exhaled slowly, "or didn't you know?"

I didn't tell her I didn't know. Neither did I tell her I considered it a silly name for a man. For a woman, yes. Or for a horse or a dog. But never, except in the South, would it be bestowed upon a man. Drinking my coffee I pictured the man who would win it or accept it. He would be handsome, I supposed, in a precious sort of way. He'd talk in a high womanish voice with broad A's sprinkled lavishly and he'd collect something. Porcelains maybe or ivories. He'd advise his wife about the new color scheme. And he'd always screw the top on the toothpaste with finicky exactness.

Was Cousin Eva's husband this sort of man, I wondered. The sort you would call Beauty. Thinking back I tried to recall what I had heard Mama say of him, realized suddenly how little she had said. "A letter from Eva today." This perhaps to Father at supper. Then wistfully, "She says the wisteria is in bloom," and Father gibing, mocking because (I know now) Mama's love for the South had defied his gibing and mocking. "And how are the fine old southern hookworms, ma'am?"

Absorbed in some book I would hear it without listening. Nevertheless my mind was erecting an image of Aunt Eva. Like Mama only younger, for Mama had been the older sister. But like Mama, busy with her house, her flowers, her husband and children. Buttoning herself into crisp gingham house dresses for the mornings, topping them in winter with a shabby sweater. Slipping, when she went out, into her "good black dress" from Macy's, or somebody's basement for $14.98. Like Mama, running a careless powder puff over her face, or unable to locate her lipstick and going without, uncaring. The Aunt Eva of my imagination was like millions of mothers engrossed with groceries and laundry and homemaking.

It was to this Aunt Eva I had sent the telegram on that dreadful night. It was she who had called me long distance the next day. "Darling," she had cried over the phone, "I'm prostrated. Simply prostrated. And I can't even come to you. Flu, darling! And the doctor absolutely forbids— But you must come to me. After everything is over, of course. You simply must. Say that you will—promise!"

Seated at the phone facing the windows where Mama's hyacinths bloomed fragrant and so alive, I had answered. Yes, I would come. As soon as I arranged about things. Mama's shabby furniture, Father's books—and what would I do about the hyacinths? They mustn't be allowed to die, too. Saying in the phone, yes, I would come, yes, I promised, yes, I would take the train she said. Yes, yes, yes.

Numbly, dumbly I had answered but my heart had swept toward her eagerly. For—like Mama's, her voice, sweet, a little husky. Like Mama, I thought, able to look into your heart and know what the heart endures.

But now, and there was cold shock in my sudden awareness that this Aunt Eva had been only an illusory figure, she didn't exist any more. The little dress buyer's chatter, ruthless as a careless, hurtling car, had swept her into oblivion. Forlornly I realized that I knew nothing of the real Aunt Eva. To me she was only the shadowy outline of a woman such as an artist might start and then, losing interest, leave unfinished, without face or character or soul.

The check in the waiter's hand recalled me. I came back to the diner, to the rain which was beginning to tap against the windows, to the little dress buyer who, when we had settled our check, made motions of departure, touched her hat with knowing hands, smoothed fresh lipstick on her mouth, talking as she smoothed, through primped-up lips. "I'm in car 52, honey. Come on back if you get lonesome. There's a couple of buyers from Loveman's—Birmingham, you know—and a shoe salesman. We're going to get up a game."

Thanking her I neither accepted nor refused. But she didn't notice. She was inspecting her mouth in her compact mirror, etching its crimson to a truer line with a taut little finger. Then she closed the compact with a snap, thrust it into her bag, closed the bag with another snap. "You're going to have a marvelous time at your aunt's, honey. If you don't you ought to have your head examined." Her eyes rolled heavenward again. "That gorgeous home—"

She pushed her chair back as if to go, but for a moment continued to sit there; the doll's eyes were less doll-like as she stared into space, were thoughtful and, it seemed to me, bleak. "It makes you wonder, don't it, honey," she asked slowly, "how some women have it all dropped in their laps without turning a finger. And the rest of us—"

She ground her cigarette in the tray, got up, stood looking down at me. "It makes you feel that there ain't no justice, don't it, honey? Some women, like your aunt, with everything. The rest of us—" Then as if afraid she had revealed too much she shrugged off seriousness with a flippant little laugh. "Oh well! I guess some are just born lucky."

I had no answer for that so I sat looking up at her. And impulsively she leaned and patted my cheek. "Maybe you're one of the lucky ones, honey. Like your Aunt Eva. Anyway, I hope so." Then before I could speak she and her high-flung hat were mincing down the aisle toward the door. And I, taking my book, made my way back to my pullman.

"You are Eva Avery's niece?"

For the second time within an hour an incredulous voice asked that question of me. I was annoyed.

I had found him occupying my section, reading my magazine, his feet propped on the opposite seat, as much at home as if he had lived there all his life. He was totally unembarrassed when he looked up and found me hesitating in the aisle. "Porter hasn't got to me yet," he announced cheerfully and without hurry removed his feet. "Sit down. Make yourself at home."

I sat across from him, rigid with resentment at what I considered impertinence. But I knew before long that I had misjudged him. He had not been impertinent, he would never in any situation be impertinent, or anything except himself. But I couldn't know that at first. So I sat straight and stiff in the absurdity of offended dignity.

He continued to read my magazine, but he wasn't stupid. Finally he became aware of my resentment.

"Say," his southern voice drawled that "say" interminably, "you don't mind my sitting here, do you?"

"Oh no!" I was regal, I was icy.

He regarded me as a small boy might regard a dog which suddenly snapped at him. Then he smiled. "Say! You're being silly, you know."

"Oh naturally!" I might have been Marie Antoinette condescending to the mob.

"I'm not trying to pick you up or anything like that, you know. It's just"—he spread his hands—"I've got to sit somewhere until the porter gets my section done up."

"Does it have to be here?"

He considered this gravely. "No," he admitted, "it doesn't *have* to be."

"There is a smoking car," I pointed out, "and probably a club car—"

"Sure." His admission was casual.

"Then why impose on me?"

He stared at me in wonder. "I declare," his voice was without guile, "you sure are unfriendly. It's a shame. You're so pretty, you know."

"I do not wish to hear—" I began, but he didn't allow me to finish.

"That you're pretty?" His laugh was gently disbelieving. "Oh come now. Of course you want to hear it."

"Really," I spluttered in anger. "I won't allow—"

He leaned toward me confidentially, his palms on his knees. "Won't you allow me to say you're pretty? But I do say it. You are, you know. Very, very pretty."

Speechless with frustration I could only stare at him belligerently. But even as I stared I felt my belligerence dissolving, vanishing. I clutched at it, I tried to revive it, but in vain. For he—well, he was nice. Not nice in any of the ways in which a girl usually thinks of a male. Not dark or mysterious, or dashing or romantic. Just big and quiet and with a gentle good humor which reduced the often ridiculous social amenities to the insignificance they deserve, and my temper to its proper level. That of a spoiled child who responds to friendliness with a tantrum. He made me feel young and gauche.

"I've been stupid and horrid." There was no belligerence in my stammering voice now. "I—I—I'm sorry."

He didn't protest, as others might have protested, that I hadn't been stupid—or horrid. Instead he said ruefully, "Well you were sort of unfriendly."

I said I hoped he would forgive me, then realized that I sounded like a bad actress in a bad play. But he didn't notice. He was genuinely surprised. "Why, shucks! There's nothing to forgive. You have a right to be that way, if you like."

"Surely you don't think I like to be horrid?"

"Well, you can't always know. People like to be the craziest things sometimes. Like mountain climbers and tree sitters. I thought maybe you liked to be—well, ornery."

"Oh you couldn't!" My smile accused him of pretense.

But he was serious. "Yes I did. I thought it was a shame too. For a girl as pretty as you—" He broke off, chuckled. "But you were cute, you know. You flew at me like a peppery little bantam chicken." The chuckle grew into a laugh. "Why, you almost scared me to death."

His laughter was contagious and suddenly I realized that I was laughing too! Laughing for the first time in many days. And as if our laughter brought healing with it the cold tight knot which I had carried was warmed and eased.

It sounds trite to say that time well spent goes swiftly, is gone before you realize its passing. Because even truth, if said too often, attains triteness. Yet it does not lessen truth's quality or cheapen its value. So, trite as it may be, it was true of time that day. It went swiftly. Looking back, I cannot say why. We talked, I know. Yet for long stretches of time we sat silent, looking out at the November rain which veiled the faces of the little towns that scurried past our windows. And somehow there was comfort in that silence, and the understanding which words, no matter what they say, can never bring.

I do not remember just when we came to names. Somehow they didn't seem important. But finally we did. He told me his. Tyler McKinnon. Distaste curled his mouth. "But for Lord's sake call me Ty. Everybody does."

I was reminded of Aunt Eva's husband and his nickname. "Is it law down here," I asked lightly, "that everyone must have a nickname? Just this morning I've learned that my uncle has one too. It's dreadful." Now it was my mouth that curled distastefully. "They call him—imagine—Beauty."

"Beauty?" He sat erect, regarded me intently. "Say! You don't mean Beauty Avery, do you?"

I told him I did, that he was my aunt's husband.

It was then that he asked, his voice as incredulous as the little dress buyer's had been, "You are Eva Avery's niece?" And when I nodded he stared at me a moment before he laughed ruefully. As if he had stumbled upon knowledge possessing the quality of amusement, but which, for some reason, failed to amuse. I wondered why.

"It seems to amuse you. Because Eva Avery is my aunt—"

His head moved in denial. "No, it doesn't amuse me. It does surprise me—sort of—"

"But why? People do have nieces, you know."

"Sure," he admitted. "It's just that—well, it would never occur to me that you and Mrs. Avery were related. You're—you're different, you know."

I thought I knew the reason for his surprise. It was because Aunt Eva, who was beautiful, should have a niece with no pretensions to beauty. And somehow, though I knew it was silly, I felt guilty. As if I might have acquired beauty, and had failed to do so.

Leaning toward him I said, "Tell me about my aunt." Then at the questioning which widened his eyes I explained. "You see, I was just three the only time I saw her. Of course I have no memory of her. Tell me, is she as beautiful as I hear she is?"

His glance met mine briefly and, I thought, somewhat warily. His hand raked his dark hair. "Yes. She's beautiful all right."

"And that is what you mean when you say we are so different?" I held my voice to lightness, tried with careless sophistication to imply that lack of beauty was unimportant.

His surprise at this was genuine. "Good Lord no! I didn't mean that at all. You see, I think you're a darned sight more beautiful than Eva—than your aunt."

I had been leaning toward him. Now I straightened and drew back. Perhaps he believed my question to be a bold bid for admiration, would consider me a cheap little female on the make. But immediately, I knew better. He only wanted to be kind as, I somehow sensed, he would always be kind. So I ignored his gallantry.

Still I persisted. "Then if the difference between us isn't beauty—what is it?"

"Oh!" His shrug was a movement of disinterest which verged on impatience. But I would not be put off. Leaning toward him again I said softly, "Please tell me about her. You see I am going to stay with her. Perhaps for a long while." Then I told him of the Aunt Eva of my imagination. Sweet, I said, and gay and comfortable. But this morning in the diner—I repeated what the little dress buyer had said of Aunt Eva, the doll-like eyes, the high-flung hat before me again. "Now," I said, "I wonder."

He listened, his eyes not upon me but on the rain-obscured landscape which ever changing yet seemed unchanged. When my voice stopped they came back to me, regarded me speculatively. Then he leaned toward me, serious, confidential.

"Say," he said. "Do you know anything about bees?"

The unexpectedness of his question shocked me into stupidity and for a moment I stared at him blankly. Then I yielded to the laughter that swept me. "Bees?" I gasped, my voice rising on the wave of my laughter. "Bees?"

But he was intent, grave, and I stifled my laughter. It would be rude of me to ridicule what was interesting or important to him. To redeem myself I clutched at the only fact I knew about bees.

"They make honey, don't they?"

His nod confirmed the fact that they made honey. "They're wonderful, you know." He spoke with absolute gravity.

"Wonderful?" Mirth threatened to engulf me again but I resisted it. "Wonderful?" I echoed. "Bees?"

"Yes. Bees."

"You mean because they make honey?" My smile was tolerant. "But they only obey a natural law. Just as we do when we breathe."

"But that's what makes them so wonderful." His eyes met mine earnestly. "The natural law. Do you know anything about their laws?"

It was stupid of me, I said, but I didn't.

"No, it isn't stupid. Why, millions of people don't know a darn thing about bees. I just happen to. When I was a kid I spent the summers on the farm. They kept bees, so I just happened to learn about them."

"We read about them back in the fifth grade." Frowning as I tried to recall what we had read. "They have a queen, don't they?"

"Yes. And let me tell you. That queen is quite a gal. Do you know that the worker bees wait on her hand and foot, comb her hair, even feed her?" His laugh was rueful. "Why, she's the only real queen left in the world. And let me tell you something else. If another queen tries to get a look-in, the queen stings her to death. Even if it's her own daughter."

"She sounds like a jealous female," I said lightly.

"Partly that," he nodded gravely, "but not entirely. You see—she's a queen bee. She can't take competition. Like some women you know."

I would not admit this. "Like women," I scoffed, "really! But that's absurd."

His eyes narrowed sagely. "No," he contradicted, "it isn't absurd. There are women like that, you know. Millions of them. It's a whole social order. Queen-Beeism. And you find them everywhere. Not just in the South—though more in the South because every little girl on every shabby little street down here is raised to believe that she's so damned wonderful that the world must be served to her on a silver platter." He broke off and, as if my quizzical smile had penetrated his consciousness, gave me an answering grin. "Say! You think I'm crazy, don't you?"

"No. I think you're more interesting than bees."

He was dubious. "Now you're kidding."

"I'm not. I'm serious." I leaned toward him again. "Listen," I

said, "I ask you to tell me about my aunt. And just when I think you're about to—you're off on bees. Which takes you back to a farm, which takes you back to your boyhood, and back to bees again. And you haven't told me the first thing about my aunt."

His hand raked his hair again. "Say! You certainly are hepped on the subject of your aunt, aren't you?"

"I told you why. I don't remember her."

"And I told you that she's beautiful, didn't I?"

"I want to know more than that. I want to know if she's real and —comfortable to live with. Or if she's the sort you have to live up to. You see," now it was I who was earnest, "she's the nearest relative I have in the world. Except for her, there is no one. You can understand, can't you, why I want to know about her?"

He surveyed me thoughtfully, "But—your folks. What about them? Your mother—your father?"

I told him then about Mama and Father and the car that had hurtled, about Aunt Eva and the long-distance call. I told it quietly, without emotion, without tears, with no intention of trying to ease my heart as people do sometimes, by pouring its pain into his. Yet, when I finished and he leaned over and laid his hand on mine, it was eased somehow.

"Listen," he said, and I had never seen eyes so steady, never heard a voice so gentle. "You haven't a thing to worry about. You'll get along fine with your Aunt Eva. Just fine! She can charm the birds right off the trees. And she'll love you."

I breathed. "Oh! Do you think she will?"

"Why, she can't help it. You're sweet, you know. Mighty sweet."

Try as I might for steadiness the smile I sent him was tremulous. "And you—you're nice," I managed.

We sat there smiling across at each other. Then a voice, raucous, loud and startlingly near shocked us from our absorption like a splash of cold water. It was only a waiter from the diner sounding the first call for lunch as he passed us. As he went on Ty and I looked at each other, amused, and broke into laughing. Then suddenly he stood and taking my hands pulled me to my feet. "Come on, sugar," he drawled, "Powder your cute nose. I'm going to set you up to the finest lunch the Southern affords."

We went down the aisle toward the diner, I feeling very small be-

hind his tallness and liking the way he walked, in leisurely fashion yet with such surety, as if it never occurred to him that he might fail to get his way. He was nice, I thought. I liked him. And it was not until we were at the table and he was ordering the "finest lunch the Southern afforded" that it dawned upon me that this unpredictable young man hadn't really told me one single thing about Aunt Eva. He had talked instead of bees. Remembering, I smiled. Crazy, I thought. But nice. I liked him.

Waiting in the bleak waiting room of Brookwood station while Ty, in the telephone booth, tried to call Aunt Eva for me, I refused to recognize the twinge of uneasiness which twisted in my stomach.

No one had met me. When the train finally slid to a stop by the concrete runway and Ty and I had stepped down, my eyes had sped on an eager search, but a futile one. Other passengers were claimed by relatives or friends, the little dress buyer by a surly dark-browed man. Passing me she had waved gaily, like an old friend, and like the others had vanished. Finally only Ty and I were standing in the bleak waiting room above our bags which the redcap had dropped beside the empty benches.

Towering at my side he looked down at me worriedly. "You're sure they expect you on this train?"

"It's the train Aunt Eva told me to take."

"Then why the hell didn't she meet you?"

I laughed at his indignation. "She will. I sent her a wire. It's just—well, she's detained. Perhaps the rain—"

His eyes went to the rain-lashed windows across the front, then came back to me. But they lacked conviction.

"And if they don't turn up," I was airy, confident, "I'll just get a taxi."

"A taxi? In this rain?" His laugh was cynical. "To take you way out there? Honey, you don't know the Atlanta taxi service."

"Is it so far?" I was less airy, less confident.

"It's one hell of a drive even in good weather. Miles beyond Buckhead."

It occurred to me that I was becoming a nuisance, that he wanted to go, yet was loath to go and leave me stranded.

"You mustn't wait any longer." I was composed, assured. "You've been so kind—but it really isn't necessary. Aunt Eva will show up in a few minutes. It's just that she's late. You know women and time." I shrugged, deprecating women and time.

He looked down at me without speaking, then wheeling suddenly went toward the telephone booth that stood against the wall. "I'll call the house," he threw over his shoulder, "and see what gives."

Through the booth's glass door I watched him insert the coin, dial and wait. Then another coin, another twist of the dial, and another wait, his hat pushed back on his head. It was then that the first small finger of doubt prodded my consciousness. Suppose, I thought—and the word was the key that freed a flock of suppositions. Suppose Aunt Eva had no memory of asking me to come (after all, she had had flu when I talked to her)—or suppose the doctor had prescribed Florida. Even now she might be basking in Florida sun. Or suppose the doctor had said, "There is no hope," and Aunt Eva was dead and the family scattered as death sometimes scatters families, like a monstrous wind blowing them to bits. What would I do? I wondered. Would I have to wait on in Brookwood Station, forever?

I visualized the future which I, with nowhere to go, would spend in Brookwood Station. I would keep house in one of the telephone booths I decided, and in hours when there were no trains, sleep on the benches. The stationmaster would allow it because I would make myself so useful. Sweep up the floor, help mothers with fretful children, answer the numberless questions which travelers ask of station attendants. I would live there until I was very old. When I died the newspapers would make a story of it. "Mysterious Woman of Brookwood Station Dies" the headlines would say. "No one met her when she arrived fifty years ago," states Stationmaster Jones, "and she had nowhere to go."

Well, at least I would have somewhere to go when I died, I thought. Then I giggled. This was fantastic and ridiculous. I was still giggling when Ty emerged from the phone booth and when he smiled across at me I changed my imaginary future. I wouldn't live in the station. I'd just let him take care of me. Somehow I knew he would. He would make me eat properly and get enough sleep and wear galoshes in bad weather. Yet he wouldn't be fussy. When he disapproved he'd just drawl, "But that's silly, you know," and he'd make *silly* sound so silly you'd be convinced.

He was still smiling as he came up to me. "All set," he said matter-of-factly and I thudded back to reality, remembering that I was a girl in a strange city whom no one had met.

I asked, "Did you get Aunt Eva?"

"She wasn't at home. I talked to Beauty."

"Beauty? Oh! My uncle?"

"Yes. He's driving in to get you."

I saw him again. The Beauty of the womanish voice, the mincing walk, and I made a little mouth, instantly was ashamed. After all I would sleep beneath his roof, eat his bread, he was driving in to get me.

Brightly I said to Ty, "Then you needn't wait any longer."

He grinned and picked up my bag. "You don't get rid of me that easy, hon. It will take Beauty an hour to make it in this rain. I told him to pick you up at my place. Belle Isle promised to send us a cab."

We crossed to the tall glass doors that ran across the front of the waiting room and waited, Ty searching the rain-splashed street for the taxi, I getting my first glimpse of Mama's Atlanta. It was not prepossessing. A sweep of mirror-wet asphalt, a bridge that spanned the cut where the train tracks ran—flanked by billboards jumbled higgledy piggledy.

Where, I wondered, was Mama's Atlanta? The white-columned mansions, the magnolias, the southern charm and loveliness of which she had talked, for which she had longed all these years?

Ty said, picking up our bags, "There's our cab," and together we plunged through the door, crossed the wet sidewalk with the rain stabbing at our faces and scurried into the shelter of the taxi which breathed at the curb. Leaning forward Ty gave the driver directions. "Keep straight out Peachtree," he was saying.

I turned to him aghast. "Is this Peachtree?" I asked, and when he said it was I turned back to the window and stared out unbelieving. This—Mama's Peachtree! Such a wondrous street as she had remembered it, had talked of it. Street of fabulous homes, of beautiful women, of young men handsome and gallant. Peopled by names which she had scattered through the years like drifting rose petals. Sallie Lou and the Conway girls! Mildred who, in white fox furs on a long ago snowy day, had looked so lovely. And all the gay young men! Linton and Buck and Bradley. Heretofore just names, meaningless to me. But I realized now all were woven into the unforgettable pattern of Mama's Peachtree Street. Where were they now? I wondered, the gallant ones, the beautiful ones. Impossible to associate them with the Peachtree Street I saw through the rain-streaked windows of a yellow cab. Its once beautiful homes were elbowed by down-at-heel shops and billboards, their beauty ravished by the grimy commercialism which had encroached upon them. They were like lovely ladies who having married questionable characters are unable to withstand the commonness in which necessity forces them to live.

Turning back to Ty I found his amused eyes upon me. "I know," he said with mock gravity. "All of your life you've heard of Peachtree Street," he chuckled. "Everybody that comes to Atlanta says that, you know. And they're always disappointed. Cheer up! It gets better."

It did. The shops, as the cab went on, dwindled and finally, as if made aware of their presumptuousness, disappeared. Wide lawns began to stretch gently toward the street. The street itself widened and wound its way proudly onward. Here and there the tall spires of handsome churches lifted toward the sky as if they too, were proud. And in the regal sweep of street and lawn the houses of brick or stone or gleaming clapboard stood aloofly as if withdrawing from what might disturb or contaminate. This, I said to myself, was Mama's Peachtree.

It had not occurred to me to wonder where Ty lived or how. Vaguely I had thought of him as belonging to that army of young men found in front offices or behind desks in unimportant jobs. But now, like the little dress buyer, I had to rescale my values. For the taxicab, slowing, swung and turned into a driveway that led to a rambling house of brick that far back from the street sprawled across its width of not too well-kept grounds. It wasn't a pretentious house. Neither was it beautiful. It was old and sturdy and plain. But it rose among the new French Provincials and pseudo-English manors with the assurance a dowager might wear among upstarts. As if their smart sophistication only emphasized her quality.

I turned to Ty to cry, "You live here?" But I caught back the words. No need, I thought, to let him know the ticket with which

I had labeled him. So I sat silent while he paid the driver, and still silent walked beside him up the wide steps to the door.

While the driver lifted our bags to the porch Ty found the right key on his keyring, and unlocking the door opened it. "Come on in, sugar," he said, "Sue will give you some tea."

"Sue?" I echoed vaguely.

"My sister," he said leading the way into the house. "A good gal."

Following him I stepped across the threshold and found myself in a world that closed out the dreary rain. A world that I had never known, of wide rooms opening one into another, with soft rugs and deep chairs and massive claw-footed furniture. Yet it was a familiar world too. For there were flowers in bowls and vases, hyacinths, pink and purple like Mama's, bloomed against a window and fire-light gleamed on books just as it had at home. It had the deep sweet sense of home which brings a house and its furniture alive, more difficult to attain than priceless old Meissen or the patina of lustrous mahogany. It explained to me the quiet surety which Ty wore like a cape.

He helped me out of my coat, hung it carefully in a small closet, then led me past the wide-flung rooms to a small one where a fire burned quietly on the hearth. At the door he paused and waited for a Negro woman of elephantine proportions who entered a door at the end of the hall and plodded toward us.

She peered at us through the gray afternoon light. "Dat you, Mr. Ty?" she called. Then, nearing us, she answered her own question. "You'se back den."

"Hello, Aunt Efola. Think you can bring some tea for this young lady? And a highball for me?"

"Reckon I can." Her small shrewd eyes ran over me. "Pretty, ain't she?" She was as impersonal as if I were a head of lettuce. "Look lak a little kitten wid dem gold streaks in her hair." She cut her eyes at Ty drolly. "Don' reckon you is aimin' to drown her, dough!" Turning, she lumbered down the hall, guttural laughter inspired by her own humor rolling back to us.

Ty called after her, "Miss Sue home?"

She called back, "She upstairs. Call her if you wants her," and lumbered through the rear door.

Ty chuckled. "There goes proof that your Mr. Lincoln didn't

free all the slaves down here, hon. Efola pops the whip over Sue and me like a Simon Legree. I'm surprised she didn't tell you she used to diaper me." He gestured toward the fire. "Go in to the fire. I'll call Sue."

I went toward the fire, breathing the fragrance of the hyacinths, sweeter, deeper in this small warm space. At the hearth I stretched my hands to the quiet blaze, and waited while Ty, going to the foot of the stairs, called, "Sue—Sue!"

A startled voice cried, "Oh, Ty!" There was a rush of footsteps along the upper hall and down the stairs, then she came into view. A slight woman, not young (for her dark hair was threaded with gray) nor pretty. Yet with dark eyes so warm, and a mouth that curved with such quiet humor that mere prettiness suddenly seemed cheap and undesirable.

In the archway of the room she paused. The "Hello there" she gave Ty was casual, his answering "Hello" equally so. "Aunt Efola says I've brought home a kitten," he told her, smiling across at me as he spoke.

She smiled at me too. "A tawny one," she said. "I like tawny ones." Her smile turned gay. "Perhaps if she's a stray and has no home, we can keep her."

Ty rushed in abruptly. "She's come down to stay at Beauty Avery's. She's Eva's niece."

Her warm dark eyes met mine but they were no longer gay. "I see." Then, "You must be Sally's daughter?"

With emotion blurring my voice I asked, "You—you knew Mama?"

"When we were girls, we were best friends. I can't tell you how grieved I am about her. Knowing her daughter is the nicest thing that could happen to me."

I stood beside the fire fighting back the tears, unable to manage words. Ty's drawling voice saved me the effort. "For Lord's sake," he said, "are we going to stand here all day? Let's sit down."

Then I was sunk in a big chair, with Sue on the couch that faced the hearth. Aunt Efola, waddling in, brought a teatray and Ty, his long legs stretched toward the five, drank his highball and began to open the pile of mail she put on the small table. Sue, talking quietly, poured the tea, flanked each cup with a tiny sandwich, and handed mine to me. She said, "Sally and I went to Boulevard School together. I lived on the Boulevard then, out beyond the old Nelson place. Of course that was before the big fire."

I remembered hearing Mama talk of the big fire. How it swept for blocks and blocks, leaping from one house to another, faster, she had said, than you could walk it. As I remembered I had a fleeting sense of life's idiocy. It saved you from disaster as if you were worth saving, then sent a casual car around a corner.

I pulled my thoughts back—I mustn't think about *that*—to Sue. She was talking, laughter crinkling her eyes. Telling now of the time she and Mama had been taken to the circus, how Mama, to the delight of the thousands of spectators had lost her little petticoat as they walked to their seats. Mama, only ten or so, had stepped from it unperturbed, had nonchalantly thrown it over her arm.

Ty broke into our laughter to say, waving the letter in his hand, that maybe he'd better get in touch with Winship. His eyes abstracted, he left the room. I turned back to Sue.

"Then you must know Aunt Eva too?"

"Oh yes." For an instant she looked down at her hands, which lay with linked fingers on her lap, then smiled across at me. "Of course she was younger than Sally and me, several years. And I didn't see much of her. Your grandmother—their mother, you know—was always dashing off to this place and that with your grandfather. She left Sally with *her* mother—your great grandmother that would be—who lived near us on the Boulevard, but she sent Eva to Macon to her husband's mother."

Wonderingly, I said, "Mama never told me that about her mother. That she left her children—like that. Why did she?"

Her face and voice were thoughtful when she answered. "Your grandmother was one of those women—oh, we see them now and then—who refuse to be responsible for anything except a man. Even her children didn't count. If your grandfather—I think he built bridges—had to go to South America, she'd park Sally with one grandmother, Eva with the other, and off she'd go. Months later she'd come back, gather up the girls, set up some sort of a home again. Before they'd get the furniture in place it was the same thing all over again."

Her words invoked a picture for me. Two small girls, Mama and

Aunt Eva, parked here and there like surplus luggage. Wrenched from their schools, their friendships and associations scattered through the years like broken toys, without permanence or security. Trying to fit themselves into strange surroundings, but never feeling sure that they did fit. For the first time I understood why Mama loved the shabby old flat, why she had clung to it through the years against all persuasion.

I said to Sue, "It must have been dreadful. For Mama and Aunt Eva."

She shrugged, her dark eyes quizzical. "Who knows? Oh, I know psychologists would say this and that. But who knows really? Your mother went to New York, met your father, and had a happy life."

"She did—she did."

"And Eva married well."

Eagerly I interrupted her, "I hear that she has everything. A lovely home, and wonderful clothes!"

Her "Yes" was brief.

"And that she is very beautiful? Tell me, is she really so beautiful?"

Her eyes were on her hands again. "Yes," her voice was quiet, "Eva is beautiful."

I rushed on, my voice light, uncaring. "Of course I don't remember the tiniest thing about her. And I can't help wondering. After all she and Mama are were sisters." Then the significance of the changed verb flowing over and engulfing me, I broke off clumsily and sat there confused, unhappy.

The glance she sent me was searching. But as if it told her what she wanted to know she began to talk again, telling as matter-of-factly as she might speak of the weather about Aunt Eva's household. There was Miss George the housekeeper, she said. One of those derelict old maids often seen in the South, earning a livelihood from a civilization which had no place for them. There was Phyl, Beauty's young sister, who made her home with Beauty since her father's death. "Hardly older than you," she said. "You'll like her." Then there were the children. Trissa, ten or so; the boy younger, four or five. And I would love the house. One of the few Atlanta houses, whatever historical novels might claim, with a really interesting history. Beauty's ancestors had bought the property long

the remoteness! And I was afraid. I wanted to cling to Ty and his sober sanity, wanted to cry out that he mustn't let me go. But of course I did nothing of the kind. I buttoned the last button on my coat.

When I would have gone, his hand on my arm detained me. "I want to tell you something," he said.

"Yes?" I said, and waited.

"I don't even want you to think about it. Unless you just want to —but I want you to know. You're going to be my girl."

I stared up at him a moment before my mind encompassed the meaning of his words. When it did I laughed. "Why—why, you're crazy!"

"No," his voice was quiet as always, "I'm not crazy."

"But you've known me only—why not even twenty-four hours—"

With his hand on my arm we started toward the front door. "Time," he said, "has nothing to do with it. I knew the minute I saw you how it was going to be. And that," he said with firm gentleness, "is the way it is."

We had reached the front door, open now, and we halted. I was vaguely conscious of a big sedan at the steps, of Beauty cold and remote at its wheel, of Sue poised on the steps, and of Ty, waiting.

I looked up into his eyes and was flustered by their grave steadiness. "But this is utterly fantastic," I said.

His face was softened by the ghost of a little smile, and the moment hung between us. Then with a meaningless little laugh I destroyed it. I did not know, as I know now, that the moment held within it the power to change my whole life. Or that with this little laugh I tried to deny my destiny. Even now, knowing what I know, I cannot regret that denial. I have learned that love, however passionate, cannot change our destiny; that it is only the gleaming thread in a pattern, the bright garden over which the arrow speeds and both shuttle and arrow must move relentlessly to complete their destined voyaging. But I have learned too that the glowing threads, the bright garden endure in the remembering heart forever, and are forever touched with splendor.

But this I couldn't know then. I was so young. So, with a meaningless little laugh I destroyed the moment. And when I had said my thanks like a schoolgirl leaving a party, I went down the steps toward the dark insolent man who waited for me.

We went like the wind. I crouched in my seat and closed my eyes as we swerved in and out of traffic, closed my ears when, stopped by red lights, my companion cursed softly but with fluent passion. I stole a look at him from beneath my lashes. The unmarred profile for all its dark splendor was as remote and bleak as the profile on a coin. He did not know I existed. Miserably I pulled at the tips of my gloves and stared at the road ahead without seeing it. I saw instead the days that loomed before me, that must be lived among people who had no need of me, who perhaps did not even want me.

We rode in silence, sweeping past the stately homes and the few apartment buildings which with pillared fronts and grilled balconies tried to justify their presence among them. On and on down the wide street that curved and straightened only to curve again, coming after awhile to a shopping district which later I would know as Buckhead—a tawdry noisy section as out of place as hoodlums invading a conservative neighborhood. After Buckhead the houses stood farther apart with stretches of pine woods between them, and still farther on there were spans of road bordered by houseless and unkept land.

Still we rode on and finally outrode the rain. But the countryside bore evidence of it still in dripping forests, in swampy fields, in sallow puddles that sprawled beneath the curbs of sidewalks. The landscape was so devoid of variety that it acted like an opiate. Unconsciously I relaxed against the seat. The weight of my tiredness dropped over me.

Then suddenly the car slowed. Rousing from an inertia that was almost sleep, I saw that Beauty leaned forward, his eyes narrow and intent. On the curve just ahead an overturned car sprawled on its back like some huge grotesque bug. Two policemen in the glistening black of their rubber coats stood above it, notebooks in their hands.

"Smashup," Beauty said curtly and more to himself than to me. "Another damned fool took that curve too fast." He slid the car forward, stopped abreast the wrecked one, and lowering the window thrust out his head.

"What happened, Andrews?" he called.

Both policemen looked up. Then one, square and squat with steely eyes beneath bristling sandy brows, sloshed across to us. He touched his cap. "Don't know exactly, Mr. Avery. Got here after it happened. Pretty soon after though. He was still alive—"

"He?" His eyes on the wrecked car Beauty pulled a package of Camels from his pocket. "Bad?" he asked as he pressed the car's lighter.

"Looked bad." Officer Andrews waved the proffered cigarette away. "Finally got him in an ambulance and on his way to a hospital. No use for her, though." He spat in the puddle at his feet. "Dead as a doornail when we got here."

Beauty, lighting his cigarette, looked up. "Woman, eh?"

"Yeah. Good-looker too." Officer Andrews consulted his notebook. "Oglesby, A. J. and wife, from Philadelphia. Figure they were passing through on their way back from Florida. Receipted hotel bills in his wallet. Took that curve too fast. Street like glass and the car skidded—hit that tree." He spat again. "Leastways that's my guess."

Beauty flipped his half-smoked cigarette into the road. "Perfect setup for it." His laugh was grim. "That curve, they ought to call it Dead Man's Curve."

Officer Andrews shook his head. "Got one named that," he said. "Closer in. Oughta call this one Suicide Curve. That's what it is, taking it too fast in wet weather—suicide." He stepped back as Beauty sped his motor. "If the damned fools would just take it a little slower—"

Then we were back on the road, Beauty remote and bleak again and I crying silently into my handkerchief, furtively so he would not see. I was thinking of another car and another man and wife, lying like limp marionettes on a cold street while strangers discussed them cold-bloodedly. Perhaps one had said of Mama, "Dead as a doornail," and her goodness and sweetness hadn't mattered at all. And Father. Just another casualty to them! His dream for a better world and all men free and unoppressed had been as unmeaning as the dreams a child might have dreamed at night.

I cried on, the tears running down my face until Beauty, without slackening his speed, turned and looked at me, his eyes bright and unchanging as those of a bird of prey. "Oh, for God's sake," he drawled the words wearily, "stop sniffling."

I tried to stop. Pressed my soaked handkerchief against my eyes, in an effort to stem the water that welled as from a spring. But as if the knot inside my breast had suddenly dissolved and must be emptied through my eyes, it continued to well. And suddenly I didn't care if I cried, or if he saw. Yet now perversely, and without effort on my part, the tears stopped. When Beauty turned and looked at me again I managed a watery smile.

"I've stopped," I said.

He asked indifferently, "What are you crying about anyway?"

"About those people back there. That were smashed up."

"Oh God!" he said, without reverence. "Two people you've never seen or heard of."

"But people," I said. "Human beings, with hearts and souls and perhaps fine dreams."

He laughed at me. "Mr. and Mrs. A. J. Oglesby," he mocked, "on their way home from Florida. Where they drank liquor in a twenty-five dollar a day suite and dressed for dinner and gambled at some swank place and went to bed. Perhaps with each other—perhaps not with each other." He threw back his head and laughed—as a dark angel might laugh, I thought, standing at the doors of hell. "Let's cry," he said, "for Mr. and Mrs. A. J. Oglesby of Philadelphia. Two shoddy greedy little people who seasoned at Palm Beach."

I hated him for the bitterness and cruelty which laughed at death. And my hate steadied me. I told him, speaking clearly, for his eyes still held that vague sleepwalker's stare. "You can't know that about them. Perhaps they were valuable, had children. Perhaps he'd taken her to Florida because they'd had to struggle for so long, and then a little money came to them. He wanted her to have a holiday. He loved her, you see. And now—"

He gave me a swift narrow glance, then turned back to the road. "I see," he said. "You're young enough to believe that life has value. It hasn't. Suppose your Mr. and Mrs. Oglesby were what you believe they were. And they're dead. So what? I'll tell you what. They'll sleep forever in the cool dark earth. Side by side, no doubt. No more struggle, no more betraying or being betrayed, no more lies and worse than lies. No more watching themselves become what they never wanted to be." His hand left the wheel, was raised in a mock salute. "Let's salute Mr. and Mrs. A. J. Oglesby," he taunted, "may they rest in peace. They got," his eyes slewed round at me, "a better break than you or me."

He swung the car from the highway, followed a lane-like unpaved road that twisted between walls of forest, and we were silent again. Within the woods the rain still dripped on, tapping from limb to limb. In the watery gray of late afternoon the land seemed sad, I thought, and somber, with a brooding melancholy never glimpsed in colder climates. Somehow it caught at your heart.

How many miles we went along that twisted muddy lane I do not know. I lost all sense of time. The day just lived stretched out like a fantastic nightmare that goes on forever. Centuries might have passed since I talked to the little dress buyer, since Ty had talked of bees, since in the doorway he had said, "That's the way it is."

Now I was conscious only of road. Straight road, curved road, smooth road, rough road. Road that swept past fields and rose to hilltops, then leveling out poured itself into valleys. Sighing, I resigned myself to more road, to an eternity of road, sank deeper in the seat, and slept.

It was almost dark when I sat up startled, as awaking in strange surroundings one is startled. Then my mind cleared. I became aware of our slowed pace. And peering, I saw that we had left the road, were circling a driveway that, coiling, ran between vast spreads of sloping lawn which rose gently to a crest. On that crest stood a house—the most beautiful house I'd ever seen. A house for which even Mama's fabulous tales had left me unprepared. It rose snow white and perfect, its white columns sweeping majestically to the roof. Crowning the crest on which it stood, its immutable design as perfect as if it stood in ancient Greece, whence its chastely beautiful lines had come. Yet, for all its heritage it belonged here.

Beauty stopped the car at the front steps and leaning, opened the door beside me. "Hop out," he ordered curtly, "I'll take the car around."

Even after I obeyed him I continued to stand beside the car, uncertain, until he said impatiently, "Go on in. Nobody's going to bite you." Speeding his engine he continued around the drive.

Then I went up the steps, crossed the wide veranda, reached the door, at the door hesitated. Should I, as Beauty had ordered, go on in? Or should I ring the bell? Tentatively, I touched the doorknob. The decision was made for me. The door swung open.

I stepped into a foyer, my eyes widening at the high-flung ceiling which swept past the second floor to the roof, at the chandelier of dripping crystals, the black and white marble floor. It was as regal as a small but perfect palace, and it made me feel in my cheap little suit and tramp of a hat like a servant girl who had blundered into the wrong door. I had a sickening picture of the clothes I'd brought, the worn skirts, the tired sweaters—my best dress which Mama had made, which had seemed so right before. I was conscious of a half-formed wish to flee before my cheap shabbiness could be exposed. But even as I wished I knew I could not flee. I had nowhere to go. So—I waited.

I did not have to wait long. A woman, obviously old for all the quick agility with which she moved, emerged from one of the rooms that opened from the foyer. She didn't see me at first, for the foyer was dim with twilight. When she did she halted, her neck craning forward like a scrawny chicken's, her eyes peering through thick-lensed spectacles.

"What do you want?" she rasped querulously as if I were an intruder. Before I could answer she prodded, "Well, who is it? Who is it?"

She spoke with sharp impatience as if she had no time to bother. But somehow I sensed that she was not as cross as she pretended. Even in the dusk I saw that her sharp little eyes were not unfriendly and were near to smiling. So smiling back, I told her who I was.

"I am Jennifer," I said.

"Child!" she said, peering, her bony hands clasped on her stomach. "You've come then? A shame nobody met you." Then she was brisk again. "Well, come on! Come on! Meet the family. At least what there is of it."

I followed her from the foyer along a corridor which turned and twisted and finally led to a room at the rear of the house. A high long room, evidently a sort of back sitting room, and as alien to the stately foyer as a poor relative dressed in shabby hand-me-downs. The rug was faced and worn, the chairs derelicts of another time, the huge leather sofa scuffed and beaten. Nevertheless I liked its shabbiness and lived-inness. I liked best of all the log fire on the big fieldstone hearth where a slim small girl with a fine grave face sat knitting, and a boy with silver-gilt hair lay on his stomach and sailed a fleet of paper boats in a foot tub.

Miss George said briskly, "You children, here's your cousin Jennifer. Say 'How do you do' to her. Then you, Trissa, show her to her room. In the left wing, next to Phyl."

The girl child left her knitting in the chair and with a sedateness which made her seem more mature than she was, crossed to where I stood. "How are you, Jennifer?" she asked quietly. The dark luminous eyes seemed almost too wide for the slim pointed face turned up to mine.

She was a tiny thing. I smiled down at her, thinking what a darling she was. Then I nodded toward the boy who had not so much as turned his head. "Is he my cousin too?" I asked.

She said he was and called to him, "Ted, come say 'How do you do' to Cousin Jennifer."

He might have been carved from stone for all the response he gave her. He did not so much as stir but watched his boats with the concentration a kitten would bestow on a pool of fish. He was so young, I thought, and probably shy with strangers. But when he slowly turned and looked at me I dismissed that thought. He appraised me, not with the frankly curious stare of childhood but with eyes so cold, so unchildlike, that I stood startled until, having swept me from head to toe, he disdained me and returned to his boats.

Then Trissa, her hand on my sleeve, was saying, "I'll show you your room, Jennifer." And we were going up a back stairway and along another corridor which also turned and twisted and which led, Trissa said as we went, to the left wing. She explained in her small gentle voice how the wings, the left and right, were the *real* house, the one Daddy's great-great-grandfather bought from the Indians, that the right wing had been the council room for the tribe. But Mother hadn't liked the house like that. She had made Daddy build on the new front with the big columns and had had the right wing all done over for her very own. She had left the little outside staircase, though, which hung at the end of the wing. See —if we leaned from this window, wasn't it cute? And so tiny. Like a play staircase, almost. Daddy said the Indians had used it when they had important business with the chief and must reach him in the dead of night.

Leaning, I followed her small pointing finger and saw the two barracklike wings of brick, white-painted now, which projected from the front portion of the house, the whole forming a huge U. Between the wings lay a bricked court, its center dominated by a lily pool, its water murky from the rain, its lily pads dank and sodden. Then I saw the little staircase that hung at the end of the opposite wing. It ran from the second floor to the ground, so small and hugging the brick of the wing so closely that it was almost invisible. Of course I was intrigued. Almost I could see the lean brown Indian runners slipping up in the dead of night, perhaps with ominous tidings for their chief, and later slipping down again.

Behind the house the land, shadowed with pines and oaks, sloped to a sallow rain-swollen river. The Chattahoochee, Trissa said. Beyond the river the forests rose again and swept on to the horizon. But between house and river I saw stables and outhouses and in a wire-fenced run a number of dogs. They were Daddy's hunters, Trissa said, and tired as I was I knew a rush of pleasure. Vague memories of hunting prints I'd seen, of books I'd read stirred in my mind. Ladies in smart habits! Men in pink coats! The horn sounding tantivy tantivy, and afterwards the hunt breakfast with huge quantities of food eaten beside open fires. The life lived here must be a good life, I thought, as Trissa and I withdrew our heads and went down the corridor.

Glancing into the rooms we passed, I saw that this wing bore no kinship to the front of the house but was almost barracklike. No fine carving here. No high-flung arches or dripping crystals. Nevertheless the rooms were spacious and high-ceilinged, their window sills so wide they could (and probably had in other days) served as seats. And if the luxury and elegance of the new part of the house was lacking, still they were comfortable. When Trissa told me this was Daddy's wing and hers and Ted's and Phyl's, I looked at her surprised, so plain it seemed. Almost like servant quarters.

Trissa said, "This is your room, Jennifer. Right next to Phyl," and led me into the room on the end of the wing. It, too, was plain. But its windows opened to space and trees on three sides, and those on the rear looked out on the Chattahoochee. From them I could see, too, the little staircase across the way. And I was glad, for I was young enough to consider it romantic.

As I took off my hat and hung my coat in the empty closet Trissa explained about the bathroom. There was only one, she said, for Phyl and Ted and herself, and now of course for me. She hoped I wouldn't mind. And in this press I'd find towels and washcloths and soap. And the water would run in the toilet bowl forever unless, when you flushed it, you jiggled the handle like this. With her small competent hands she demonstrated.

Back in my room she said she would go down now. She expected I would like to have a hot bath and time to change. Then I must come down to the sitting room again. Follow this hall, she pointed, and turn left, then right, and left again and I would come to the back stairs. She went out, closing the door gently.

While my bath ran I unlocked my bag which had been put in my room, and unpacked my good dress, placing it on a hanger so it would shake into smoothness. As I hung it in the closet it recaptured something of the charm which, in the elegant foyer, had turned cheap and shoddy. I was remembering Mama's face as we selected the material, hearing her voice saying, "Of course we really shouldn't pay so much." But paying it, and bringing the same reverence to its making that an artist would bring to the creation of a masterpiece.

Now smoothing it over my thinness I loved it again. Told myself almost fiercely that it was a *nice* dress, that even Aunt Eva, who had "marvelous" clothes would admire its plain goodness, its smart leather belt. Perhaps she would exclaim—after she had kissed me of course—"Jennifer, such a stunning dress! It must be custom made!" Then I would tell her Mama had made it, and she would say she couldn't believe it, would declare that Mama was wonderful. And we would talk of how really wonderful Mama was.

I gave my hair a last brushing, put on lipstick, took a last look in the mirror, hating as always the smattering of freckles across my nose. Then I turned off the lights and started out to find my way to the sitting room.

I wasn't good at it. Perhaps my very first turn was a wrong

one, for I found myself wandering from one corridor into another, as completely at sea as Columbus had been on his uncharted voyage. Like Columbus I landed on a spot I didn't even know existed: a little balcony with a fragile grilled balustrade which overhung the foyer.

For a moment I lingered, impressed anew by the elegance, gazing at the jeweled chandelier which turning slightly but forever, tinkled delicately like lovely ghostly laughter. I visualized the wonderful parties Aunt Eva probably gave. Beautiful women in sumptuous gowns sweeping across the marble floor with courtly men in black and white scattered like exclamation points among them.

Standing there I was as goggle-eyed as a child for whom a fairytale comes alive. Then that fairytale, like all fairytales, was shattered. The front door opened and slammed to. Feet, definitely of this earth, entered the foyer. I heard a woman's voice. Eagerly, I lifted my head. Perhaps Aunt Eva, I thought. But when she emerged from under the concealing balcony I knew otherwise. This was a young woman, younger than Aunt Eva could possibly be, no more than twenty-five or six. And she was not beautiful. The dark hair was drawn plainly from her thin face. The flannel shirt and worn jodhpurs were shabby. There was not even a striving for beauty. No, this couldn't be Aunt Eva; she must be Phyl—Beauty's sister.

Impulsively I leaned forward, intending with an easy little laugh to cry hello and ask the way to the back stairs. But when I heard a man's voice call "Wait, Phyl" the impulse was stillborn. Suddenly —and despising my shyness—I wanted only to avoid explanations and introductions. I stepped back, and pressing my body against the wall waited for them to go.

They didn't go. Phyl stopped in the center of the foyer and the man, moving with an animal-like quietness, came up with her. For a second they faced each other almost defiantly. Then he said, and he spoke as quietly as he moved, "You're wrong about this, Phyl."

She cried out: "I'm not! I'm not. I don't want her to know!"

Without moving he asked levelly, "But what about Beauty?"

Her head moved in swift negation: "Or Beauty either! Oh he wouldn't mean to let it slip, but he would when—when—"

He asked, still levelly, "When he's drunk, you mean?"

She turned on him fiercely, "All right, when he's drunk." Her riding crop beat a restless tattoo on her boot. "I tell you, Jud," she began. Then her frail shoulders moved despairingly. "Oh Jud! You know Eva as well as I do."

"Yes." The word was wooden as he said it. He might have been carved from wood as he stood there. But suddenly with a shrug he yielded. "Okay," he said. "We'll do it your way. We won't tell her —or anybody. Just slip off one day." His laugh was grim. "Makes me pretty much of a heel with Beauty though. After all he's my friend —and my job."

"Oh, Beauty!" Her voice was listless now and sad. "It's like worrying about a dead man."

"Don't forget. The corpse owns the mill."

Her fierceness came alive again. "The mill! The mill! I'm sick of the mill."

His brown hand reached and touched her cheek. "Okay," he placated, "okay." Then as if his touch had pressed the spring of her emotion she was in his arms, her arms were clutched around his neck, her dark head was buried in his shoulder. The very curve of her body told me that within her was a capacity for loving so great that it was terrible. I could not bear to look. I turned my eyes away.

When I looked again they had gone on, had turned into the corridor that led from the foyer. Phyl's voice receding as they went drifted back to me. "I'm sorry," she was saying, "it's just that Eva is such a—" The rest of the sentence, with their footsteps, was lost to me.

Furtively I left the little balcony, started on my search for the back stairs again. But they and their discovery had sunk into unimportance. I was absorbed instead with that last sentence of Phyl's, and the word which had escaped me. "If Eva wasn't such a—" she had said. Such a—what? I wondered. Like a little girl with her grammar lesson I tried to complete the sentence. Could it have been "such a *darling*"? And must something be kept secret lest it cause darling Eva pain or worry? Or could it have been "such a—bitch"? Instantly I refused the word. It was as out of place in this house as swine in the parlor.

Yet as I descended the back stairs, which I found almost without effort, the word "bitch" would not be denied. Suppose, I thought, Phyl *had* said "such a bitch." Suppose Aunt Eva was a vicious woman, driving her husband to drunkenness, her young sister-in-law to a hole-and-corner love affair. I told myself it was too unbelievable, the sort of thing that happened only in books or movies. Nevertheless I remembered the few hundreds of Father's insurance thankfully. For the first time I recognized them for what they were, what Father had meant them to be. Not just an insignificant sum but, if necessary, the price of escape.

I was back in the sitting room with Phyl and the children, Phyl and I exchanging the small meaningless remarks of first acquaintance as we waited. Miss George wandered in and out to complain of delayed dinner, to wonder when on earth Eva would get home and asking Phyl querulously if she hadn't better let Tom serve. Dinner would be ruined, not fit to eat—

Phyl, still wearing the shabby jodhpurs and shirt, was detached. Miss George must do as she thought best, she said. Which left Miss George's problem unsolved. She continued to worry at it like a distracted hen.

"You know as well as I do that fried chicken isn't fit to eat when it's cold."

Phyl smiled at her. "Then I'd have dinner now."

"Oh, you would?" Miss George was tart. "And have Eva fit to be tied if *her* dinner is cold?"

"Then wait for her," Phyl veered amiably. "Perhaps she'll come soon."

"And Tom swollen up like a poisoned pup because he wants to get off early tonight. Guess he's scared he won't get his share of that rotgut whisky."

I sat on the window seat feeling that a life reduced to the sole consideration of when we ate was incomprehensible. Sadly I recalled our suppers in the flat. The fragrance of Mama's vegetable soup, the richness of her pot roast preceding her gay "Come and eat!" Father and I getting out of our chairs by the sitting-room fire, and with our books under our arms trailing into the snug little kitchen. Mama chattering as she served us of the happenings of her day, her canary's frenzied singing providing background music for the janitor's lumbago or her argument with the milkman. Afterwards, Father and I doing the dishes over Mama's protest. Father saying, "In a democracy, Sally, there is an equal division of labor as well as of privilege. Damn it, woman! Get out of this kitchen."

The thread of my remembrance was snapped by the reappearance of Miss George. "I'm going to feed Trissa and Ted, and get them to bed." Her announcement, as portentous as a declaration of war, was not, it developed, so foolish as it seemed. For Ted's going created a minor crisis. His first coolly contemptuous refusal I took for the usual childish opposition to bed. But it grew into something which while equally cool, equally contemptuous, was less childlike. Getting up, he stood facing the room, his small back to the fire, and surveyed the rest of us with quiet arrogance.

Miss George rasped worriedly, "Now Ted! It's past your bedtime! You know how your mother—" And Trissa pleaded lovingly, "I'll read you a story, Ted," but without result. Motionless, he stared at them with cool disdain, his ice-blue eyes implacable. I was both amused and amazed, yet impatient too. Ridiculous, I thought, that without so much as speaking he could hold the harassed Miss George and the beseeching little Trissa at bay. Undoubtedly he was a little devil for all his cherubic beauty.

The crisis was resolved by Phyl, who having watched the scene now ended it. "Let him stay, Miss George." She inserted the words quietly between Miss George's fretting and Trissa's pleading. "Don't you see?"

Miss George's patience was raveling. "I see all right," she retorted. "He thinks he can ride roughshod over—"

Phyl's quiet voice interrupted again. "He's waiting for his mother." And prosaic as the words were, they held some magic which vanquished Miss George. Without another word she stalked from the room. Ted returned to his boats. And I took up my vigil of waiting again.

But suddenly it was over. We heard the faint slam of a door and Trissa from the big chair smiled across at me. "There's Mama," she said. Listening I heard a rush of quick light footsteps, which somehow gave an impression of slender feet, high-arched and moving with exquisite grace. Then I heard her voice, speaking to someone she passed, a maid perhaps, or Miss George. A soft voice and

Southern, yet without the laziness so often heard in Southern voices and with a huskiness which made it vibrant and alive; and so like Mama's.

Instinctively I straightened. Then aware that I had tensed, tried to relax again. But it was impossible. For it struck me suddenly that the color and shape of my life for weeks, perhaps for months to come, hung on this meeting. And that now that it was here I dreaded it as much as I desired it. I sat with my eyes on the doorway. And I felt uncertain and self-conscious, like someone waiting to be interviewed for a job.

Then suddenly she was framed within it, poised there with deliberate grace as a stage star might wait for anticipated applause. Only for a moment, a moment in which I received a swift impression of slenderness, of leaf-brown hair, of wide brown eyes which circled the room and came at last to me.

"Jennifer!" Her voice made my name a sound of breathless delight. Then she was coming toward me swiftly, smiling as she came. Automatically, as she neared me, I stood up. I waited stiff and awkward as a schoolboy. Then she was beside me, was gathering me into her warm and perfumed embrace.

"Darling!" The sweet husky voice throbbed the word. "I was frantic because I couldn't meet you. *Simply* frantic! Have they looked after you?"

Stammering, I said not meeting me hadn't mattered, that they had looked after me; she was not to worry.

Her arms dropped away and stepping back she surveyed me, the brown eyes traveling over my figure, a little smile quirking her mouth. Then her gloved hand reached. Her finger lifted my chin.

"But darling!" She spoke slowly. Her eyes were wide and wondering. "Why, why—you're pretty! I never dreamed! Why didn't Sally write me?"

Holding my chin she continued to regard me almost as if she found me unbelievable. Then her hand dropped lightly to my shoulder. "But darling," her voice still warm, still sweet, was now somehow gently accusing, "where *did* you get that tacky little dress?"

We were at dinner, at last. I, on Aunt Eva's right, Phyl on her left, Beauty still remote, still aloof at the other end of the table which, for just the four of us seemed somewhat long and awkward. But Aunt Eva, her voice beating like music against the quiet room, vanquished the awkwardness as she talked of the wrecked car, which she too had seen, of the rain, of the tiresome party which had kept her from meeting me. Carrying, I soon realized, the burden of talk, unaided. Phyl across from me, sat unspeaking, so pale, so exhausted, that I wondered if she were really frail or if the thinness, the hollowed cheeks, only gave her a false fragility. As for Beauty, he made no pretense either of conversation or eating. His entire attention was centered on the decanter by his place and the emptying and refilling of his glass.

With small remarks I tried to help Aunt Eva carry her burden of talk, but without success. Every word I uttered seemed dull and weighted. So, despairing, I sat ill at ease and tongue-tied, unable to understand the sense of strain. It was, I thought, as if Aunt Eva's light, laughing voice danced over tension, and I wondered why. Could it come from her awareness of Beauty's steady drinking? Somehow I knew she was aware though nothing in her gentle vivacity suggested it. Or could young Ted's behavior before dinner have caused it? When Miss George had reappeared to take him and Trissa off to bed he had clung, screaming his passionate protest, not to Aunt Eva but to Phyl. A ridiculous scene, I told myself. One which a sound spanking would have settled. Yet when Phyl loosened the frantic hands from about her knees and, lifting him, bore him from the room, I was less sure. When she passed me I saw the small child's face; it was not the face of temper but of utter desolation. Little Trissa saying her ladylike good-nights appeared almost as desolate. Impulsively, I drew her close and kissed her on the cheek.

When they had gone I turned to Aunt Eva fearing she too would be upset. If she was, she did not betray it. My admiration for her, a proud lady transcending petty considerations, grew. She was poised before the mirror over the bookshelves (which held everything excepting books) touching her hair with her dancer's hands. She had such lovely hair, I thought. Not the rigid waves which speak blatantly of the beauty shop but hair fluffed with such artlessness that it formed a shining aura about her small proud head.

In the mirror our eyes met and spinning lightly, she faced me with a throaty little laugh. "Ah Jen! You're thinking that I am a vain silly woman. Now aren't you?"

"I'm thinking how—beautiful you are," I told her awkwardly.

This time the throaty little laugh was as self-conscious and as charming as a child's. Turning to Beauty who stood at the hearth she put her hands on his shoulders and tiptoeing dropped a brief kiss on the ravaged cheek. "Do you hear her? Beautiful, she says."

He placed his highball glass on the mantelpiece and with his face inscrutable, deliberately moved her hands from his shoulders. Then he looked across at me with a harsh laugh. "Jennifer sings for her supper," he said and reached for his glass again. As we went in to dinner I was uncomfortable and embarrassed. Not for myself, for common sense told me Beauty could have no reason for hurting me, but for Aunt Eva. I could not believe, despite the amused little laugh with which she answered him, that she had been amused.

Yet—and I thought her wonderful—she transcended his rudeness. While we ate the fried chicken, the rice and gravy, the tiny buttered biscuits which white-coated Tom served, her sweet husky voice was gay, her three-noted little laugh, happy. Circling like a winging bird her voice came back to her distress at not meeting me.

Again I insisted that it hadn't mattered. At first I said, trying for careless laughter, at first I had worried. Oh, just a little! But Ty had called the house, had talked to Beauty. Beauty had been kind enough to drive in and get me—and here I was.

She broke into my sentence, asked, her hand playing with the pearls at her throat, "But, Jen, I don't understand! Do you mean no one met you at the station? That you had to call the house?"

Again I protested. It hadn't mattered, I said.

Her hands lifted in a gesture of bewilderment. "But darling—" Her eyes circled toward Beauty. "Beauty," she was gently reproving, "you didn't meet Jen?"

Without so much as looking her way he drained his wine glass, refilled it slowly. Then his eyes met hers with half-laughing insolence. "Why should I have met her? I didn't know she was expected."

Aunt Eva's luminous puzzled eyes circled from his to Phyl. "But Phyl?" she asked, waited. Then as Phyl sat unspeaking, "Dearest, I asked you to tell Beauty."

Phyl said quietly, "No, Eva. You did no such thing."

The brown eyes widened with distress. "But darling! I did. Don't you remember? I stopped at the sitting-room door on my way out and asked you to tell Beauty that Jen would arrive at four." She surveyed Phyl concernedly. "You *do* remember now? Don't you, darling?"

Phyl's eyes staring back at her were curiously hard. Then suddenly she laughed. A sweet high laugh tinged with shrillness. "You don't really expect me to remember? Do you, Eva?"

"But dearest!" Real concern now. The patient concern you bestow on a backward child. "You *must* remember. Listen, Phyl." She spoke measuredly with each word emphasized as you speak to one of poor understanding. "You were in the back sitting room with the children, reading them a story. I—"

Beauty's voice, ugly and demanding, cut across her words, "Oh hell! Break it up! Don't try to cover up for me, Phyl." The hateful laughter shone in his eyes again. "I'm the guilty party. Phyl gave me the message. I—" he picked up his glass, "I forgot." He lifted his glass with mock gallantry. "Ladies, my apologies and my alibi."

A pause hung voiceless in the room, shattered after a half-moment by Aunt Eva's throaty little laugh, her voice gay again and caressing. "Ah, Jen! Aren't we silly? When nothing matters except—" her hand reached for and found mine, enclosed it, "—that you're here." She leaned toward me, her eyes mischievous. "But Jen! You met Ty McKinnon! Darling, such luck! One of the richest young men in the state, you know."

Amazed, I said I didn't know.

"But he is, darling. And so good-looking. And such a splendid family. And all the McKinnon money, Jen," her voice was warm, intimate. "Tell me, did you like him?"

Yes, I said. I had liked him, his sister too. They had been so kind.

Her eyes widened. "His sister? Oh! You met Sue?"

I explained that Beauty had picked me up at their house. She listened, smiling faintly, thoughtfully. Like a child who stumbles upon a delightful secret.

"And you like Sue, darling?" Her voice was tender now, as if my liking Sue pleased her. "Beauty," her eyes swept down the table toward him, "did you hear? Jen likes Sue."

He didn't deign to answer. Unperturbed she came back to me. "Sue," she told me gently, "is our local legend."

"Legend?" I looked up, puzzled.

"Yes, darling. Every town in the South has one you know: beautiful girl, jilted on her wedding eve, still waiting for her unfaithful lover to return. Sue is Atlanta's legend. The bridegroom-to-be, the very night before the wedding—a simply tremendous wedding too—eloped with a—a beautiful wench." Pensively, she added, "Poor Sue! All those years she's waited for him—" her voice trailed into nothingness.

Suddenly Phyl, who had sat with eyes intent on her plate, hardly seeming aware of the rest of us, pushed back her chair abruptly and rose. Her "Excuse me" was so stifled, so choked that I looked up quickly wondering if she were ill. She looked ill. Her face, as she turned to leave the room, was tight and still, her eyes wide, almost unseeing. Aunt Eva's tender, "Do go to bed, dearest. You look simply dreadful," invoked no response. Phyl did not turn or answer, but went swiftly from the room.

Aunt Eva sighed and her attention came back to me. She dropped her elbows on the table, cupped her little chin in her hands. "Now, darling," her smile was teasing, her voice intimate again, "tell Beauty and me all about Ty and Sue."

Because I wanted to please her I groped for something I could tell of Ty and Sue that I hadn't told. They had been kind, I had liked them—what more was there to say? But I was spared the effort, for now Beauty pushed back his chair and stood. Not abruptly as Phyl had done, but without hurry. Neither did he hurry from the table. Instead he bowed in our direction as the villain in a melodrama would bow, with elaborate and taunting courtesy. "Ladies," he said, the gallantry of his words belied by the mocking laughter in his eyes, "I am desolated to leave your charming company." He reached down and plucked the decanter from the table. "But frankly I prefer company that gives me more pleasure." And grasping the decanter in his hand as nonchalantly as if it were a cane or an umbrella, he strolled from the room.

It was so rude, so obviously intended to humiliate, that I glanced at Aunt Eva apprehensively. Her smile was no less gay, her manner no less serene. Yet I had no faith in that gaiety, that serenity. They were the cloak, I thought, with which she covered her humiliation. It dawned upon me that for her the whole meal had constituted a struggle against bad manners and ugliness, a struggle in which the weapons of sweetness and charm had not availed.

I wanted to tell her I understood, that I thought her wonderful, but words with which to say it would not come. It was she who found the right words. "Darling," she said, "you must forgive Beauty. He's so attractive, so charming when he's himself. Tonight he isn't himself, and really," with the throaty little laugh, "I shouldn't have teased him."

"Teased him?" I echoed blankly.

"About Sue McKinnon, darling. Didn't you know? It was Beauty who left her waiting—practically at the church—and eloped with a beautiful wench? And *I* was the beautiful wench?"

I looked at her dumbfounded. "No. I—didn't know."

"It's true, darling. It really is. It was simply dreadful—for Sue, I mean." The wine-brown eyes, half gay, half grave questioned mine. "Was it so horrible of Beauty, Jen?"

Slowly I said, "You must have loved each other terribly."

The slim brows lifted, the eyes staring into space were blank, unhappy. Then warmth flowed back into them. They were velvety again. And her soft laughter was triumphant. "Darling," she said, "he was mad about me. Simply mad."

I waked in the morning to a splash of water in the patio, to the dry cackling of Miss George's voice, to November's gold-edged sunshine streaming into my room. Jumping up I ran to the windows and looked out.

The world I saw was wonderful. The trees which in yesterday's rain had looked sere and drear rose like a sweep of fire, their russets and reds and golds flaming wherever you looked. Below in the patio Miss George, her black dress hidden by a voluminous gingham apron, leaned to feed two huge gray geese from a pan, her voice as she scolded so like theirs that I laughed. "You Sudie! You Sam!" She slapped one long reaching neck aside, then the other. "Wait your turn. And you Tom!" Without so much as turning her head she spoke to the old Negro who languidly swept before the kitchen door. "Get about breakfast. You're slow as molasses in the wintertime." Then to the geese which continued to stretch their necks toward the pan, "That's all. Now, get! Go on! Get! Get!" And waving her apron she charged them, shooing them from the patio into the yard beyond, her berating voice mingling with theirs in raucous discord.

This accomplished, she pattered after Tom into the kitchen, and the place fell into quiet. Yet not quiet. From the stableyard came the sound of galloping hooves. In the dog run the dogs barked ecstatically. And Sam and Sudie wending their single-file way across the land continued to sound their strident cry. To my ears—ears attuned to the symphony of elevated and subway, the million-throated voice of automobile—it sounded strange but, perhaps because of that strangeness, beautiful. Suddenly I felt alive, as if this was living. I couldn't dress quickly enough in my eagerness to be a part of it.

As I left my room Phyl emerged from hers and with a friendly good morning waited for me to come up with her. Together we went along the corridor and down the stairs. She seemed quite another person this morning. Gay and relaxed; and with no hint of the pale tenseness she had shown last night at the dinner table.

Apparently we were the first up. The little breakfast room was deserted when we entered. Nevertheless the percolator perked merrily on the table, the toaster was flanked by bread and butter and on the built-in buffet a warmer held bacon and scrambled eggs.

It was fun to help ourselves, to wait for the toast to pop from the toaster, to eat with the trees just outside the window, the checkered glimmer of sunlight on the table. I told Phyl so.

Pouring our coffee she asked, "You've always lived in New York, haven't you, Jen?"

I told her I had and that never before had I eaten breakfast with trees looking in at me. It was true. And I began to have a half-formed realization of why Mama had loved her South. The space, the trees, the peace. Unattainable in a city where a thousand families must occupy the space which here belonged to one.

I only said laughing as we took our places at the table, "I'm starving. And I slept like something—" cringing at the word 'dead' I avoided it, "—like a log."

She smiled across at me. "I'm glad. I was afraid Ted and his nightmare might have disturbed you."

I tasted my eggs, discovered that I was hungry. "Oh! Did Ted have a nightmare?"

She nodded. "It's a wonder he didn't wake you. He screams like he's being murdered."

"Does he have them often?"

"Yes." Her face was suddenly thoughtful. "Too often."

Her thoughtfulness told me that she felt concern. More, in my opinion, than a child's nightmare warranted. I recalled a nightmare I had had as a small girl when I too had waked up screaming. How Father, explaining the reason for the dream, said the young have a dreadful feeling of insecurity. Feeling very wise I repeated to Phyl what he had said.

Her dark eyes met mine quietly. Yes, she said. Insecurity—

Eating my eggs I wondered why small Ted should feel insecure. If he were an underprivileged child, or neglected or let go hungry or beaten, then there would be reason. But he was none of these. He was one of the lucky ones.

Drinking my coffee I said, "He adores his mother, doesn't he?"

"Yes." She spoke briefly, almost abstractedly and rising picked up her riding crop as she spoke, stood flexing it in her hands. Then she turned back to me. "Do you ride, Jen?" she asked lightly.

Almost apologetic I said no—I didn't ride. In New York there had been no opportunity. Of course there were riding academies where you hired a horse and let him walk you about the park. But—I just never had.

"You'll have to learn. You'd love it."

Doubtfully I said I didn't know about that.

"Come walk to the stables with me," she suggested, "and meet the horses. Perhaps you'll decide you'd like to ride."

We went out the back door, crossed the patio and walked across the golden-lighted lawn where even the tree shadows were gold-edged. I thought of New York at this hour. The mass of small automatons scurrying between tall buildings, plunging into subways with blind unreasoning haste. The dank subway platforms, the frenzied trains starting—stopping! The dark tape of humanity coiling in and out of their doors, like a tireless serpent.

Here it was so still, so peaceful, and so fresh. As if the rain of yesterday had washed everything—land and trees, the crystalline sky

—into new being. A day for happiness, I thought. Remembering what Sue had said—that I must try and be happy—I told myself that I must try.

At the dog run the dogs greeted us vociferously, leaping against the wire of the enclosure madly until Phyl bestowed upon each—two beagles, a liver-and-white pointer and a setter—tidbits she'd brought. Then we went on to the stables where, and with utmost gravity, she introduced me to the horses. This, she said, her hand on the russet neck of a slender little mare, was Mimi. The hunter in the next stall was Beau. The mare I loved at once. She was gentle. But Beau, a magnificent animal, his white fetlock startling against the black satin of his coat, was another matter. He regarded the mare, as she nuzzled us, with disdain, tossing his head. His hooves beat a restless tattoo on the floor as if he considered us poor weak things worthy only of contempt.

Phyl swung a saddle over the mare and tightened the straps, talking as she worked. Beau, she said, belonged to Beauty and was a hellion. But Beauty loved him—Beauty loved all animals. Sometimes she believed more than people—except for his children of course. Animals ran true, he said. When they didn't, you put them out of the way. Laughing at my shocked face she led the mare from the stable. Outside, she swung into the saddle. "Don't take me too seriously, Jen." She smiled down at me. "Or Beauty either. He talks a lot of nonsense." Then lifting her hand in good-by she and the mare were flying toward the drive which led to the road.

I made my way back to the house tasting the day light and dry on my lips. A day for happiness, I thought again. I must try and be happy. After all, that was what Mama and Father would want for me. Suddenly I felt as if they had sent this—the gentle sun, the high-arched sky, the peace and stillness—this *happy-being* day to me. Like a gift they might have lain in my hands. Feeling this made it easier to accept the always frightening gift of happiness.

In the house again I ran into Miss George, the tarantella of her scolding unabated. This time it beat against Mellie, the soft little colored maid who listened, apparently speechless with awe but who—when Miss George wasn't looking—winked at me over the tray she held.

"If you didn't go gallivanting Saturday nights—stay up till all hours drinking rotgut licker, you might—mind you I say *might* get to work on time on Sunday. You know Miss Eva is fit to be tied if—her coffee—you Mellie! Get that tray upstairs."

Impulsively I intercepted her, asked if I might carry the tray to Aunt Eva.

Mellie said, her voice like syrup, "I don't mind, Miss Jen," and Miss George peering at me over her glasses rasped, "You, Jen! You'd better not start that. First thing you know she'll have you waiting on her hand and foot."

It wasn't to save Mellie, I explained, smiling at Mellie. It was, well—I would really like to. I directed a smile at Miss George. Please, I plead.

In the end Mellie handed over the tray and Miss George, stalking like a grenadier, conducted me to the foyer where she pointed to a door on the left side of the little balcony. "That's her door," she said grimly and marched off toward the back of the house.

Carefully I ascended the curving stairs, my eyes taking in the delicate porcelain, the fine lace mat, the silver tray cool and smooth as silk against my hand. All worthy of a princess, I thought, and even as I thought it I remembered Mama's little cream pitcher. Four inches tall, of lovely grayed blue, costing only a dollar or two in some little shop, a tiny fraction of the cost of these. Yet somehow I didn't doubt even then which was really valuable. Even then, I knew.

My first knock was gentle and invoked no response. So—but still gently—I knocked again and waited patiently, as a page might wait his lady's pleasure. Then, when there was still no response, I turned the knob and opened the door.

At first I was dazzled by the room and could only stand gazing. I had not dreamed that there were rooms like this, except in movies of course—or perhaps, palaces. It was a beautiful room. So beautiful that it overwhelmed me, left me incapable of realizing any individual part of it. I was only conscious of exquisite color, of dripping crystal, of varitoned silk sweeping at windows, of an entire wall of mirror which with reflection intensified the total loveliness. It wasn't a practical room. You couldn't conceive of hanging stockings to dry or turning a hem in it. It was created only for beauty. The toil of craftsmen, the whirring of looms, the loading and unloading of ship and train and van, the labor and sweat of thousands had been required to produce it, to gather here in one space this shrine for Aunt Eva's loveliness.

On the bed Aunt Eva was asleep, the leaf-brown hair feathering against the pillow, one white arm flung high over her head. Crossing noiselessly I stood beside the bed and looked down at her. She was worthy of the room, I thought—and seemed so young. No line marred the soft melancholy of her sleeping face, the breast revealed by the frothy lace of her nightgown was small and round and lifting, a young girl's breast. Yet somehow I knew there was no summer in her heart.

Quietly I said her name and she awakened. Not as others awake with languor and luxurious stretching and eyes sleep-blurred. But springing up as a doe sleeping in a forest might spring at some slight sound, with head raised warily and wide alert eyes.

When she saw me the smiling vivacity slipped over the melancholy of sleep like a mask.

"Ah Jen!" She smiled up at me. "You've brought my coffee. How darling of you!" Then as I started to place the tray on her lap, "No—no—no! Not yet, darling! I'm a fright!"

Reaching in a drawer of the bedside table she brought out an enameled box and opening it revealed a dressing kit complete with mirror and numerous vials and boxes. With sure deft hands she dipped into them. Touched her cheeks and lips with color, smoothed the satin skin with powder, brushed her loosened hair into its accustomed aura.

She replaced the kit in the drawer, smiled up at me. "Now," she cried gaily, "I want my coffee."

While she drank the black coffee she questioned me. Had I slept well? Did I sleep late? Oh—up early? What time? Heavens! And I got up? What on earth had I found to amuse me at that horrible hour?

Sitting on the foot of her bed I told her; of my early breakfast with Phyl, of my visit to the stables and dog run, of meeting the horses, my recital meaningless except for the pleasure it gave me. Chattering, it occurred to me that she was bored, that her thoughts strayed elsewhere. Somewhat abruptly I brought my chatter to an end.

She smiled at me over the edge of her cup. Asked, "Darling! You like Phyl?"

Oh yes! I said. I liked her.

"And what did you two find to talk about so early in the morning?"

I tried to recall what we had talked about. Laughing, said it couldn't have been important for I didn't remember—but it had been fun—

She refilled her cup from the tiny urn. "I'm glad you like Phyl, Jen. You'll be good for her, I think. She isn't very well, you know."

I had wondered about that, I said. Last night at dinner she had seemed, at least to me, tense and high-strung, not well. But she was all right this morning. Gay and relaxed.

"She's like that, darling." Her tiny shrug deprecated Phyl's moodiness. "A wonderful person when she's well." Laughing softly she stretched luxuriously. "I'm glad she feels better. She gets such weird ideas when she feels badly. And hates everyone. Including me."

Unable to believe that I protested. "Oh, Aunt Eva, she doesn't!"

She was amused at my disbelief. "But, yes, darling. But heavens! Don't take it so seriously."

"But how can she?" I did take it seriously. "When you give her a home? When you're so—so sweet to her?"

"That's part of it, Jen. Living here I mean. When her father died she wanted to stay on in the house in town. She wanted to be free—she said. But of course Beauty wouldn't have that and, since John Avery left Beauty in charge of everything—"

"But why can't she be contented here? This lovely place. And her horse! And the children! She seems to love the children so."

She toyed with the spoon on her saucer, her eyes, shadowed by her lashes, watching her hand. "Yes." The admission was tinged with reluctance. "She does adore the children. That makes another problem, Jen. She adores them—too much. It's not—not good for them. Especially Ted." Her eyes lifted met mine gravely. "Perhaps I'd better explain about Phyl, darling."

"Explain?" I wondered if I sounded as vague as I felt. What was there to explain about Phyl? I wondered. Phyl, slim and dark-haired! Loving children! And dogs and horses.

Aunt Eva's eyes were on her hand again. "Phyl," she spoke almost haltingly as if she weighed her words, "Phyl isn't well, Jen. We, Beauty and I, are concerned about her. You see her father was ill a long time before—he died." She paused a moment, then added quietly, "Mentally ill. We fear that Phyl—"

I cried out aghast, "Oh no!"

She continued, disregarding my cry. "We didn't realize—that illness in John Avery until—well almost at the last. Then we did realize. He forgot things. The simplest things." She lifted her hands, gestured hopelessly. "Naturally when Phyl—that message I asked her to give Beauty about your arrival—just one instance, darling. You see—she had no memory of it."

I cried out, "But Beauty said—"

Her nod intercepted the thought I would have expressed. "I know," she said gently. "You see we try—oh so hard—to keep Phyl from realizing. We kept it from John Avery for a long time. But at the last he knew. And he went in the bathroom and—shot himself."

I stared at her with sick eyes. Thinking, this too added to Beauty's drinking. And my sympathy for Phyl, deep as it was, was submerged by sympathy for Aunt Eva. I stammered. "It's terrible for Phyl. But so—so terrible for you."

Her hands lifted again in the small gesture of futility. "It's just one of those things, darling. I could let myself brood, I suppose. But —I just can't. I simply have to rise above it." Thoughtfully she raised her cup, drank the last of her coffee, put the cup down, and automatically I rose and reached for the tray.

She caught my hand, held it close and warm and loving between both of hers. "Jen." The soft wide eyes looked up at me. "You mustn't ever leave me. You must stay with me—always."

I was swept by a rush of love. "Oh, Aunt Eva! Do you like me?"

She threw back her head with the three enchanting little notes of laughter. "Darling!" she cried. "But I adore you. And, Jen." She was serious again. "I need you."

I was wrenched by a gratefulness so close to pain that it hurt. *She needed me.* With those three words she won not only my love but an allegiance which, I swore to myself, would be undying. I did not know (I was too young to know, too inexperienced) she had used the lure by which we are all irresistibly trapped. Or that in our need to be needed we often invest with too much meaning casual words which have no meaning, except to hide the fraud of the heart.

So, not knowing, I stood there, my hand in hers until she cried out that she had a perfectly beastly luncheon at the club—she hated awfully to leave me—but it was one of those things, and she had to rush like mad or she'd be late. And would I be a darling and run her bath?

I ran her bath, marveling at the bathroom with its delicate opaline tints that made it like the underside of a seashell. All pale and expensive loveliness. Touched the huge velvety towels with their pompous monogram! Sniffed the fragrance of soap and bath salts! Felt that to walk on the pale lovely rugs was sacrilege. Looked with wondering eyes at the dressing room which led from the bath; lovely too, but as efficient as an operating room, with its wardrobes and its dressing table of glass set against mirror which reflected the dozens of jars and bottles and boxes. While the water ran into the tub I inspected them. Creams for face and neck, for throat and eyes, for arms and feet. Cleansing cream, day cream, night cream, nourishing cream. Orange cream, cucumber cream! Lotions too! For skin, for throat, for eyes, for hands, for body, for elbows. Powders in every shade. Tiny box after box of rouge running the scale from pale pink to fuchsia, and nail polish as colorful and as varied. Then the implements of beauty. Tiny brushes, tiny clippers! Soft down puffs by the score in a plastic case. All done in the pale pink which Elizabeth Arden has made her own. All created to bestow beauty on women yet unable, I knew, to bestow one iota where there was none.

Then there were the perfumes. *Dangerous Moment*, *Love Me*, *Allure*, and a dozen others revealing by their names the thought behind their creation, their selling, their buying. Squat bottles, tall bottles. Black bottles, gold and crystal bottles. Worthy containers—at least in the manufacturers' opinion—to hold the magic formulas of distilled sex.

While the water ran in the tub I ventured into the room which opened off the dressing room, a long room with the same wide window sills I had found in mine. These—the window sills—told me what it was; the right wing of the original house, which according to Trissa, her mama had taken for her own—had had done over. Perhaps because its basically simple lines refused ornateness it was less ornate than the rest of Aunt Eva's apartment. Yet it was lovely too. Its appointments were obviously expensive but it failed to impress as the other room had impressed. That one might have housed a goddess; this bore evidence of being used by a woman occupied with earthly things. The little desk was untidy with its confusion of letters and bills and papers. Sofa cushions sprawled on the floor. Magazines—*Vogue* and *Harper's Bazaar* and *Town and Country*—were scattered helter-skelter on floor and chairs. And across the surface of a small carved table a blood-red stain—nail lacquer no doubt—had streaked its ragged path and hardened into permanence.

At the end of room I saw a door, and realizing that it must open on the little staircase, I was unable to resist my curiosity. Crossing I tried to open it. But without success. It was locked and bolted, its bolt so rusted I could not so much as budge it. Perhaps it had been locked for years, I reasoned—maybe since the last lean brown runner had, departing, closed it behind him before he slipped down the staircase in the night.

"Darling."

Aunt Eva's voice tore the fabric of my reverie and I turned, guiltily. She stood in the doorway wrapped in a sea-green robe. When remorsefully I asked if the bath had run over she laughed at me delightedly. "No! No! No! Darling, I turned it off. Jen—do you like my sitting room?"

I told her I liked it. Especially the little staircase at the end. She brushed it away with a careless "Oh that" and her eyes swept the room. "It's in a frightful mess." Her laugh was a child's apologetic laugh. "But I don't care." The little laugh again. "I simply won't allow Miss George to put her foot in the door. She's such a—a snooper. And of course Mellie doesn't half do it."

Eagerly I asked if I might keep it for her. Her answer was another careless laugh. "We'll see, darling. Really I hate for anyone—" she broke off her eyes widening. "But darling! I'm forgetting. Somebody wants you on the phone. Take it in my room. And don't go down. I won't be in my bath a minute—"

Wondering who could be calling me I went back to her room and crossing to the telephone beside her bed, picked up the receiver. "Hello" I said.

"Hello, sugar." It was Ty, his voice drawling, casual. "How you doing?"

"Oh Ty," I cried out his name happily, "hello."

He repeated his salutation with absolute gravity. "Hello. How's my girl?"

"Your girl?" I sounded blank. "I wouldn't know. Who is she?"

He ignored my question. "I've been wondering about you. How are you getting along with your Aunt Eva?"

He was sweet, I thought; sweet to remember that only yesterday I was wondering and worrying.

"Oh Ty!" I said. "I'm just crazy about her. She's wonderful!"

His voice was as steady as my memory of it. "That's fine. Just fine. Now listen, hon. On Thanksgiving we're going to have what we call the Nine O'Clock Ball. Now listen, hon—"

He talked on and while he talked Aunt Eva, wrapped in the sea-green robe, emerged from the bathroom and unaware of my watching eyes paused before the length of mirror that ran along the opposite wall. Twirling languidly, she studied her reflection. Surveyed her figure at this angle and that one as she twirled with tilted head and drooping eyes, her hands now lifted gracefully, then dropping to run caressingly down her slim thighs. Watching, I smiled to myself; not with derision, but with tenderness. Who could blame her, I thought, for loving the woman the mirror gave back to her?

Ty said, "I'll see you," and rang off, and I replaced the receiver in its cradle. Then Aunt Eva turned toward me, and finding my eyes upon her laughed guiltily but enchantingly, like a child surprised at the cookie jar.

"Darling! Don't tell me that was Ty McKinnon?"

I said that it was Ty. That he had invited me to go to something called the Nine O'Clock Ball with him. She surveyed me with amazement.

"The Nine O'Clock? Jen, every debutante in Atlanta will want to tear your hair!"

Dismayed I asked why.

"Why? Because he's the most eligible young man in town. Probably has bids to dozens of tables, and"—she laughed delightedly—"and he brushes them off—for you. I love it!"

I plopped in a chair feeling a little numb with surprise while she sat at the dressing table and did her face, using the creams, the rouge, the minute brushes and soft puffs with the same delicate precision with which a surgeon wields lancet and scalpel. As she worked she talked of the Nine O'Clock Ball. It was a tradition in Atlanta, she said. Everybody who was anybody took a table and had guests and of course there was always a mad rush for the few men in Atlanta who were both rich and attractive. She and Beauty were going of course. Louella was having a table for her sticky cousins from Milwaukee who were ghastly bores. So they, she and Beauty, would drive me in and save Ty the long ride to pick me up. "But, Jen," suddenly she left the dressing table and crossing stood over me, "what on earth will you wear?"

I said uncomfortably that I didn't know. Would my good dress, the one with leather belt do?

"Heavens, darling! That dress?" Annoyance threaded the light voice. "Really! Sally should have seen that you had decent clothes. After all—"

I intercepted her, said quietly, "Mama couldn't spend much on clothes, Aunt Eva."

"But darling, you should have at least a couple of really good dresses. Why, this dress," she designated one which waited on its hanger, "cost only 79.95. Anybody can afford 79.95."

"There are millions who can't, Aunt Eva."

Her shrug dismissed the millions who couldn't. "I just don't believe it. And it's their own fault if they can't."

My protest was half laughter. "Aunt Eva! You don't believe that."

With answering laughter she admitted her unreasonableness and taking the waiting dress from its hanger slipped it over her head. Then she was intent on the mirror again. Pulling seams straight with tender finger tips, settling shoulder lines trimly, the caressing palms running down her thighs once more. When at last the dress pleased her, she lifted her hat from its box. A minute hat and simple, but with expensiveness woven into every thread. With wary hands she adjusted it. Back a fraction—still another. Then front the tiniest bit, but—right. Then the accessories. Bracelets, one of diamonds, the other of sapphires, jangling up her arm. The wrist watch, diamonds too, clasped about her wrist. Pearls fastened about the slender throat. Perfume behind her ears, on her shoulders, at the back of her neck, its fragrance, as she sprayed, filling the room.

Another long scrutiny before the mirror, then picking up bag and gloves she turned to go. But passing me she stopped, looked down at me. "Jen," she said.

"Yes, Aunt Eva?"

"Make up your mind"—she was dead serious—"that you want the best things in life and get them. You can, you know. Any woman can, if she uses her head." Narrowing, her brown eyes stared at the wall over my head. "And don't think I'm talking nonsense." Her voice was edged with conviction. "I'm not. A woman can get what she wants." For a moment she stood motionless, her eyes gleaming with something not unlike triumph, as if she reviewed a past in which she had got what she wanted. Then she smiled down at me. "I know," she said softly, and with the husky little laugh came back to the present. "Remember it, darling. You can get *anything* you want. Even Ty McKinnon."

I would have told her that wanting Ty McKinnon was the furthermost thing from my thoughts, but I had no opportunity. With a glance at her wrist she exclaimed that she must rush like mad—that already she was late—would I bring her coat—the mink—from the wardrobe? And where did she leave her car keys?

I laid the mink coat on her shoulders and her hand groping in her handbag for the car keys she started from the room. At the door she paused, looked back over her shoulder. "And, oh yes, darling! Tomorrow we'll go shopping. You've simply got to have some decent clothes—after all."

She was gone. I heard the tap of her high-arched feet on the stairs and across the foyer, followed by the slam of the door. A moment later the car's engine raced and slackened and its wheels screamed as it flashed down the drive toward the road.

We drove into town early on Monday and went shopping at Wendells, the little dress buyer's store. A gray and rose Wendells instead of the mauve and rose I had imagined, otherwise identical with women's shops everywhere. With spacious carpeted floors and sleek black-gowned saleswomen posed as carefully, and as lifelessly, as the mannequins which displayed the clothes that must be sold.

As we stepped from the elevator the little dress buyer rushed to meet us, her welcome as effusive as if we were long-lost relatives. When she had related for Aunt Eva's benefit the story of our dining car meeting she led us to a mirrored fitting room where, after Aunt Eva was comfortably ensconced with a Coca-Cola, she brought dress after dress for her approval, twirling them on their hangers as reverently as if they were made of star dust. But when Aunt Eva carelessly, as if it were of no consequence said, "We want a really good dress for her, Miss Rose—Ty McKinnon is taking her to the Nine O'Clock," she transferred the reverence to me. Slipping a dress over my head she whispered, "Didn't I tell you? On the train? That you're one of the lucky ones?"

Stepping back she surveyed the atrocity in which she had enveloped me. "Perfect!" she breathed.

Aunt Eva was charming, she was friendly. She was also firm. "Not good for Jen at all. It simply isn't her type."

Miss Rose's smile was brightly determined, her voice humble. What did Mrs. Avery have in mind?

Aunt Eva's gesture was vague. "Something terribly smart. Ingénue-ish—but sophisticated."

Privately I considered it a large order, but Miss Rose produced it. A filmy floating thing as unadorned as a new fall of snow but with knowing in its off-shoulder line. In it I felt like the garlanded calf which wasn't important. Aunt Eva liked it.

While the fitter, gray-haired and sweet, knelt to adjust the hem, Aunt Eva and Miss Rose, with the aid of various stock girls who ran back and forth tirelessly, chose other clothes for me. A black dress, plain but "terribly smart," Aunt Eva said. A black coat equally plain. A small black hat that perched far back on my head. Handbag and shoes! Stockings and underwear! Soft pale sweaters, skirts with which to wear them—a fleecy polo coat to top them. While they chose I stood and accepted and was fitted. I was as opinionless as a mannequin, but cringed at the money spent. "We will go shopping," Aunt Eva had said and naïvely I had thought of shopping as Mama and I had done it. Going from store to store. Selecting, comparing. Telling the salesgirl that we'd come back, knowing that the budget must be juggled before decision could be made. Not like that with Aunt Eva; Aunt Eva bought generously, magnificently, the words "Charge it" and "Put it on my account" slipping from her lips easily and with assurance. I was impressed. I was awed. If she had ordered a ring for my nose I would have accepted it. And worn it.

Trailing in her wake, as she went from one department to another, was not unlike trailing in the wake of royalty. Saleswomen, with eye on future commissions no doubt, deserted less profitable customers to rush and serve her with arch and brittle smiles: "Good morning, Mrs. Avery! I want you to see the lingerie that just came in —it's too lovely—" or "I told the girls the minute I saw it. Only Mrs. Avery can wear this hat—"

Their flattery was blatant, and so obvious that I looked at Aunt Eva amused, expecting to receive an amused glance in return. She wasn't amused. She drank it in as eagerly as a starving man accepts food, seemingly unaware that for each bit of crass flattery bestowed upon *her lovely hair, her lovely skin, her lovely figure*—she paid; and the price exacted was the merchandise which they sold her shrewdly and with calculation. A dozen pairs of stockings instead of two. An entire line of cosmetics instead of the cream she requested. They used scare tactics. "The last in your color" or "Heavens only knows when we'll get *these* again" like a velvet club, and "suggested selling" like an opiate deadening her discrimination, stripping her of resistance.

I was thankful when it was over. When at last we left Wendells, and walking to the parking lot, got into the car and turned toward home. But I was troubled too. Counting to myself worriedly, I realized the money Aunt Eva had spent on me. Its total more than the few hundreds of Father's insurance. Unhappy, embarrassed I mentioned it, asked if I might partly repay her now and pay the remainder when I had found a job—or something—

She regarded me with wide surprised eyes. "Repay me? Jen—the very idea! Darling, surely you don't think—"

I protested that she had bought too many, spent too much. She brushed my protestations aside. "Darling, you'll be asked places. You'll meet my friends. I'd die if you didn't have the right clothes. After all—"

Staring at the road ahead, uncomfortable as the recipient of unwanted gifts is uncomfortable, a tiny splinter of doubt slipped into my mind. Would she, I wondered, have troubled about my clothes if there had been no friends to see me? Ashamed, I thrust the thought down, down, out of consciousness. I told myself staunchly that she was sweet, she was generous, she was loving; and I—what was Ty's word—I was a heel.

Sometimes I think whoever coined the axiom regarding first impressions stupid, whoever accepts it more so. Your first impression of a family is no more than a photograph such as your friend might show you of her husband's family. Its characters are only paper dolls and like paper dolls reveal only one side. It takes living with them, seeing them involved in the tangle of everyday life, to give them dimension, to prove that they are neither the saints in best clothes and camera smiles which the photographer managed to capture; nor the devils which your friend, being an in-law, would have you believe. They are ordinary everyday people who eat and sleep and go to the bathroom, capable of kindness and cruelty, of laughter and tears, and since they are human beings, with a sprinkling of both saint and devil in their make-up.

Before the passing of a single week I recognized the impression I had carried to bed on the night of my arrival at Aunt Eva's as adolescent and naïve, my resolution to stand like a flaming sword between her and the drunken Beauty as vainglorious as the dreams of a schoolgirl caught in the uneasy passion of her first crush. The days that slid one into another projected other sides of Beauty which obscured—at least for a time—the first one. There was the Beauty who, emerging from drunkenness, spent hours in stable and dog run, busy with the horses and dogs; who rode the black hunter with the white fetlock recklessly as if fleeing from some fiend who pursued him; or in leather jacket, with shotgun under his arm, followed his dogs into the woods at dawn, returning at dusk with quail and dove and sometimes wild duck which he dumped in the back court and which later old Tom brought to table deliciously brown and succulent.

He was as aloof, as remote, this Beauty, as the other; and as solitary. He came and went his secret way almost unspeaking. Yet he wasn't rude as he had been rude in drunkenness. And if his courtesy was threaded with irony, it was courtesy nevertheless. Passing him in the hall with Aunt Eva's morning coffee the quietude of his "Good morning, Jen" would deceive me until I saw the half-mocking smile with which he surveyed the tray I held. One such time he paused and asked, "What? No butter for the royal breakfast?"—and I glanced up at him quickly, dubiously—perhaps he was drinking again. And I saw that I had misjudged him; but before I could explain that Aunt Eva didn't take butter—that butter was fattening—he had gone on, his face bleak and aloof once more.

There was another Beauty who was neither bleak nor aloof. The one who spent hours with his children. Then he seemed almost young, and gay and tender. Helping Miss George with some task about the house I would hear their laughter ring out at stable or dog run so infectiously that I was tempted to desert my task and join them. Sometimes the three of them would disappear into the autumn woods and be gone for hours, reappearing at dusk with Trissa and Ted chattering like magpies, telling how Queenie, the liver bitch—was Trissa's story related with utter nonchalance—had flushed a covey, but Ramble had held as if carved from rock.

Sometimes as the children had their early breakfast in the little breakfast room with Phyl, who drove Trissa to school, urging her to eat, she would be tardy, it was quarter after eight—Beauty without warning would descend upon them announcing that this morning *he* would drive Trissa to school, that Ted must come along and keep him company. He'd bundle them into coats, singing slightly bawdy songs as he buttoned, sending them into shrieks of delight. Then the rush out of the back door! Piling into the front seat of the car! The car swinging down the drive, the horn sounding stridently while Phyl and I watched from the window. At such times I wondered if he tried to compensate to the children for their loneliness, because they were lonely. No other children lived near enough for companionship and though Trissa often talked of the girls at Miss Cherry's School, they never came to the house nor did she go to theirs. On rare occasions she was invited to a birthday party, and resplendent in white dress would be driven into town, clasping her tissue-wrapped present, her wide dark eyes luminous with anticipated delight. They would be weary eyes when she returned, and somewhat disillusioned, as if she had learned, as grownups learn, that parties are not the answer for loneliness.

It takes time to clear blurred first impressions. So none of this at first had form for me, or meaning. But as time went on I began to perceive the relationships that made up the household, to realize that in the way of families it was not a single design but several, each following its separate course yet at times attaining at least for the casual beholder the effect of unity. There was the house itself, foundation for all the life that went on within it, with Miss George the centrifugal force from which all labor emanated. Ordering and directing old Tom the cook and Mellie the maid, the tireless changing of linens, the laundry sent out, laundry returned and put away. Pursuing dust into corners, the washing of windows, the sudsbath for the crystal chandeliers. Stale flowers thrown out, fresh ones arranged. Food ordered, food checked and stored away in frigidaire or freezer. Food prepared, food cooked, food served and eaten or stored away again. It was a pattern that spun relentlessly, defying old Tom's periodic sprees and Mellie's frequent absences, which with Miss George at the helm would defy flood and storm and even death.

Phyl and the children formed another pattern; Beauty's solitary life still another. And though the two merged often, just as often Beauty—as if his pursuing fiend had finally caught up with him—plunged into drunkenness again, keeping to his room in the left wing, his bottle and whatever bleak thoughts he followed, his only company. When this happened Ted would go back to his paper ships. Trissa rosy from outdoors back to her knitting beside the fire. Sometimes as she sat in the big chair, her slim little hands moving with delicate precision, I saw a pensive and resigned melancholy on the fine grave face. As if she had already learned to accept whatever life might force upon her. And I was saddened. She was too young for resignation.

It did not then strike me as strange that the pattern of Aunt Eva's life should be such a thing apart, should so rarely and so lightly touch the others. It seemed natural and right that she should keep to the rooms she had had redone for herself—that her privacy should be inviolate. Even had it seemed strange I would have told myself that she was the lovely princess, that she kept to her tower because there, and only there, could she escape the ugliness which waited for her below. Yet when she did descend she transcended that ugliness and brought loveliness with her. Watching as she strolled through the lower rooms—but always with her light and resolute step—I would see her move a chair but the fraction of an inch and bring the whole room into complete balance; or her hands would hover above a bowl of flowers but an instant and the arrangement, stiff and awkward before, would achieve perfection.

She had a flair for perfection, I learned. At dinner, which was almost the only meal she ate with the family (she breakfasted in bed and usually lunched away from home) she would sit at the head of the table, the candlelight laying a patina of gold on the soft brown hair and warming her eyes to the color of sherry. Her lovely husky voice would spin a web of talk, her hand as she talked playing with the inevitable pearls at her throat. Nevertheless she would see and later mention to Miss George that the roast had been overdone or the silver in need of cleaning or the lace cloth had been not *quite* centered. She would mention it casually, the smile she flashed at Miss George warm with friendliness; and I was indignant at one such time when Miss George, taking care that Aunt Eva did not see, sent an amused glance toward Phyl, the corners of her withered mouth pulled down with derision.

Even when I carried Aunt Eva's coffee at nine her day, filled with luncheons and bridge and fittings and hairdresser, had started. I would find her propped against her pillows, the telephone on her lap. "I simply can't accept the dress, Miss Rose (or Miss Grace or Miss Nell). The seams are definitely crooked. I'll bring it in and let your fitter see what she can do." Or perhaps she had her hairdresser on the wire. "Really, Marie, the wave you gave me is impossible. I'll come by today at five and let you try—"

Hearing, I would wonder if all the women in the world obsessed with straight seams and right hair-dos were merely trying, as I thought she tried, to fill a gap in their lives. Impossible to believe her obsession was anything except escape; as unimportant as the shoddy toys for which an unhappy child might reach.

Gradually I became familiar with the pattern of her days. Coffee, her only concession to breakfast, was at nine. Then the telephone. Arranging with Sara Lou or Louella or Harriet how the day would be spent, the discussion of where they would lunch as lengthy and as weighty as a diplomatic session. *The food was better here—but* then everybody who was anybody went there. The discussion was interspersed with enlivening bits of gossip. One woman had looked a frump, with all that money too; and another had looked but simply stunning and how she did it on her dinky little income. Harmless enough for the most part, it was the sort of thing disseminated by women over morning telephones everywhere. Yet some of it was not so harmless. I heard, and at great length, of Lillian (Lillian who I was never to know) whose second husband had died suddenly—the second to die suddenly, mind you, and how lucky! For both had left her scads of money. After all you couldn't help but wonder, especially when everybody in Atlanta knew that she'd been carrying on like mad with—

Telephoning done, she would get up, slip her feet into petit point mules, pull a chiffon robe about her slimness, preening before the mirror as she tied it. Sometimes she'd cry with the artless candor of a child, "I'm pretty, aren't I, Jen?" When I told her gravely, because I meant it, that she was lovely she'd throw the small proud head back with the throaty three-noted laugh. "I can't help it if I'm vain. Can I?"

While she bathed I brought order to the lovely confusion she left in a trail behind her. Put the mules in the shoe bag, the fragile nightgown in its satin case. I loved doing it despite Miss George's grumbled warning "She'll run your legs off if you let her." Against Aunt Eva's "I need you," it had no power.

After a few days it came to be routine that as she sat at the dressing table and "fixed" her face she would dictate thank-you notes and I would write them for her. "Mrs. J. Anthony Pierce," she would say, smoothing cream into her lucent skin. "Heavens! That bore! Just say 'Thank you for a lovely evening,' Jen. It was too ghastly, darling. Not one attractive man!"

There were days though when there were no notes to be written. On one such day as she sat at her dressing table she commanded playfully, "Talk to me, Jen. I'm bored to tears." Obediently I groped in my mind for a subject which might interest her—mentioned the question of civil rights which was receiving headline attention in the papers and had inspired an article by one Ralph McGill, whose thoughtful columns I read and liked. But she would have none of it. "No, no, no!" she cried. "It's too absurd, all this fuss about Negroes! Not that I dislike Negroes. I suppose there are actually some good ones. But I certainly don't want to sit next to them in a restaurant. After all—"

Intent on her make-up she didn't see my shocked stare of disbelief or realize the anger which—remembering Father who seemingly incapable of fury could become furious at discrimination against any man—swept me. Then I saw her reflection in the mirror and my anger receded. This was the South, I told myself. She was the product of the South. As logical to expect honeysuckle to concern itself with the rotting house on which it climbed. I searched for another topic.

Every day wherever she went the moment of departure created a small tempest. She would take a last scrutiny in the mirror, then, assured that the "really good dress," the chic hat, the mink coat, the diamond bracelets were as they should be, would tell me to have Tom bring the car around. She would descend the stairs swiftly crying that she was "terribly late"; pause to drop brief kisses on Ted and Trissa and start out the door groping in her handbag as she went for the car keys. She'd exclaim "My keys! My keys!"—she knew she had put them in the bag—and where on earth could they be? And the family would concentrate on a search for the keys. Trissa would run up to Aunt Eva's room. Miss George and I would look into possible hiding places frantically, the hunt prolonged until poised in the door she would cry, "I've got them! I've got them! Imagine! In my bag all the time!" With another hurried good-by she'd rush out to the car. We'd hear the car door slam, the scream of her tires on the gravel drive as she headed for the highway. Then the house would settle to quiet again.

Her departures, her frantic last-minute cry of "My keys! My keys!" were, I perceived, part of the family design which gradually became as familiar to me as the shape of my hand. It started, that design, with early breakfast for Phyl, the children and me, with Phyl and Trissa dashing off to school, Ted and I watching them go. Afterward he and I would go to the sitting room. I, to wait until nine when I must carry Aunt Eva's coffee, Ted to play his solitary games. Pretending to read the *Constitution* I would watch him as he moved his toy soldiers or sailed his fleet of paper ships, and it struck me that he was a strange unchildlike child; that he played, not as other children play, but with motionless face and withdrawn eyes as if his game absorbed only the surface of his mind and held so little interest that behind his eyes his thoughts continued to weave somberly. He was a strange child in other ways too. With his silver-gilt hair and ice-blue eyes he had the cherubic charm which silly women run to enfold with small ecstatic cries. I doubt if the silliest of them would dare, after one glance from his contemptuous eyes, enfold Ted. Passing him one day I, unable to resist the curls which shone like liquid amber in the sun, reached and playfully tousled them. He withdrew from my hand with such regal arrogance (as if I had intruded) that I was startled into discomfiture. Later I spoke of it to Phyl somewhat ruefully. "He acts as if he resents affection," I said. Her quiet answer puzzled me. "All of his life," she said quietly, "he's been searching for affection."

His nightmares were part of the pattern too. So much a part that I became accustomed to the frantic scream curdling against the night, to Phyl's bare feet speeding to his room, to her crooning voice as it banished his fear. Sometimes wrenched from sleep I too would go to his room. I would find little Trissa white-faced and subdued watching from her bed and Ted, his eyes bright and frantic, clinging to Phyl, as if in Phyl lay his only salvation.

One such night I watched with Phyl until Ted and Trissa had dropped off to sleep again. Then quietly we went into her room where as if exhausted she sank onto the side of the bed. Standing above her, my arms crossed over my chest, for I was cold, I remarked idly that it was really too bad that he had to have so many of these things. Could it be, I asked, that he ate too heavy a dinner at night?

She shook her head wearily. "No. We're careful about that."

"Do you have any idea what does cause them?"

She only shook her head again.

"It's probably because he is overimaginative." My voice made light of it. "And keeps things bottled up within himself."

"Perhaps," she said. "Perhaps."

"I wonder what he dreams that frightens him so? Do you know if he's ever been frightened? With ghosts, or scary stories?"

Again she moved her head in negation. "No. It isn't that sort of a dream."

"Do you mean," I asked slowly, "he dreams just one dream?"

With a nod of assent she said, "The same dream. Over and over."

"The same dream? Oh! A recurrent dream." Shivering in my nightgown I tried to remember what Professor Weigand had said in psychology class of recurrent dreams. Of Phyl I asked, "What is the dream?"

Folding her elbows on the foot of the bed she rested her chin on them and stared into space. "He dreams he is in the car—"

"Oh surely!" I was skeptical. "He isn't frightened of a car?"

"It isn't the car that frightens him." She was impatient with me. "It's when the car begins to slide down the drive."

"I see," I said and I did. I could understand how a small boy might—alone in the car and it sliding—be frightened.

Phyl continued to stare into space. "In the dream it is dark, he says. And the car goes faster and faster. He sees the river coming nearer and nearer—"

I said, "Yes"—waited for her to go on.

She stood up then and shook her shoulders as if to rid them of a burden. "That's it."

"You mean that is all of the dream?"

"That's all. Just before the car reaches the river he screams and wakes."

I stood there in my nightgown, no longer eager to talk glibly of my psychology teacher and recurrent dreams. Professor Weigand's dry pedantic voice was in my ears again. "The dream of falling," it was saying, "is a symbol of the death wish. Let us take the case of Miss X—" Did Ted's dream of sliding, sliding symbolize the death wish? Surely not. Why would young Ted wish to die? Yet even as I thought it his face flashed before me, its strange stillness, the eyes with their cold brightness—a light, I suddenly realized, that you see in the eyes of those who endure pain.

Shivering with something deeper than cold I asked Phyl haltingly, "Why should Ted dream a dream like that?"

She came and stood before me and I saw that the thin face had hardened, that the eyes were wide and unhappy. "It's Eva's fault. All of it. The dreams and the bottled-up things and his—his unhappiness."

Incredulously I asked, "Aunt Eva's fault?" I was indignant and defensive. "That's ridiculous!"

"Is it?" She threw the words at me. "Well, stay here long enough. You'll see."

"But how *could* it be her fault? Why, she's sweet with him."

"Sweet!" Her mouth curled. "Oh yes, she's sweet! She's sweet with everybody."

For a moment we faced each other, almost angrily. Then she slumped as if the defiance had been drawn from her body. With a despairing gesture of her hand she turned to get into bed. "You must go to bed too, Jen. You'll be dead in the morning."

Inanely I said yes, I must. And telling her good-night I returned to my room and bed; but not to sleep. For a long time I lay straining into the dark, my thoughts jumbled and confused. Ted's nightmares! Phyl's eyes! Somber, brooding, or glazed with hostility. And what Phyl had said of Aunt Eva. It was not until I recalled what Aunt Eva told me of Phyl. "She hates everybody when she feels badly—me most of all," that the confusion began to clear. Phyl didn't feel well. She hated everybody, including Aunt Eva. Aunt Eva was right. Phyl adored Ted too much. Only a neurotic, I thought drowsily as I floated off to sleep, would blame Aunt Eva for his nightmares. Darling Aunt Eva!

Next morning Ted's nightmare, in the way of night terrors, sank into the unimportance which to me it seemed to merit. I felt somewhat ridiculous because I had dramatized what was neither strange nor dramatic. Children everywhere had nightmares. Doting sisters were often jealous of their brothers' wives. In every family there were behavior patterns which varied from what we are accustomed to think of as "normal." Surely I did not expect Aunt Eva's household to escape them. I must accept them and try to adapt my own life to them.

However, try as I might, I was unable at first to fit into any of the various patterns of the house. I fluctuated from one to another, not really belonging, yet without pattern of my own. Mornings I devoted to Aunt Eva: carried her coffee, ran her bath, straightened her room; writing, as she dressed, her thank-you notes, sensing that with these small services I pleased her. When she had gone, after the inevitable search for "the keys," which just as inevitably she found in her bag, I would drift to the sitting room; perhaps wander aimlessly in the yard kicking the leaves which blanketed the ground; or go to my room to putter at trivial tasks, conscious whatever I did that it was only a way of speeding time which seemed endless. But as time went on I gradually began to weave a pattern of my own. Miss George yielding to my constant offering allowed me to iron Aunt Eva's fragile underwear or wash out sweaters for the children, or on days when Mellie failed to appear I set the table for dinner. Her permission was reluctant though. "You're not a servant," she told me tartly. "Don't start being one."

It was in those first patternless days however that Phyl and I became friends. Often in the afternoons we'd walk, with Trissa and Ted, in the woods that surrounded the place or along the unpaved road that led away from Atlanta. Phyl and I sauntered along while Trissa and Ted with the inexhaustible energy of children would race to see who could first touch a certain tree or futilely chase the bright-eyed, scampering squirrels. As we strolled Phyl and I would talk—the idle sort of talk with which women beguile time. About Thomas Wolfe and Erskine Caldwell and William Faulkner, mixed in a hodge-podge with the right way to fry chicken and the position of the Negro in the South, sharpened with a seasoning of Russia and communism. A bewildering welter, but through it we came somehow to understanding and liking.

One day, a gray day with a hint of winter in its sharpened air, we came of course to the subject of love. I asked Phyl if she'd ever been in love. She parried my question with one of her own. "Have you?"

Doubtfully I said I didn't know. There had been a chap—oh terribly young, hardly more than a boy—in Father's class at the University. Father had asked him for tea one Sunday afternoon. And after that he came almost every Sunday. He and I (his name was Paul) had walked in Central Park and gone to the Metropolitan Museum and to occasional concerts at Carnegie Hall. I had been, well, fond of him. But love? Honestly I didn't know.

"Then it wasn't love." Phyl was firm. "When it's love—you know it."

But how did you know? I queried. After all there was love and there was the biological urge. How could you tell which was which? Did love come first? Or the urge?

She laughed her high sweet laugh. "Jen, that's like asking which comes first, the chicken or the egg."

"You know an awful lot about it?" I was accusing. "Have you been in love?"

Yes, she said, she had.

I remembered the man I had seen with her in the foyer the afternoon of my arrival—the man who had held her in his arms. "You are in love now, aren't you?" I half teased. She only laughed but I would not be put off. "I saw him—and you."

"What are you talking about?" she demanded sharply. But still pretending to tease, I wouldn't tell. I only nodded wisely as one who possessed a great secret. "I thought him terribly attractive," I said slyly.

She stopped and faced me. "When did you see him?" she asked quietly and something in her voice warned me that I must tease no more. I told her then about that first afternoon. How I had hidden on the little balcony, too shy to call to them; had waited until they'd gone. As I told, I knew from the guarded expression that slipped over her face that she too remembered, that now she wondered how much I had seen and heard.

When I had finished, somewhat lamely, we began to walk again, but in silence, mine uncomfortable. I felt like a Peeping Tom who inadvertently reveals that he has seen what he was never meant to see. Phyl seemed equally uncomfortable. She walked with her eyes down, and her face was thoughtful.

Our silence held until Ted and Trissa ran back to inform us with great excitement that they'd almost caught a squirrel. When they had run ahead again, she spoke.

"He is Judson Poole," she said monotonously, without expression, "raised—Atlanta would say—on the wrong side of the tracks. He went to work in Father's mills when he was sixteen. He was smart and ambitious and Father liked him. He sent him to the University just as he did Beauty, and Jud has been like one of the family. Even lived with us, until a year or so ago. Then he moved away to live by himself. To a house," her hand pointed, "down the road. He doesn't come to our place now—at least not often. Only when he wants to talk business with Beauty. He runs the mills for Beauty, you see."

"I see," I said lamely.

We walked on in silence. Until suddenly she halted and faced me. "Jen," she said.

"Yes, Phyl?"

"I don't know what you saw or heard that afternoon when you were on the balcony. But do you think—whatever it was—you could just forget it?"

"Why of course, Phyl."

"I hate to ask it of you. I know how fond you are of—of Eva. But please. Don't mention it to Eva."

"I won't," I promised, and even as I promised felt a twinge of guilt as if in promising I was disloyal to Aunt Eva. Stupidly I tried to make amends for that disloyalty. "I wish you wouldn't feel as you do about Aunt Eva, Phyl." I made my voice gentle and reasoning. "She's awfully fond of you."

Her hand dropped away from my arm and the almost indiscernible shadow that slipped over her face warned me. "Not that I'll tell her, Phyl," I reassured her hastily. "I won't, I promise."

She said, "Thank you, Jen," and we continued down the road in the gray November afternoon and after a while began to talk again. But I had a feeling of frustration and chagrin, as if a door had been half opened, then closed again in my face.

Father told me of talking with a man of great age who said that when you're very old and look back at your life, it is like looking down on a desolate and empty plain peopled by shadows. The few people and incidents you really remember stand out like great trees. "We say," he told Father, " 'I remember when I was four,' but we really remember only one person, or one day, or one incident that happened during the year when we were four. All the other days have vanished into limbo."

Perhaps the old man spoke truly, for that first Thanksgiving Day at Aunt Eva's remains as firmly placed in my memory as a green tree on a plain. Perhaps because it was the beginning of so many things, the first act of a play that was to move inevitably to its end; perhaps also because it was the day on which I began to grow up.

It was a wonderful day, bright and cold and with leaves sifting slowly to the earth outside. Inside the fires crackled on the hearths when at eight I went down wanting coffee. As I ate my solitary eggs and bacon in the breakfast room, Miss George bustled about baking pies in the kitchen while Old Tom stuffed the turkey, and the spicy fragrance of mincemeat and pumpkin and cloves and ginger permeated the air. I felt the little stir of excitement which as a child I had felt on special days.

It was not, it developed, very special. Phyl came down in the shabby shirt and jodhpurs as I drank the last of my coffee. In a few moments she was gone on Mimi, the little mare. Trissa and Ted, after their breakfasts, put on coats and caps and went into the yard. And a few moments later Beauty, in leather jacket and with his gun under his arm, disappeared into the woods, Queenie the liver bitch sniffing at his heels.

Through the window I watched Ted and Trissa as their eyes followed him with longing. Wondering why he had left them behind, I went out the back door to where they played. When I had inspected the "pretty rocks" they had gathered and had admired them sufficiently I casually asked them why they had not gone with their father. Trissa's eyes looked troubled. "He said he had to do something special this morning," she evaded, adding valiantly, "but he said he'd take us with him this afternoon."

I left them to take up Aunt Eva's coffee, stopping in the kitchen to get the tray Mellie was preparing. Miss George, whipping cream, her tongue whirring as fast as the beater, prodded Old Tom to make haste. But he continued to move about the kitchen with his leisured and regal mien, paying as much attention to Miss George as he would to an annoying fly. In the exploding skyrocket of her words I gathered that we would eat Thanksgiving dinner not at the traditional hour of seven but at two o'clock.

I turned a surprised gaze her way. Did she know, I asked, that Aunt Eva had a very special luncheon at the club, that she couldn't be here for Thanksgiving dinner if we ate at two.

She gave me one of her wry glances. "I know." Her voice was tart. "I got my orders."

I took the tray and going into the breakfast room filled the small coffee urn from the large one. When I turned I saw that Miss George had followed me and stood, her hands folded on her stomach.

"Child," she said, "I didn't mean to speak so sharp. You must overlook what a crotchety old woman does and says."

I laughed at her with affection. Her peering eyes were sad and bewildered and her voice, as she continued, was sad too. "I don't know what's happening to the world," she said. "Wild horses couldn't have dragged my mother away from home on Thanksgiving."

Lightly I pointed out that the world was changing, that life was different. She shook her head. "No," she said, "you couldn't use that as an excuse." She looked at me shrewdly. "I'll bet your mother stayed home on Thanksgiving."

It opened up for me the memory of Thanksgiving in the old flat. Mama cooking the turkey, Father making the salad and building up the fire on the hearth to glowing perfection. Some student of Father's (who, Father suspected, wouldn't have Thanksgiving turkey otherwise) would be the only guest. The centerpiece of artificial fruit and gourds taken from the closet shelf where it lay tissue wrapped all year was brought out for this special day. There would be wine with dinner, usually sparkling burgundy with Father making a ceremony of its chilling and explaining to the impressed young student that whatever connoisseurs might say, burgundy was the wine for turkey. After dinner, sitting before the fire with the bowl of nuts and passing the single pair of nutcrackers from one to the other, we listened to the radio, to a symphony or maybe a football game. At dusk we had cold turkey sandwiches in the kitchen and mustard pickles, and the last of the plum pudding. None of it was expensive or "smart," but it was beautiful because it was warm with love.

Only when I saw that my tears were dropping on the lace mat, leaving a damp spot, did I come back to the present. I looked at Miss George remorsefully. But with "You, Jen! Go on, take the tray to her. I'm an old fool," she marched back into the kitchen, and I went toward the stairs.

Aunt Eva, her eyes bright with excitement, replaced the telephone receiver in its cradle as I entered. "Darling," she cried, "I just heard the most stupendous news from Harriet. Monk Lyons is in town! And he'll be at the Nine O'Clock tonight."

Putting the tray on her lap I asked who Monk Lyons might be.

She laughed up at me, making a little "mouth." "Jen, really—you are *too* naïve. Imagine not knowing who Monk Lyons is."

"Should I know?" I asked.

"Of course. He's known everywhere. In New York and Washington and—everywhere."

I sat on the foot of her bed. "Because he's famous—or notorious?" I teased. Her little laugh was mischievous. "A little of both, darling. He's the Atlanta boy who really made good. He's on all sorts of boards in Washington and friendly with the President. And of course he's horribly rich—but horribly." Pensively she added, "All because of Ty McKinnon's great-grandfather."

I looked at her wide-eyed. "Why Ty McKinnon?"

"Because Ty McKinnon's great-grandfather invented a tacky little soft drink and made all that money. Because of Monk Lyons."

I was becoming confused and I said so.

She explained, "It's like this, darling. Ty's great-grandfather invented the tacky little drink, but Monk Lyons bought stock in it and promoted it. And now," she spread her hands, "it's *terrific.* Simply terrific. They drink it all over the world."

"Like Coca-Cola?" I suggested and she said yes like Coca-Cola. Not as good as Coca-Cola but that didn't matter. For Monk Lyons and millions of dollars in advertising had actually choked it down people's throats. And now—her eyes sparkled—he would be at the Nine O'Clock tonight, probably at Ty's table.

Inwardly I thought "Oh dear," and wished I could stay at home. Until now I hadn't minded the Nine O'Clock Ball, had really looked forward to it. After all it was my first ball. I had imagined Ty and me at a little table for two where I wouldn't feel shy or awkward. But now all changed. Instead it would be a party. With Monk Lyons and Sue of course—and Lord knows who else. If only I didn't have to go, could develop a headache or flu. I suggested it but Aunt Eva laughed.

"You're crazy, Jen. Why you'll be the envy of every woman at the Nine O'Clock. With Ty McKinnon! And Monk Lyons. Darling, if you could only realize how Atlanta women simply scramble to get Monk for dinners. And that old frump of a mother."

"Mother?" I was doubly fearful now. "Monk Lyons' mother?"

"Yes, darling. Aunt Min! Everyone in Atlanta calls her that. They used to live here, you know. And she's down here with Monk. So she'll be at Ty's table too. Be very careful with her, Jen. She has a tongue like carbolic acid." Her coffee finished, she handed me her tray. "Darling, will you run my bath like an angel? I certainly don't want to be late for this luncheon. There's no telling—"

No telling *what?* I was never to know for her voice died. And unhappily I went to turn on her bath. I was seeing myself at the Nine O'Clock at Ty's party, awkward and saying the wrong things and bored to death. I thought of the new dress hanging in my closet. So miraculous when it came! Now transformed suddenly into a costume for execution. Watching the tub fill I wondered if drowning was dreadfully uncomfortable.

Even when Aunt Eva had gone with the usual flurry about her keys and with promises to be home early, my spirits refused to rise. Thanksgiving dinner for all its deliciousness might have been—for me—the last meal of the condemned. Listlessly I heard Phyl tell Beauty as he carved the turkey that she and Judson Poole were going to ride after dinner, that Judson might stop in for supper and keep her company while we were at the ball. I was envious. She would stay at home and sit by the fire with Judson and not have to worry about saying and doing the proper thing.

Beauty was piling turkey and dressing and cranberry sauce on the plates while Old Tom served. He suggested that Phyl must ask Judson to stay the night. "There's a couple of things I want to talk over with him."

"You can talk them over when you get home," Phyl said almost crossly. "You know Judson doesn't like to stay overnight."

He lifted his eyebrows at her. "I may not be in condition when I get home. The only way I can take the Nine O'Clock is to—" He broke off, looked at Ted and Trissa who sat on either side of him, was suddenly gay. "Here, you rascals. If we're going to the woods after dinner you'll have to eat up."

With happy giggles they complied and for a little all of us were busy with food. Then Phyl asked with elaborate casualness. "By the way, Beauty! Did you attend to—that matter this morning?"

With equal casualness Beauty said that he had; but little Trissa, ever sensitive to what went on about her, asked anxiously, "What matter, Daddy?"

At her question he laid down his fork and his face was thoughtful, his hand flexing and unflexing on the arm of his chair. Then very gently he said, "I had to shoot Queenie."

Ted and Trissa turned shocked faces toward him. "Shoot Queenie?" Trissa's mouth trembled. "Oh Daddy! No. Oh you loved her so—"

"Trissa," I could hardly believe the gentleness in his voice. "You know why I had to do it. You saw her when she had that last fit."

Phyl said sharply, "You shouldn't have told them. They're too young."

Beauty spooning more cranberry sauce on the children's plates said quietly, "They're not too young to know when a dog is sick and can't be cured it must be put out of the way. Before it passes the taint on." He turned first to Ted, then to Trissa. "You understand that, don't you?"

Trissa gave him a tremulous "Yes, Daddy. It's just that Queenie was so—so beautiful."

Old Tom bearing the plum pudding with its aura of flickering flame consigned the liver bitch, for the time anyway, to oblivion. Beauty, as he served it, looked over at me. "When we go to the woods," he said gravely, "I think Jen had better go with us. I think she has the Nine O'Clock jitters." A disease, he explained when the children demanded to know, that attacked people when they were very young and very foolish. As he explained, he laughed at me down the table.

We went to the woods, Beauty and the children and me, with the dogs, except for Queenie of course, trailing us. None mentioned her as we scuffled through the thick-piled leaves. Beauty, at the insistence of the children, sang little songs. Strange songs with a weird primitive beat. Songs which, Beauty said, had come down through his family from slave days. Listening I was fascinated not only by the songs but by the folk stories in which they played a part.

"O—didn't you kill Mr. Kingdeer's goats?
Sho nuf', sho nuf', yes I did."

He brought the story of Mr. Kingdeer to an end, was instantly besieged by Trissa and Ted for another. So he told of Mr. Terrapin who owed his escape from the soup kettle to the song he sang for the admiring Negro cook:

"Git dat tangle to kill dat Oo-o
Git dat tangle to kill dat Oo-o."

Both stories and songs were forgotten however when coming to a spot where the Chattahoochee, sallow and sullen, coiled about a tiny cove. Beauty asked if we didn't want to build a fire. Ted and Trissa were delighted. With great industry they began to run hither and thither gathering dead wood while Beauty, clearing a circle of its leaves, placed small dry twigs together and lighted them, adding larger twigs and wood as the fire grew. When, with a great snapping, it was burning brightly he sprawled beside it, a child cupped in each arm. I across from them guarded the fire, held it with a stout stick within its destined circle.

At first we were too intent on the fire for talk and Trissa's dark eyes were dream-shadowed. Then Ted, as if bored with the stillness, pulled away from Beauty's arm and sat erect. "Sing 'My Lady,' Daddy," he ordered.

So Beauty sang "My Lady" while the fire crackled and the leaves floated groundward and the Chattahoochee murmured.

"My lady—my lady with eyes so blue
And heart that is cold as April dew
Oh my! Oh my! Oh my!
My lady for whom I would die."

It was a plaintive little melody and he sang it softly, gently, his eyes—dream-shadowed too—fixed on the flames.

"My lady's a cheat and a liar too
She lies when the truth would better do
Oh my! Oh my! Oh my!
My lady for whom I would die."

His voice sank, died and his eyes, still intent on the flames, drooped with brooding thoughtfulness. Then Ted, his head tilted like a robin's, peered up at him. "Go on, Daddy. Sing the rest."

He came out of his absorption to laugh down at Ted. "Okay, Son."

"My lady is warm when she wants my gold
But when she can't get it, so cold, so cold
Oh my! Oh my! Oh my!
My lady for whom I would die."

Ted, content against Beauty's shoulder again, said, "He's going to kill her now. Go on, Daddy—"

"Some day I'll kill her and deep, so deep
I'll bury my lady and then I'll sleep
Oh my! Oh my! Oh my!
My lady for whom I would die."

His voice died again, we were unspeaking again, except for the rustle of the leaves and the unchanging voice of the river. Then I saw that Ted was crying—not his customary passionate protest, but a dreadful noiseless slipping of tears down his face and with his eyes wide and unseeing like the eyes of the blind. Beauty following my glance saw too; and sitting erect he pulled Ted about and looked into his face narrowly. "What's the matter, Son?" He spoke sharply. His voice was almost rough.

The tear-streaked face turned up to his blindly. "I can't help it, Daddy. It hurts so. When the lady has to die."

His father held him close, and his eyes staring across at me were as unseeing as Ted's. Then he said quietly, "She's only a lady in a story, Son. Let's forget about her. Let's—" Suddenly he was gay and teasing. "—let's talk about Jen. She's unhappy too. Because she has to go to a ball. It proves, Son, what silly things can make a woman unhappy." His laugh was rollicking, as if on it he would lift Ted above pain.

Trissa, as always, tried to help, cried out excitedly, "Oh Jen! You're not! Why you'll have a wonderful time. You ought to see her new dress, Daddy. It's out of this world."

"I'm sure it is." He met Trissa's seriousness with equal seriousness.

"But, Jen." Trissa struck by a sudden thought rose to her knees and looked across at me earnestly. "Flowers!" She turned to Beauty worriedly. "Daddy, she must have flowers."

"She must indeed!" Beauty agreed darkly.

"You could send her some," Trissa suggested tentatively.

Beauty's nod was impressive. "I could indeed. But I hardly think it necessary, Trissa. Undoubtedly Ty McKinnon is peddling his soft drink on street corners this very minute so he can send Jen flowers."

Trissa clasping her hands ecstatically sank back. "Oh, Jen will look—" she searched for a word, found—"*scrumptious*, won't she, Daddy?"

"I'm sure of it." He still played at being serious. "I'm sure that she'll put on the new dress and do her hair a new way and put on her war paint—and look exactly like every other woman at the ball."

I laughed across the fire at him. "You sound as if you consider that an unworthy accomplishment."

"I do. I like you much better as you are. In your sweater and skirt, and your hair a little blown. You are you. Not a sawdust doll. They come a dime a dozen. Now you, if you had the sense to know it, belong to a rarer species."

His manner toward me was exactly the same he would use toward Trissa—or any child; and a vague discontent stirred deep, deep inside me. When would I be old enough to be treated like a grownup? I wondered. How did one grow up? I did not know that before this day was done I would have started to grow up; and that then, much as I might desire it, I could never be a child again.

The air was colder. The big rosy apple of a sun was slipping down the western sky. Beauty, rousing, said we must put out the fire and go. He sent the children running to whistle up the dogs which had roamed off. Kneeling, he and I began to beat the fire into oblivion. He with a dead branch, I with a slab of rock I found close by, together annihilated each small persistent flame, watching lest it revive. We heard the children's voices thin and sweet in the distance as they called the dogs. But prowling restlessly as if they were searching for something, the dogs refused to come. Otherwise the cathedral stillness was unbroken.

Beauty, pausing in his battle with the flames, watched the dogs for a second. "They are looking for Queenie," he said quietly. "I buried her just around that curve." His eyes were hot with pain. And I remembered what Phyl had said of him: "He loves all animals. Sometimes I think more than people."

Impulsively I cried, "How could you bear to shoot her?"

He looked at me surprised. "Why, I had to. The vets couldn't help her. You see, it was an inherited thing—"

"But couldn't you just have penned her up? Did you have to shoot her?"

"Don't you understand? She would have passed it on. When you get a thing like that, a bad thing bred so deep in the blood and bone it can't be got out, a quick bullet is the only way."

He turned his attention to the fire again, smothered a last eager little tongue. Only a bed of charred wood and ashes remained. Still he continued to kneel there.

I looked at him surprised. "The fire is out."

"Yes," he said. "I was just wishing—" he broke off, finally went on. "If all fires could only be smothered as easily."

The bleak far-away look in his eyes told me that his thoughts had moved to a plane where mine could not follow, so kneeling there beside him I was silent. Then he stood and taking my hands, pulled me up beside him. For a moment he held my hands, looked into my eyes steadily. At something, some dark force, some potency I saw in his, I was seized by an inward trembling that crept from my legs up my thighs, even to my breasts. Then abruptly he freed my hands and we were walking through the leaves toward the children; he silent and intent, I shrinking lest in walking he should touch me, but rapt and blinded as if I had stumbled from the dark into a dazzling light.

The children ran to meet us. Chattering like birds they held up twigs of dogwood heavy with scarlet berries. Beauty took one and laughing turned and clumsily, as a man is clumsy, thrust it in my hair. Then whistling to the dogs, who came obediently now, he turned toward the house.

On the carved chest in the foyer we found a florist's box with, to Trissa's delight, my name upon it. With her and Beauty and Ted watching I opened it and lifted the three huge pink camellias from its tissue. Trissa could manage only, "Oh Jen!" But Beauty's eyes were mocking. "I see that Nova Covas sold well today. Or am I mistaken?"

"You are not mistaken." I read the card which said *For my girl, from Ty*. Silly Ty, but nice. And taking the box of camellias I marched to the kitchen to put them in the frigidaire. But when I went to my room I put the twig of dogwood in a glass of water and stood it on my bedside table. I would see it there the last thing at night and the first thing each morning.

I brushed my hair, smoothed lipstick on my mouth and went down to the sitting room again hoping, though I wouldn't admit it, that Beauty and the children would still be there. But they weren't. The room was empty except for Judson Poole who stood beside the hearth, his back to the fire. His quick eyes slid over me indifferently when I entered. His voice was indifferent too. "You're Jen, I suppose."

I told him that I was. "And you're Judson Poole. I've heard Phyl speak of you."

He had no comment for this and, as if he disdained the trivial talk which courtesy demanded, began to turn the pages of the magazine he held. Obviously, he wished to be rid of me. Yet it caused me no more embarrassment or awkwardness than if he had been an animal. Somehow he reminded me of an animal. A stag perhaps—or a leopard. Strong and bright-eyed and absolved from man-made custom and law. I would not have been surprised to learn that he lived in a cave and foraged for his food.

I asked him where the others were, Beauty and Phyl and the children. He looked up from his magazine long enough to tell me Phyl was changing in her room, Beauty making drinks in the kitchen. The children? He didn't know. Probably outdoors.

They were. For when I crossed and sat on the window seat at the end of the room I heard their voices, sweet and shrill, through the windowpane. But I didn't see them. I saw nothing as I stared out of the window. I was absorbed by the new thoughts and new emotions which moiled within me, which had moiled since that moment in the woods. It was as if that dark potency I'd seen in Beauty's eyes had raised a curtain from over a corner of my mind and revealed that of which I had not even been aware, dared not be aware. Now I was aware of the way he came through a door, of his mocking laughter, of his gentleness that had a traitor touch. Aware that when he drank in his room a sickening darkness crouched over the house.

I was aware now. And waiting on the window seat for him to come in the door again I could have died with shame.

It wasn't Beauty who next came in the door. It was Aunt Eva. She paused within it peering (I had often thought she needed glasses) at the hearth. Then she saw Judson Poole and with a tiny exclamation went toward him lightly. "Jud." Her voice sang his name, a muted song, sung for him alone. Poised before him, she—or so it seemed to me—curved toward him. "You've come back," she said softly.

Apparently unaffected by her welcome he moved away, waved his hand toward the window seat and me. "Been getting acquainted with your niece," he said dryly.

She wheeled and peering, saw me. For just a second I thought she was annoyed. But her face crumpled with startled laughter. "Darling," she cried, "I didn't see you." Moving swiftly she touched a lamp chain and filled the room with mellow glow. "No wonder. Why the dark?"

There was no need to tell her why even if I could. For Beauty came in the door with a tray of drinks, the children tagging at his heels. Promptly Aunt Eva forgot me. She must drop soft kisses on their cheeks, darting from Beauty to Ted, from Ted to Trissa like a restless butterfly, declaring as she darted that she was a wreck—she simply must lie down before she changed, or she'd look like a hag at the Nine O'Clock.

She started to leave the room but in the door paused and looked back at Jud, who regarded her through noncommittal eyes. "You're staying for supper, Jud?"

Beauty, giving Jud a drink, answered her. He had asked Jud to stay the night, he said. They had business to talk over. Talking, he served Trissa and Ted small glasses of chocolate milk.

Aunt Eva's eyes which had circled to him as he spoke came back to Jud. "How nice." The words were meant for Jud. "Like old times." Gravely she added, "'The wonderful old times."

For another moment she stood in the doorway looking back at him but he didn't speak, didn't even look her way, and she laughed her soft three-noted laugh. Then calling that I had better think about dressing for the Nine O'Clock, she went along the corridor toward the stairs. Soon I followed her; but reluctantly. I wanted to stay in the shabby room with its open fire, with the children and Jud and Beauty. Suddenly it had become the most wonderful room in the world.

Dressed I looked in the mirror at the tall girl with the upswept hair and the white dress which floated mistily. At her bare shoulders rising from the knowing neckline. She was slim, her freckles were hidden by powder and rouge, her mouth curved red and alluring. I liked her. But she was a stranger and had no kinship with me.

Even little Trissa, perched on the side of the bed, realized it. She cried, bouncing in excessive admiration, "Jen, you're scrumptious. Like Cinderella after the godmother—but you don't look like you at all."

Pinning Ty's camellias on my bodice I thought: this is my first ball, my first ball dress. It is the sort of thing you tell your grandchildren about. I pictured myself, old and withered, telling a little girl, like Trissa perhaps, or a blond cherub like Ted, "It was such a beautiful dress. White and floating. My beau sent me pink camellias to wear." I would add, "I was terribly happy and excited." But that would be a little lie. No matter how old I might come to be I would never forget that on the night of my first ball I was neither happy nor excited. I was terrified of all the secret thoughts which Beauty's eyes had uncovered for me; shameful thoughts of the body and vague conceptions of the delights the body might hold. They were terrible thoughts and I was ashamed. Yet I thought them beautiful.

Trissa said, "Aren't you ready to go down?" And I said yes—I was ready. I picked up the velvet cape Aunt Eva had loaned me, knowing it would please her, asked Trissa to carry it for me. Then we went down to the back sitting room to wait for Aunt Eva.

When we entered all of them, Beauty and Jud and Phyl, looked up. Jud's shocked voice ejaculated "My God!" but Phyl, snuggled in a chair with Ted, smiled at me and her "You're lovely, Jen!" was warm. Beauty at the hearth with the inevitable glass in his hand said nothing, but only quirked his brows at me.

The new Jen had a self-confidence however that the old one had lacked. So, smiling I dropped a little curtsy before him. "Do I please you?" I asked saucily.

"Well," he drawled his words lazily, "you look older. And very grown-up."

"But a dime a dozen?" I reminded him.

"As you are—a dime a dozen."

His carping could not spoil my moment of triumph—somehow I knew he did not mean it. Nevertheless the triumph was short-lived. Aunt Eva came in the room; and against the perfection of her gown, more bronze than gold, and the tiny mink jacket with its wide sleeves, I was just a girl in her first party dress, awkward and immature; and she realized it. After a first swift glance she, ignoring the others, crossed to where I stood. And bidding me stand correctly, straightened the lines of my skirt, settled the off-shoulder line, unpinned and repinned the camellias at another angle. Apparently she was oblivious to the others, unconscious of their watching eyes, but I wasn't. I saw Jud's bored and cynical, Phyl's bright with a hostility which puzzled me and Beauty's coolly speculative above his ironic smile.

Trissa standing at my elbow and of course absorbed cried, "Oh Jen! You look simply scrumptious! When you were young, Mama, were you as pretty as Jen?"

If Aunt Eva, pinning an errant lock of hair, heard she did not answer.

But Trissa's admiration continued to effervesce. "I hope I'm beautiful like Jen when I grow up." Wistfulness edged the small voice.

I wished she'd stop. I knew I was blushing, yet I put my hand on her shoulder quietly, pressed it. "You're sweet, Trissa. And beautiful."

Aunt Eva, at last done with me, stepped back, surveyed me appraisingly and sighed. "Well—" She spread her hands as if admitting defeat. Then at last she looked down at Trissa. "You'll have to be clever, darling. The Avery women are never beauties. And you are a born Avery."

The light went out of Trissa's eager face and she stood motionless. Then quietly she walked toward the door. I wanted to follow her—comfort her, but it was unnecessary. Beauty moving swiftly seized her in his arms, swept her high into the air. His baritone voice rang out lustily:

"My lady's a cheat and a liar too
She lies when the truth would better do.
Oh my! Oh my! Oh my!
My lady for whom I would die."

Trissa, her laugh gurgling, her hurt forgotten, nuzzled her face against his. "Daddy! You're crazy! You think I'm beautiful, don't you, Daddy?"

"Oh my! Oh my! Oh my!" sang Beauty, "My lady for whom I would die."

He was still singing the song as the car turned out of the driveway and headed for Atlanta. I wished he wouldn't. It was not the gentle singing which the children had heard in the woods. It was hateful and mocking and was meant, I knew, to annoy Aunt Eva. If he accomplished his purpose she gave no evidence of it. As the car flashed along the road she turned back to me at intervals. Was I comfortable? Did Beauty's fast driving frighten me? Her face was serene, her eyes shone like topazes in the dark. Then Beauty's singing stopped and she forgot me. He was quarreling with her. Apparently, from what I could gather, because she had told Trissa she could never be beautiful. I stared out of the window, tried to pierce the dark which enveloped the roadside, tried to close out the low storming of his voice, but I could not close it out.

Aunt Eva's voice could be heard now, Aunt Eva saying with sweet reasonableness, "We must be practical, Beauty. It will be tragic for her to grow up expecting to be beautiful when she won't be."

"By God, she should be made to feel that she is." Beauty's voice again, followed by a grim laugh. "But you'll take damned good care that she doesn't, won't you? You want her to feel plain and awkward, so you can steal the show, lord it over her, feed your hideous vanity on her. By God, don't you do it to my Trissa! Save your bitchery for your own kind. Or I'll wring your God-damned neck."

Huddled in the back seat I heard and was sickened, dreading what he would say or do next. There was no need to worry. As suddenly as it had begun the quarrel was over. Aunt Eva remembered me again, asked if I was all right, her voice and manner as sweetly solicitous as before. The car swept along. There was consciousness of nothing except its rush against the night between the walls of trees, and Beauty's storming voice might never have been. The car was a void in which Aunt Eva's head, highlighted by the glow from the dashboard, rose shining and proud from the dark like a flower.

Then we, in a line of other cars, were crawling toward the entrance of the club, finally gaining it. The doorman opened the door and Beauty got out. Every inch the courtly gentleman, his hand reached gallantly to Aunt Eva, then to me. Aunt Eva's nod to the doorman might have been the recognition of royalty, her little bow to this or that one in the crowd was regal—the bow of a lovely and proud lady. We were, I realized startled, merely nice people attending the Nine O'Clock Ball.

I suppose the words "The Ball" have ever held a special magic for women. You picture a glasslike dance floor stretching into space, a magnificent stairway rising majestically, huge chandeliers of crystal casting a fairylike glow over the beautiful women and handsome men who waltz lightly, exquisitely to the strains of muted music—probably the "Blue Danube"—the sort of ball you see in movies of old Vienna or of the Old South.

The Nine O'Clock wasn't at all like my—or Hollywood's—picture. There was no great shining dance floor, no high-flung stairway, no huge dripping chandeliers of crystal. Neither were all the women beautiful. And the courtly men, absorbed by the path which led from ballroom to bar and back again, had no time whatever to spare to courtliness.

Ty, as casual, as nice as my memory of him, led me through the jumble of tables and faces which rimmed the dance floor toward his table, our progress a series of starts and stops as he was slapped on the shoulder by men and invariably asked, "How you doing?" or was cooed at by older women or frankly pawed by younger ones. To each he gravely introduced me. The men, in the way of men, accepted me smilingly and said polite things. Not so with the women. They were gracious, they uttered the small banalities due a stranger charmingly. But their eyes, as they said them, slipped over me surreptitiously, weighing my virtues and my weaknesses as if, it occurred to me, we were opponents in a future struggle.

Passing Aunt Eva's table we must stop again. "Darling," this was Aunt Eva, "you must know Louella and Hazel—"

Standing above her, trying to smile naturally, I said "How do you do?" to Louella and Hazel; to their husbands who at our approach had risen gallantly; then waited while Ty, casually and so easily, said the proper things. Then my eyes met Beauty's. He hadn't risen but continued to sit carelessly in his chair, a glass of course in his hand, and smiled across the table at me.

"Are you having fun?" he asked, his brows lifted.

I threw him the stock answer. "Wonderful! Are you?"

He raised his glass significantly. "With the help of God and enough liquor, it's improving."

We went on then, Ty and I, with Aunt Eva's voice following us. "Do give my love to Aunt Min." Vaguely I wondered who Aunt Min might be, then remembered. She was Monk Lyons' mother—Monk Lyons who sat on boards in Washington, who was a personal friend of the President's. And they would be at Ty's table. I had a sudden picture of the shabby sitting room at home, of Phyl and Jud before the fire, Jud perhaps with his arms about her. Both closed in and snug and warm with love. A woman's strident voice sang out in passing, "But it's only ten o'clock!" And I thought *only ten o'clock!* Oh God!

Then we were at Ty's table. Sue, her eyes warm and friendly, smiled across the centerpiece of russet and gold chrysanthemums and said, "Hello, there." I was saying again for the how many hundredth time, "How do you do." This time to Monk Lyons, a ponderous man in beautiful clothes, his eyes myopic in a bored face, and to his mother, Aunt Min, tiny and old but with an indomitable nose riding the sea of her wrinkles.

When eleven o'clock came the ball had acquired some of the magic with which my imagination had vested it. Dinner had been served and eaten, then was snatched away by the harried waiters. Voices had dropped to the pleasant busy hum of a beehive. Even the music (they were playing "Night and Day") was muted. Dancing with Ty, I told him that I was having a wonderful time. I meant it sincerely. I was.

But he said skeptically, "Now you're kidding."

"I'm not. Can't you tell by my eyes?"

He leaned back as we danced so he could look at my eyes analytically. "It could be the champagne, you know."

"But one glass couldn't make me feel like this."

"How do you feel?" He held me tighter.

"Oh, happy! And excited. And as if—suddenly—I was beautiful."

"You're not *that* beautiful." His voice was dry.

Laughing, I insisted I knew better. I *was* beautiful. And I even, but perhaps this was the wine, half believed it. Until Aunt Eva danced by. Aunt Eva dancing with a tall silver-haired man. Then my belief in my own beauty faded. Aunt Eva was the beautiful one. Dancing lightly but with deliberate grace she was, in the gold-bronze gown, not a woman but a lovely eager light which reduced me and other women to shadows and drew all eyes as irresistibly as candlelight draws insects. The men in the stag line, old men and young, decent men and lecherous, watched her as they leaned against the wall. Those who sat out the dances at the tables watched her. Even the eyes of the other dancers followed her as they wheeled. And lounging in a door, his hands thrust deep into his pockets, Beauty watched her, his eyes as they followed the small proud head and the gleaming gown unhappy and lost. Seeing, I was unhappy too, and lost. The ball was stripped of its magic.

Dully I asked Ty as we went back to our table if he knew the tall silver-haired man who had been dancing with Aunt Eva. Turning, he looked, told me gravely, "That's Atlanta's industrial maggot."

"Atlanta's what?" I gasped.

He chuckled. "That's what Aunt Efola calls every successful man. Of course she means *magnate*."

I giggled, which of course was what he wanted, but when we reached our table I tried to recapture dignity once more. Aunt Eva was there, leaning over Aunt Min with charming deference and telling her how nice it was to see her again. But trying also, I knew, to charm Monk Lyons with her veiled, provocative eyes—apparently without success. Imperturbably he smoked his cigarette in an absurdly long holder and while Aunt Eva and Miss Min exchanged pleasantries he murmured to Sue. I somewhat illogically was resentful. Aunt Eva was sweet, she had done a gracious thing by coming over to speak to Miss Min, and as she talked, her eyes turning from one to the other were soft, appealing. But Monk Lyons was indifferent. Yet when she left, and walking with her light but resolute step went back to her own table, I mistrusted that indifference, for his bored myopic eyes slid after her, narrowed and speculative.

Aunt Min, drinking Scotch highballs as if she were not nearly seventy, said flatly that Eva Avery was a beautiful woman. My—she shook her head regretfully—what a couple she and Beauty made before he got himself scarred up in that car. And so soon after they married too.

Monk drawled, "Probably drunk when he did it."

"No, you're wrong about that, Monk." This was Ty being Ty, casual, but defending. "Beauty didn't drink then. That came later."

Aunt Min said slowly, thoughtfully, "I've never been able to figure it out. Of course there were rumors—"

And Ty's quiet voice inserted deftly, "We're forgetting. Jen is Beauty's niece." Then I felt Aunt Min's shriveled hand on mine, Aunt Min saying remorsefully, "Vultures will pick at old bones, my lamb. Forgive me." Her voice cackled sharply, suddenly, "Ah, speak of the devil." Turning, I found Beauty at my side. Beauty bowing, asking if he might have this dance.

We danced. And as we danced the magic which I had counted lost returned, and I knew why. I was ashamed, grieved because of the necessity of shame, but still the splendor would not be denied. It was because his arms held me closer than need be, because the dark head bent over mine, because his eyes, when I could bear to look, were tender. I didn't speak—I didn't want to speak, for fear that words might shatter the thing which breathed between us. I thought how wonderful to die and go to heaven if heaven could be this: dancing and dancing in his arms forever.

A foolish thought, of course, and one which proved its impossibility all too soon. With a triumphant clash the music stopped and his arms released me. While the others clapped and begged for more we stood there gazing at each other. Then Beauty said a quiet "Thank you." As the crowd surged toward the tables he moved as if to go. But he didn't go. For another half-moment we stood there. And he said again, "Thank you, thank you, my *darling*." Then before I realized the significance of the word—such a wonderful word, and so different as he said it from Aunt Eva's careless use of it—he was leading me back to our table. He was laughing and talking with Aunt Min as he pulled out my chair, he was asking Monk what went on in Washington. I pretended to listen, I laughed when I thought I should laugh. I told Ty, yes, I'd adore a drink, and when the waiter brought it I drank it. But I neither saw not heard nor tasted. I was still dancing with Beauty, his arms were holding me close, the *dahdah-dahdahda* of the music was neither the beat of the drums nor the wail of the horns. It was Beauty's voice saying, "Thank you, my *darling*."

Ty drove me home. Calmly, sensibly. Careful about traffic lights though there was no traffic, never going faster than thirty miles an hour, his manner of driving resembling Beauty's as much as a tractor resembles a meteor. And I wasn't grateful. I had wanted to leave with Aunt Eva and Beauty, who had gone an hour ago; I was furious with the supine will which had yielded to Ty's persuasion. I wished now I had resisted, had gone in that other speeding, reckless car, where at least I could have heard his voice and from the rear seat watched the profile I loved.

Loved! The word slipped easily, too easily into my consciousness. I sat up startled.

Ty asked, "What is it, hon?"

"Nothing," I told him. "Nothing. I just had a thought." What if I told him what that thought had been? Said to him casually, lightly, "I've just realized it. I'm in love. With my aunt's husband." Instead I told myself that I was mad. I had no right to love him. I *couldn't* love him. It was only fascination. It was because he was older, because he was unattainable. I dragged out all the worn and tattered reasons for not loving, using them to unsell my heart.

Ty was talking, saying, "I've given you time to get sort of settled. But now I'm warning you, I want to see you damned often. You're my girl, you know—or have you forgotten?"

Wearily I said, "Oh Ty! Please—"

He went right on. "I'll want you to come in town for lunch, and dinner. We've got things to do. The Cyclorama and Stone Mountain and the Henry Grady monument. And you've got to learn about Atlanta's notable ancestors."

My protest was with laughter now.

"Yes, ma'am, you've got to catch up with the notable ancestors. Everybody in Atlanta has them, you know." His voice took on the unctuous drawl of a Kentucky colonel. "Why suh, Grandpappy fought with Gen'l Lee at Shiloh. Or Chickamauga or Bull Run. And my grandpappy, I'd have you know suh, owned a thousand slaves. My grandmammy never so much as put on her own stockings. And when the damyankees came she buried the silver in the yard and hitched up the bays to the kerridge and drove to the battlefield and found my grandpappy and brought him home."

I was laughing, of course. And he grinned at me in the dark. "You needn't laugh," he said severely. "You'll hear it over and over—when you marry me."

I sat erect again, regarded him with startled eyes. "Marry you?" I was firm. "Ty, you are too ridiculous."

He braked the car, waited on the deserted corner for the green light. Then he said, "Ridiculous?" And I was struck by some inflection he gave the word. I glanced at him quickly, at the eyes fixed so steadily on the road. I thought, "Why, he cares." And I felt a tiny tug of sympathy for him. He was sweet and maybe hurt because of me.

If he was he concealed it. He said, and his voice was devoid of emotion, was its usual friendly self, "Madame, you are talking with a man who all of his life has avoided mentioning marriage. When I do, it may be absurd, but it isn't ridiculous."

"I'm sorry." And I was. Sorry too, suddenly, that I didn't love him. It would solve everything. I saw myself married to Ty, untroubled and with laughter trailing through my days. Living in the big shabby house with Sue, with books and flowers at the window, reading by the fire at night. A comfortable life, a placid life and secure.

But Ty was talking again, saying, "You've got to marry sooner or later. And—I'm crazy about you, Jen. You like me too. Or," he waited a breath, then with something unsure in his voice, "or do you?"

"Oh Ty! Of course I like you."

"Then what's the argument? We'll get along just fine. Winters we'll live with Sue in town and summers we'll stay at the farm. You can learn about bees at the farm." He whistled. "Say! That reminds me. I bought you a present today."

Thrusting his hand in the pocket of the car he brought out two books and put them on my lap. "Happened to see them in Davison's bookshop. Picked 'em up for you."

I took them in the dark, peered at them, trying to read their titles. Ty said, "Don't you know you'll ruin your eyes?" He was disapproving. "I'll tell you what they are. They're about bees."

"Bees! Oh Ty!" I laughed again.

"Now wait a minute. They're interesting. And instructive—"

"I know." I was humble. "You're sweet to buy them for me." I hoped I sounded grateful.

He turned the car into the driveway, guided it up the rise which led to the house, and came to a stop at the front steps. "We're home, baby," he said.

I put my hand on the handle of the door, then turned back and faced him. "Ty, I had such a wonderful time. I can't tell you—"

He slid his arm about my shoulders, pulled me over to him and kissed me on the mouth. A brief kiss and gentle. "Don't try and tell me, Funny Face. You're tired to death. Go on in and go to bed. And sweet dreams."

I waited on the porch until the car had turned up the road again and headed toward Atlanta, then opened the door and quietly stepped inside. But halfway across the foyer I stopped and listened, hearing voices in the sitting room. Beauty, I thought, and Aunt Eva. And Phyl and Jud. Perhaps gathered around the fire holding a post-mortem over the Nine O'Clock.

But when I paused in the door I knew it was no party. Phyl sat in the big chair, white-faced and tense. Jud standing above her was, I realized, belligerently protective. Beauty leaning against the mantelpiece gazed into the fire. And on the hearthrug stood Aunt Eva, erect and proud and smiling faintly, the fire lighting the gold-bronze dress to radiance.

It was she who saw me hovering in the door. Who called, "Come in, darling. Such exciting news for you!"

I advanced into the room tentatively. "News?"

"Darling, but real news. They've only just told us. Phyl and Jud, you know. They—they are getting married."

I glanced at Phyl and Jud, ready with proper congratulations but neither of them looked my way and my "How nice" sounded inane and inadequate. Questioningly I turned to Aunt Eva, to Beauty. But they didn't know I existed.

Phyl, who had continued to stare trancelike into space, moved suddenly and gestured with her hand, almost as if hearing something she could not bear to hear. She, with her hand, repulsed it. "Oh Jud!" It wasn't protest, it was acceptance of defeat. "I asked you not to."

His bright eyes that looked flat in his face were cold. "I did though. I'm fed up."

"Fed up?" It was Aunt Eva, her soft voice edged with hurt. "Fed up with what, Jud?"

He wheeled on her. "With the deal Phyl gets. You know what that deal is." He was contemptuous.

Her luminous smile persisted. Her voice retained its hurt softness. "I think I do, Jud."

He faced her, her soft smile, sullenly. "Okay," he said. "Then we understand each other."

We stood there, all of us, so motionless we might have been a tableau, a tableau which was suddenly dissolved. Finally Beauty, stirring, moved to Phyl and laid a hand on her shoulder. "Go to bed, Phyl." His voice was quiet, and docilely, as if dazed, she obeyed. I heard Jud telling Beauty they'd have their talk about the mill in the morning. Without saying good-night he went too.

With their going the tension, which had held the room, lessened. Beauty with a sigh that was half yawn dropped into the nearest chair. Aunt Eva stifled her yawn with her crimson-tipped fingers. "I'm dead!" She smiled at me. "Simply dead. I must—I really must go to bed."

She moved to Beauty's chair and leaning lay her cheek against his. "Night, darling," she murmured like a sleepy child, then drifted from the room, calling back to me, "Come to bed, Jen. Imagine, it's nearly three o'clock."

I called that I was coming, but I didn't go at once. I waited. I wanted Beauty to look at me—desperately wanted him to look at me. But he didn't. With his hands hanging loosely before him he sat in the big chair and stared into the fire.

I couldn't sleep. My mind was a mad carousel whirling endlessly, flashing the events and faces of the night before me with weary recapitulation. The ball, and Ty, and Monk Lyons. Trissa, the light gone from her dark eyes. Aunt Eva always dancing, always shining. Phyl and Jud and Sue—how quiet Sue had been. And

Beauty saying, "Thank you, my darling." I would doze and they would fade into some limbo for the time, then the carousel would start again, whirling, whirling.

I counted sheep. I said the multiplication tables. I tried to recall my last experiment in chemistry. I counted sheep again, this time black ones, and found myself even wider awake than before. I despaired, reached up and switched on my lamp. Groped beneath the bedside table for a book. Settled my pillows, opened it.

It was a dull book, at least it seemed so then. It told of love lightly, breezily, almost you saw the author's tongue in his cheek. You knew on the first page it would end happily and you couldn't believe in it. Love wasn't happy. At least not always. Love could be a black dread possessing you, an unbearable waiting with nothing resolved, like going on and on through a dark tunnel, knowing there was light somewhere but knowing too you could never gain it.

This wouldn't do, I told myself firmly. I must find a book. Not about love but a matter-of-fact book, an informative book. I thought of the books on bees which Ty had bought for me. Interesting and instructive, he had said. Then I remembered. I had left them in the sitting room, on the small table near the door. I would put on my robe and go get them.

I went down the back stairs noiselessly so no one would be disturbed, thinking how strange even a familiar house can be at night. Yet how aware one was of the people in the house even when they slept. Tonight, or so it seemed to me, the house was troubled. The small creakings, the soft stirrings might have been the house turning restlessly in its sleep. And no wonder! Groping my way down the dark stairs I thought of Phyl and her wide dark eyes, of Jud's sullen face, of Beauty and his lost and unhappy look, and of Aunt Eva caught and ground between them, yet so shining—bright. Never, I swore it to myself, would I do anything to hurt her.

As I padded down the corridor toward the sitting room I heard the faint far-away twitter of the first birds that told me it was near to daybreak. But the corridor was a fathomless well of black and only the dying reflection of the sitting-room fire lighted my way.

Just outside the door I paused. Reached to touch the light switch. In midair stopped my arm suddenly, as powerless to move it as if it had turned to stone. Aunt Eva was in the room. Aunt Eva, not in the gleaming gold-bronze gown in which I had last seen her, but wearing the seagreen nightrobe, its fragility covering yet revealing the slim and lovely body, the girl's uplifted breast. And from the chair where Phyl had sat Judson Poole looked up at her with his bright secret eyes.

I knew that I should go but I didn't go. I was unwilling to believe what I saw or the ugly thoughts which swam beneath the surface of my mind like sluggish fish in a pool. Impossible—almost I cried out the word—that the scene should mean what it seemed to mean.

And then Aunt Eva spoke and all the pretense with which I had tried to persuade myself was shattered. I knew now that I had not doubted, really. It was impossible not to understand immediately the meaning of Aunt Eva's garb, the sway of her body as she stood upon the hearth, or the tone of her voice, hushed as the whispering of the dying fire.

"Come back, darling."

He continued to look up at her unmoving. "It's no good, Eva. I'm going to marry Phyl."

"I know, darling." Her voice was at once tolerant, yet urgent. "But that doesn't mean that we—" She broke off as he got up suddenly, and waited, her face turned toward him. She hardly stirred, but I saw him tense, as if he prepared to withstand an actual physical force. His words were flat and without warmth.

"You won't get me again, Eva. I have to live with myself. I've loathed myself too damned long. Well, I won't go through that particular hell again. I've got you out of my blood. I can look Beauty in the face again. And I love Phyl. You may as well leave me alone."

She listened, her proud head tipped slightly, the firelight gleaming on her hair and silhouetting the slim body through the fragile robe. When he had done she smiled faintly and I heard the soft sigh of her breath, saw the breasts move beneath the robe. "Darling," she breathed. The topaze eyes gleamed catlike in the reddish glow of the coals. "I'm not out of your blood. And you're not out of your hell."

Her arms slid oh so gently around his neck. I saw the shining little teeth between the crimson of her parted lips. The muscles between his shoulders knotted beneath his dark coat, and his head strained back above her hair. Then with a violence that came from his defeat he took her, not quietly nor gently but with a violence that seemed rather to belong more to an act of hatred and destruction than to passion. And, because watching I seemed to share his shame and his self-contempt at being vanquished, I turned away.

Even in slipping along the darkness of the hall I was still careful not to be heard, careful to avoid sharing by betrayal of my presence the ugliness of his defeat, as if by concealing my discovery of the truth I could avoid admitting that it could be true. But it was true. Even in the darkness and in flight from them, I knew that I would be unable to avoid this knowledge. And at the last, before I crept like a thief up to my room, I heard behind me, soft but clear, Aunt Eva's small three-noted laugh, husky now and wanton—and conquering.

Two

IT must have been almost seven when finally I slept. As I drifted off I heard Miss George's pattering feet in the patio and the sound of her voice raised in venomless scolding as she fed the geese. It followed me to the vague space which lies between reality and sleep. Then, as all else, it was submerged in the wave of exhaustion which rose and engulfed me.

When I awoke I had no awareness of time or of anything. Inertly I lay there, a limp rag doll with sleep-drugged eyes that traveled almost unseeing to the patterned sunlight on the wall, to the leaf-stripped boughs traced against my windowpane, and came at last to the sprig of dogwood on my bedside table. Then my heart quivered awake. The memory of last night was on me again and the realization that today was not as yesterday, that everything was changed.

But as I got up and dressed I had a strange feeling of apathy. Not merely weariness and too little sleep but a complete apathy toward life. As if, while I slept, a hard shell closing about the core of my sensibilities had raised a barrier between me and hurt, and made it impossible that I should ever cry again. Even the happenings of last night seemed unreal and dreamlike, without power to affect me. Except of course for Beauty. This morning only Beauty and the sprig of dogwood berries seemed to matter. And it occurred to me as I brushed my hair that perhaps this—the discovery of the existence of evil—was "growing up."

This feeling of apathy persisted in the days that followed. Even when I perceived that the surface of life was unchanged and went on as before, there was no surpise in the perception—or wonder. I listened to the talk of Phyl's marriage to Jud, the little jokes, the laughter, the teasing warnings to consider before it was too late. It was the sort of talk which families invariably make and if sometimes, remembering the ugly scene I had been witness to and Eva's

"I'm not out of your blood," I was seized by the feeling that it was all a grotesque joke, I kept it to myself. I knew that Phyl and Jud had started work on Jud's small plain house, which stood down the road, on week-ends painting walls and woodwork, coming home at dusk paint-smeared, their conversation at dinner revolving around color schemes and hand-rubbed oak. Aunt Eva smiling her faint smile listened, her hand worrying at the pearls at her throat, and with nothing in her alternations of gentle vivacity and smiling serenity to suggest anything except interest and affection. Yet there were times when, as Phyl talked of her French kitchen or her herb garden, I caught a flicker of amusement in Aunt Eva's eyes, and I was disturbed; disturbed too when Phyl having left the room on some small errand I would see Aunt Eva turn to Jud, her luminous eyes wide and pensive and seeking. Though pretending not to see he would stare into space stolidly, but there were times when he did see and his gaze returning hers was wooden and unsmiling and, I thought, defiant.

In my apathy I was uncaring. Deliberately I would push away the thoughts which the incident had set in motion. I didn't care, I told myself; didn't care what Eva did, or Jud, as long as Phyl had no knowledge of it. There was only one who had the power to affect me and he was remote and aloof again. The Nine O'Clock might never have been, I might never have danced with him, his "Thank you, my darling" might have been a dream. And so to me the days went past, dull and unlighted. Desolately I went into town and lunched with Ty at the tall dignified Capital City Club. Afterward we went in his car to a place called Grant Park to see the Cyclorama. Another afternoon—this one days later, though how many days I cannot know—he drove me out the Boulevard where Mama and Sue had lived as small girls. But if I had hoped to glimpse the dear and childish ghost of Mama wandering there the hope was futile. Now it was a shabby street of down-at-heel apartment houses and nondescript stores and shops. On the huge plot of land where, Ty said, the old Nelson place had stood, a huge hospital sprawled. And Boulevard school was no more.

Ty was kind, he was gay, and sometimes we were very silly and laughed a lot at our silliness. There were times too, as on the train that day, when we were serious and talked. It was then that I told him that Phyl and Jud were to be married, and how hard they were working on the house, and about Sam and Sudie, the geese; but I did not tell him that Beauty was drinking in his room again. The knowledge rode beside me, an uninvited guest, as Ty "showed" me Atlanta, and wherever I went it was my dark companion.

On one such afternoon Ty had driven me first along wide curving roads where stood the handsome houses which had won for Atlanta its reputation for beautiful homes, then down Decatur Street and through the Negro sections where the shambling shanties huddled pitifully—"So I might really *know* Atlanta," he said. Returning home just before dusk and entering the foyer abruptly, I ran into Aunt Eva as she ushered a stranger to the door. He was a young man not over thirty and dapper; and one who, even had I failed to see the neat black bag which he held, I would have recognized as a doctor. He wore the owlish spectacles with wide flat tortoise-shell frames which young doctors affect, and with his elegant line of mustache was the very picture of a coming young professional man. Nevertheless for all his grave sedateness he was playing the gallant to Eva's charm. When at my somewhat unceremonious entrance they turned, there was that moment of startled silence which follows unexpected interruption, a moment in which he hid the silly fatuous smile beneath professional suavity. Then Eva cried, "You're home, darling! Doctor Peeples, my niece. Jen, Dr. Peeples." The charming little laugh. "The *famous* Dr. Peeples, darling."

Dr. Peeples was obviously flattered. Even the clearing of his throat was pompous. And when Eva, being charming and admiring, Eva so grateful to the brilliant young doctor, said softly, "You've relieved my mind tremendously, Doctor. Naturally I've been so anxious, but now—" her eyes met his, all confiding, trusting appeal, and almost I could hear him purr.

I inserted a deflating note into the pretty scene. "Is someone ill?" I asked. "Or is this just a social call?"

"Darling," Eva's velvet eyes were not quite so velvety. "It's about Ted. Those terrible nightmares! Dr. Peeples," her eyes were velvet again as they went from me to him; "he's been so helpful and so kind."

He left finally and I went toward the corridor which led to the back stairs, but when Eva's voice called me, I halted and retraced my steps to the foyer. She had started up the front stairs, but now with her hand on the balustrade paused and looked at me over her shoulder. "Darling, will you come up to my room for just a minute? I've got that dull dinner and I'll have to rush like mad, and I simply must talk to you—"

I followed the slender figure which moved with such light grace up the stairs, marveling that the shining head should lift with its customary pride. Still wearing my coat and hat, I entered the room behind her and waited. She drifted from one lamp to another, touching them and bringing the room into a glow of light. Then going to the wall of mirror she gazed into it with probing eyes. "Darling," the soft little laugh of admission, "that Dr. Peeples! Really he was too absurd! Why, you would think he'd never seen a beautiful woman before."

Without smiling or speaking I waited for her to come to her reason for asking me to come up. But she had forgotten it—at least for the time. She picked up her hairbrush and, still posturing, brushed her hair. "And such an important young doctor too. The very best people have him. Of course he doesn't make house calls ordinarily but," the little laugh, "he did—for me. And he's rather charming, don't you think? In a boyish way."

I ignored Dr. Peeples' boyish charm. "What did he say about Ted?" I asked flatly.

She put the hairbrush down thoughtfully and faced me. "Just what I've said all along, Jen. That it's Phyl who is bad for Ted. Neurotic, Dr. Peeples said, and (what was the word he used) 'obsessed'—not quite *normal.*" She uttered the word lightly but somehow managing to invest it with frightening abnormality. "That she should adore him so—"

Listening, I received a swift impression of her repeating to the fatuous young doctor the things she believed, and he, bemused and fatuous, accepting them and giving back to her the diagnosis—and the remedy—she desired. As if, I thought ruefully, anything could be done about loving too much.

Undressing, preening before the mirror as she removed her dress, her slip, she related what Dr. Peeples had said, what he had advised. It was best, he had said, that Ted, well, should be less with Phyl and that someone who would be firmer handle him.

She unhooked the silken bra, stepped from the lacy panties.

Ted must not be given in to, Dr. Peeples said. After all, the nightmares were only his way of getting attention; they must not be made too much of. And of course that was exactly what Phyl did—made too much of them. She rushed to him and held him in her arms and was altogether too, too silly over him. It was the worst possible thing for him, the very worst. . . .

I thought of Ted clinging to Phyl, his eyes bright and frantic, as if in Phyl lay his only salvation. I asked what Dr. Peeples had recommended be done about it.

"That's what I want to talk to you about, darling. I wonder if you'll take over Ted—for me. I'll move Phyl down the corridor into the spare room on Beauty's corridor, you know, and put the children next to you. When he has his nightmares Phyl won't even hear."

"But won't she wonder why she must be moved?" I asked slowly.

"Of course, darling. And of course she'll think I do it just to hurt her. She does get such weird ideas—"

I wondered if the idea was so weird. After all, why not let things remain as they were until Phyl married Jud? Surely the forced separation from Phyl would harm Ted more than the nightmares. When she married—well, that would be a natural thing, Phyl marrying, going to live in her own house.

I said as much. And Aunt Eva listened, standing before the mirror utterly naked, lifting her dancer's hands, arching her nudity, surveying it with admiring eyes. "Darling," she murmured when I finished, "if I could only be sure of that."

I didn't know what it was she was unsure of. "Sure of what?"

Pirouetting languidly she reached her scarlet-tipped hand for the robe on a nearby chair. "That Phyl *will* be married—"

I looked at her, puzzled and surprised. "But of course she will. As soon as the house is ready." I broke off at some stealthy movement I saw in her eyes. "Why do you say that?"

She pulled the robe about her slimness, tied its silken cord, adjusted its filmy folds tautly over the virginal breasts, then regarded herself in the mirror again. "After all, Jen," a tiny shrug, "Phyl isn't awfully attractive, you know."

I said coolly that I thought her very attractive. Fine and sincere and—I grasped for a word—good.

Whirling, Aunt Eva stared at me, her eyes mischievous. Then throwing back her head she laughed delightedly. "Jen! You sweet innocent! As if men give a hoot for those things."

Tilting my chin I inquired levelly if she could tell me what men did give a hoot for? She laughed again. Charmingly, her head drooping gently, her eyes impish, she said: "Of course, darling—sex appeal! That's what a man wants. And really, darling, if a woman has it she can get away with murder." The three-noted little laugh sounded again, edged with guilt. "And he doesn't care."

I told her I wasn't sure about that. Men—I was speaking of intelligent men, I said; fine men, men with ideals—surely they asked more of a woman than being just—I floundered, unable to express what I would have said.

She looked at me archly. "Than being," she queried slyly, "good in bed? No, darling. If a woman is good in bed she can be wrong in everything else and it doesn't matter to a man. She only needs to snap her fingers," with her own fingers she demonstrated lightly, "and he'll come running." The little laugh was threaded with victory. "*I know*, darling."

I thought of Beauty. Did he come running when she snapped her fingers? Did Jud? Would the dapper Doctor Peeples? And Monk Lyons? Suddenly I was sickened. I saw the slim body, the uplifted breasts, the velvet eyes, as strumpetry. It differed from the crude strumpetry flaunted by ladies of easy virtue only because it was infinitely more cunning and far more expensive. Creamed and perfumed and beautifully dressed, brought to its ultimate perfection not because of any joy it would give the beholder but because it was merchandise—merchandise to be sold in the market place coldly and with calculation as a strumpet's passion is always cold and calculating beneath its imitation of living warmth.

I sat there, my eyes fastened upon her, not seeing Aunt Eva, seeing instead a stranger. Then a glance at her wrist watch and she was Aunt Eva again. She cried out, heavens, it simply couldn't be that late. She'd have to rush like mad—really she hadn't dreamed—and she simply mustn't be late for *this* dinner. The Motleys were so sticky about time. And would I run her bath like a darling?

I ran her bath. Turned on the hot water, sprinkled her favorite bath salts into the tub, waited while their fragrance rose and enveloped me. Then I tested the water's warmth with my hand. It wasn't as hot as she liked it; she would be annoyed, would declare she'd simply have to speak to Miss George—they used too much hot water in the kitchen. But suddenly the fact Aunt Eva's bath water was not of exactly the right temperature was no longer a matter of infinite importance. Suddenly I just didn't care.

I was alone that night. Jud and Phyl had gone somewhere earlier in the day and at dinnertime had not returned. Trissa and Ted and I ate ours in the breakfast room and I read to them by the sitting-room fire afterward until Miss George came to take them off to bed. Then I sat before the fire alone, hearing the wind—it had turned cold during the day—whine around the house. My thoughts wheeled like a fog-bound plane seeking a landing place and not finding it. I thought of Beauty drinking alone in his room and there was darkness in that thought. Darkness too when I thought of the Nine O'Clock and his "Thank you, my darling!" Now I knew it had meant nothing. It had been one of the silly insincere things which men when drunk say to any woman. He loved Aunt Eva. He would come running if she snapped her fingers. She had said so. He was a fool, I thought, and I a greater fool.

Suddenly, the thought which had murmured one thing over and over unwearied and persistently in the back of my mind, resolved itself. I must go away. To stay would mean only pain because (how bleak this thought and hopeless) no one really cared. Beauty didn't care. Aunt Eva? Once I had believed in her affection. Now with cold clarity I knew.

Where would I go? I asked myself. What would I do? I didn't know. I would get some sort of a job, I supposed. Women did. I thought of Miss Rose, the little dress buyer at Wendells, of the millions of other women in stores and offices. But they were there only because they knew some job or other and were allowed to occupy a niche because they could perform some task competently. What could I do? Sell books in a bookshop perhaps. I saw myself in a bookshop, trying to force Steinbeck and Faulkner and Thomas Wolfe on women who preferred *True Confessions*.

I thought of Ty, Ty sweet and friendly and loving me. I asked myself why I couldn't let Ty be the answer? But even as my mind framed the question, I knew the answer. A man with a scarred face and mocking eyes who, in a room in the left wing, sought escape from something he found unbearable.

Now Miss George came in the door, came to stand before me at the hearth, her hands crossed on her stomach. She peered at me through her thick-lensed glasses. "Child," she said, "why don't you go on to bed?"

I laughed up at her. "But it's only nine-thirty! And I'm not sleepy. Why don't you stay and talk to me?"

She sat on the edge of a chair in gingerly fashion, as if she begrudged herself this leisure. "I'm tired." She sounded tired. "Been scraping out kitchen shelves. I don't know what's wrong with folks today. That Tom! Every pot and pan put away with a scum of grease."

"I know," I said.

She went on monotonously. "There used to be such a thing as duty. You did your duty." Her head moved dejectedly. "But not this day in time. Do as little as you can get away with. That's the ticket now." She got up. "I'll go on to bed. I'm mighty poor company. No use to bother you with my worries. You're young."

"You don't bother me." I smiled up at her. "But go on to bed. You do look tired."

She yawned, her bony hand stifling it. "And tomorrow another hard day. Moving the children into Phyl's room, moving Phyl into the spare room down the other corridor." She looked at me sharply. "Do you know why?"

I told her I thought it had to do with Ted's nightmares. Aunt Eva talked to Dr. Peeples. The move, I believed, came from some suggestion he had made.

She said dryly, "I saw him. That whippersnapper of a doctor!" She cackled sharply. "In his pretty suit and his bug-eye specs and that little dab of a mustache." Her mouth dropped into lines of derision. "I wouldn't let him treat a dog of mine. But that Eva," the nod was wise, "she knew she'd get him to say what she wanted him to say."

I asked slowly, "Miss George, what is wrong with Ted?"

She peered at me and her eyes were sad again. "Child, I'm not a psychiatrist like that bug-eye little doctor, but I tell you this. It's the thing that's wrong with lots of children these days. Children are smart. They know things."

"But what does Ted know?"

"The same things you know. That he wants love. And doesn't get it from—" Her voice stopped.

I asked, "You mean, from his mother?"

"That's what I mean. He's never had from her—or Trissa either —what children want from mothers. She—" her mouth curled— "couldn't be bothered. They were cared for by nurses and maids or whoever she could get, at least until John Avery died and Phyl came. Trissa's a good little thing and she learned to accept it. But Ted, why when he was no more than a baby he'd run screaming through the house like a frantic creature, not like a child, somehow. Then when he was three or so he stole things. And always something of hers. Once her chinchilla muff, another time an evening bag. But Phyl cured him of that. She knew why he did it, you see. She understood. She's been more the children's mother than Eva ever has."

"But why is Aunt Eva like that?" My perplexed eyes sought hers. "Mama wasn't. Why, Mama lived for Father and me."

"I know." Her eyes looked off into space. "The way I figure, Jen, the men can blame themselves."

"The men?" I was skeptical.

"It's like this, child. It used to be that man was master. And he kept the woman in her place. At home. To keep her there contented he told her she was too delicate, too fine to rastle with common things. Poor fool! He came to believe it himself. 'Nothing too good for my wife'—oh child, I've heard it all my life. And women used it, the very thing he'd taught 'em, to get what they wanted from him. Silk stockings and fur coats and servants and cars. And too good to wash a dish or hang out a tubful of clothes. Them? Oh no! They're too la-de-da."

She broke off and we were silent. I gazed into the fire wondering if she were right, if men in subjection to a false ideal had built a Frankenstein which they must forever bear on their tired shoulders, a loathsome parasite whose insatiable greed demanded their toil, their sweat, their souls. Vaguely I recalled pictures I had seen in the society pages of Sunday papers, in rotogravure sections, in sophisticated magazines. Mrs. So and So, attractive member of the International Set; Miss So and So wintering on the Riviera or at Palm Beach. The Duchess of This, or Lady That. What they wore, what they ate, how many husbands they had married and divorced, who they were married to now, who they were divorcing, who they would marry when divorced. I had a swift vision of an army of predatory women stalking across the land on the prowl for richer husbands, finer fur coats, more impressive mansions; beautifully dressed always, perfumed and bejeweled, but somehow evil. They were akin to the fatal women of mythology—the Medusas, the Loreleis. Luring men with their beauty and charm, eager to sacrifice them to the avarice which was the mainspring of their lives. And I wondered too, if the rest of us—the workers, the toilers, the "socially" unimportant—hadn't come to accept them as the lucky ones, the ideal of all we would like to be. How else explain the millions of "really good" dresses that were not so good, the fur coats which were something less than fur, the synthetic diamond bracelets and simulated pearls imitating that in which there was nothing genuine or real or worthy of reproduction?

Miss George stirred and I came back to the fire. She said tonelessly, "Child, I've got to go to bed. And don't you sit up too late. You need your sleep too."

Smiling at her I said I wouldn't sit up too late. But when she had gone I continued to sit before the fire, lost in thought again. Not drifting thought now though, or aimless, but purposeful. I *would* go away. I *would* find a job—some sort of job with which I could support myself and win my self-respect. I would not be a parasite, feeding on the first convenient life that offered. Ashamed, I realized that my vague desire that I could bring myself to marry Ty had been just that; wanting his protection, the safety he would give me, the freedom from responsibility which as his wife I would have; visualizing myself as Mrs. Tyler McKinnon, attractive member of Atlanta's younger married set. Summering here, wintering there, entertaining at bridge or at small amusing dinners; wearing good tweeds and expensive casual shoes, serving on this or that committee, trying to convince myself that I was of some use to myself or to the world. Photograph, I thought grimly, of a parasite.

The front door opened. I heard Phyl's high clear voice sing out "Goodnight, pal!" and a moment later she came into the sitting room like a breath of crisp air. I had never seen her so alive. Soft color bloomed on her cheeks, her eyes were gay; she looked happy. Seeing me she cried, "Still up, Jen? How nice," slipped from her coat, scaled her hat neatly to rest on the window seat. She laughed, "Good shot," and crossing to the fire held her hands towards the warmth. "It's turning cold as the devil," she said. "Really cold. Winter is here."

"It apparently agrees with you," I told her, "I never saw you look so—so lovely."

Turning she leaned and cupped my cheeks between her thin cold hands. "Ah, Jen! You're sweet. And," she laughed teasingly into my eyes, "a nice person too. But—I'll tell you a secret—"

I said, "I love secrets."

"Better still, you can keep them. I haven't forgotten you kept one for me. And then," she straightened and laughed wryly, "Jud gave it away. He would. But," she threw out her arms in a sudden gesture of happiness, "it's just as well. Perhaps better."

I said musingly, "I've always wondered just why Jud did give it away. I came in on the end of things, you know. I never quite understood—what happened."

Recollecting, she nodded. "Nothing very important—the thing that happened, I mean. Eva and Beauty came home from the Nine O'Clock and I mentioned that Ted had had a nightmare and something she said—Oh, I don't even remember what she said, but as if I were to blame for Ted's nightmares. Anyway it made Jud furious. So he told them. Although I had begged him not to."

"But why not, Phyl? Even if they disapproved you are twenty-one, you know. There's nothing they could do."

For a second she stared into the fire. Her face, I thought, was unhappy. Then she moved restlessly. "It's just," she began, then broke off. "Oh, you don't know Eva, Jen—her way of spoiling things. Not by anything big or important or outright. But little poisonous suggestive hints that could be perfectly innocent—or deadly. Once, Jen—oh, years ago now—there was someone else that loved me." Her laugh was ragged. "She spoiled that. He was so young, you see, and so impressed with Eva. Naturally he took the little things she kept hinting about seriously. Father, you know, and his illness and how he died, and I wasn't too strong, and he must be so careful of me. So," she spread her hands resignedly.

"But she can't do that now." I made my voice practical. "Jud knows about your father and that you are perfectly all right, so there's no poison she can spill." Even as I said it I was remembering, hearing Aunt Eva's voice saying, "And you're not out of your hell, darling," but I pushed the memory down into oblivion. Everything would be all right. Phyl would be happy, she would never know those words had been said, and because she didn't know the words, ugly as they had been, were stripped of their importance.

Now she laughed her high sweet laugh and cried, "Oh Jen! I haven't told you my secret, have I?"

Smiling at her I admitted she hadn't. "Tell me now."

Her smile was mysterious. "You said when I came in that I looked different, didn't you?"

"I said you looked lovely."

She grinned. "That's different, isn't it? And you said something about winter agreeing with me. Well, it isn't winter that makes me different tonight, Jen." She lay a finger on her lips, said quietly, "Remember, no one is to know but you." Leaning toward me, her voice dropped almost to whispering. "Jud and I were married this afternoon."

I cried out, "Oh, Phyl—how wonderful!"

Her finger cautioned me to quiet again. "We drove to Marietta to the dearest old minister. But we won't tell a soul, except you, until the house is finished and we can move in."

Getting up, I went to her, put my arms about her and kissed her. I told her how glad I was. And I was glad. For her happiness was a living thing. Her eyes were living too and radiant, as if she walked joyously toward a dream, long dreamed and now at last come true.

Excited as women are always excited by romance, I asked, "But what made you decide? To do it this way?"

She laughed her high sweet laugh. "Oh, blame it on Jud. He's nagged and nagged. Ever since we told Eva and Beauty. At first I said no. I wanted to get the house fit to live in. Really, Jen, you can't imagine how impossible it was, the floors with cracks you could see through. And br'r, so cold!" The light dimmed in her face. "Then there is Ted and Trissa—and Beauty." She paused and stood gazing into the fire. I knew, happy as she was, that she was not free of pain. Then suddenly she was gay again. "But Jud—he's such a persistent devil. He kept after me. 'Why wait,' he said, 'let's marry now—today'." She laughed, a deprecating note in her laughter. "I told him I thought he was afraid."

I repeated, "Afraid?" tentatively.

"Uh-huh. That something would happen to prevent—" She laughed again, but this time somewhat too quickly, as if with her laugh she would cover a dark upthrusting thought. "Of course I only teased him."

"Of course," I said and for an instant we were silent. Then I spoke: "I must give you a present. Something you want."

She pulled a pack of Luckies from the pocket of her woollen dress and taking two cigarettes handed one to me. "Jen," she spoke quietly now and with a serious undertone, "do you really want to give me a present?"

"Of course. Oh, not a grand piano or a new car. You'll have to get those on a quiz program. But I do want to give you something, something you'd really like to have."

"You can." She spoke slowly. "Something I'd really like to have."

"Then tell me what it is, Phyl. When I go in town Friday for dinner with Ty, I'll—"

She put her hand on mine. "You can't buy it, Jen."

Gravely, because she was grave, I asked, "What is it, Phyl?"

"That you will love Ted and Trissa and Beauty for me."

I stared at her. "Love Ted and Trissa and . . ." I repeated, and on that last name halted.

"Yes, Jen. Love them." She moved close, put her hands on my shoulders, looked deeply into my eyes. "Jen, when I go they'll have nobody. They're my children. My lost children." She added softly, "Beauty too—"

I said, "I know."

She went on. "You don't know how hard it is," her gesturing hand moved as if to push away remembrance, "to leave them. For so long I've tried, oh! to make them feel loved and wanted and important." Her hands tightened on my shoulders. "You've got to do it for me, Jen. You've got to. They need you, Trissa and Ted, and most of all—Beauty."

Dry-mouthed I whispered his name. "Beauty?"

"Yes, Beauty. He needs you too. You see, Jen, I know."

"You know?"

"Yes. That Beauty loves you."

I twisted from beneath her hands. "You can't know what isn't true, Phyl."

"It's true." Her voice was grave and steady. "Oh, Jen, do you think I haven't seen it, when you come in a room? Or heard it when he speaks to you?"

"But I tell you, you're wrong. He speaks to me as he would to Trissa or Ted."

"Yes." She was half smiling, but not gaily. "He loves them too. Oh, Jen!" She held me when I would have moved away. "Don't run away from it like that."

I faced her then. "How can I *not* run away from it, Phyl? There—there is Eva—"

"Yes," she said, "there's Eva. But love, Jen, must be faith too. Faith that everything will work out as it should."

I said, not meeting her eyes, that I wished I could believe that. But I couldn't.

"But you don't know. Once—oh, I shouldn't tell you this, but once I thought that Jud—cared for someone else, that he would never care for me. But he did, you see."

"And did you have faith *then?*"

She laughed. "No. I was miserable. I was in hell. But what I'm trying to say, Jen, is that it *can* happen. Perhaps it will for you too."

I said, "I wonder," and for a moment we stood there silent while the fire died slowly and the wind like a tired spirit sighed around the house. Then Phyl said matter-of-factly, "I must go to bed. I'm starting to paint my kitchen tomorrow, early. It's going to be the cutest kitchen, Jen. It has an open fireplace, you know, and I'm going to put chintz chairs beside it."

Crossing to the window seat she picked up her hat and coat and went to the door, then turned to lift her hand in the good-by gesture she used when she galloped off on Mimi. The sound of her sensible heels echoed along the corridor. She had gone without once asking if I would give her the wedding present which she had told me she desired. As if somehow she knew, without telling, that I would.

And of course I would.

Next morning the change of rooms was accomplished by Miss George with the aid of Old Tom and Mellie and me, and I spent the afternoon taking clothes from drawers and closets and settling them in other drawers and closets. I was careful to arrange Phyl's to her liking so her changed quarters would not be too unpleasant a surprise. For it had dawned upon me as I worked that she knew nothing of the move. She had been off getting married the afternoon before; she knew nothing of Dr. Peeples' visit and advice; she had left early this morning to start painting her kitchen. There had been no opportunity for her to know.

Trissa and Ted, interested observers as we worked, I placated. I told them as if it were an event of great excitement that Phyl was going to be married to Jud, that she would live in Jud's cute little house down the road, that we would go down there—oh, every day, and have tea with Phyl. Nevertheless, their chattering which had rung along the corridor all morning was too suddenly hushed, and their small faces too suddenly still. If Beauty were only himself, I thought, and there with "Mr. Kingdeer's Goats" and "Git dat tangle to kill dat Oo-o!" he could lift them to gaiety again. But he wasn't. And I must compensate for the lack. Trissa was easily diverted. I had only to ask her to help, and she set to the task of sorting her and Ted's clothes which had been piled helter-skelter on the bed, delightedly. Ted was more difficult. Impervious to suggestion he sulked until with a turned-down chair and a comforter I built a tent into which he immediately disappeared and from which he refused to emerge until he was literally dragged forth to eat his dinner. For the time however he was entertained and Phyl's going was pushed into that never-never land of children, the future.

Each time I went down the corridor which led to Phyl's new room I had to pass Beauty's closed door, and each passing constituted a struggle between my better judgment and an almost overpowering desire, a struggle in which caution was the victor until, Phyl's room finished, I started up the corridor the last time. Then caution was vanquished by the longing to see him—to hear his voice. Halting before his door, I knocked. And when he called "Come in," I opened the door.

I do not know what I had expected to find, for I had no experience and but small knowledge of drunkenness. But what I found lightened the darkness which I had carried with me these last days. For he was very much as he had been on that first day when he had picked me up at Ty and Sue's. He sat on a couch as he had then, he wore old slacks and a shirt tieless and open at the throat, and as on that other day he held a glass in his hand. The only evidence of the many solitary hours he had spent in the monklike room was the number of empty whisky bottles ranged in geometrical design on the window sills. That and the sleepwalker's stare I saw in his eyes as he looked across at me. For an instant I wondered if he even saw or, seeing, recognized me.

Clinging to the doorknob I stood there meeting his gaze resolutely. Then his shifted. Leaning he refilled his glass from the bottle which stood on the floor beside him. The unchanging, unlit eyes came back and watched me as he drank again. While he drank I waited, aware of the separateness which divided us, my thoughts reaching toward him achingly as if I hoped with thought to dissolve that separateness. Yet hopelessly, because he was not even aware of it. And still waiting.

His eyes left me as he leaned and filled his glass, then, as before, came back, his brows lifted above the sleepwalker's stare. "Have you come to quarrel with me about my drinking?"

I moved my head in denial but I didn't speak.

He laughed derisively. "You don't even ask me to give it up?"

Again I moved my head in denial. And he laughed again. "You are an exceptional female if you don't want to reform me. But I warn you. You can't, and I'll tell you why. I drink because it lets me believe in luck again. And that a woman might love me. Why, I even have the illusion that I might—*might*, I say—make a decision that matters."

Something cold and dark took my heart in its hands and I cried out without volition, "No—no!" I could not bear to look at him seated there, proud and arrogant in his defeat. He laughed dark laughter and strange; and I shrank from its darkness and strangeness as I would from a festering wound and with closed eyes leaned my head against the edge of the door.

" 'Give strong drink unto him that is ready to perish and wine unto those that be of heavy heart.' " His chanting sardonic voice made a travesty of the beautiful words. " 'Let him forget his poverty and remember his misery no more. The afflicted are to be comforted'—that's what one Lemuel has to say of drink."

He broke off and I raised my eyes. But he had only stopped to fill his glass once more. He gulped the whisky and looked across at me with his hawk's eyes. " 'How beautiful are thy feet with shoes, O prince's daughter . . . Thy two breasts are like two young roes that are twins.' "

My eyes pleaded with his across the space between us. I whispered, "Don't—please don't." But I could have saved my plea, for the mocking voice went on, " 'Many waters cannot quench love neither can floods drown it. O my dove . . . let me hear thy sweet voice, for sweet is thy voice . . . the little foxes spoil the vines . . .' " He drained the last of his drink, and explained with owlish wisdom, "Song of Solomon." Then his attention was on the pouring of the liquor again.

Leaning against the door I was laughing and crying too. He sat, gazing at me, his hand with its lean, strong fingers turning his glass so that the amber whisky caught the light from the windows.

"You find mine—and Lemuel's—reasons for drinking amusing?"

I shook my head. "I haven't asked for reasons."

"Nevertheless I think I'll give you one—out of, shall we say, a decent respect for the opinions of womankind?"

He stood and walking somewhat unsteadily to a small table beside his narrow cot where the covers were meticulously spread and folded, as a man makes his bed, he set the glass on the table and turned to me again, the mocking smile still in his eyes.

"This explanation concerns a young man. Myself, of course. But it's easier to talk about him as if he were someone else, somebody who might be dead. Like most young men, he fell in love."

"Don't." I spoke the word involuntarily, thinking I would hear of his love for Eva and that I did not want to hear. But he went on unheeding.

"He fell in love and all in all he was a luckier young man than most. For one thing, his father was a successful man. He went to the schools he chose, belonged to the right clubs. He even had a few friends. Shall I tell you more about him?"

I still stood against the door, but now my head was bent, my eyes stared at the floor and I did not answer. He laughed shortly.

"He was lucky," he went on, "and, God save the mark, he was something of an idealist. He had ambition and even a few ideas. He knew the South, knew that with natural advantages which compared well with those in any other part of the country, the South was still in bondage to the North. He knew that coal and iron lay next to one another in the hills around Birmingham, but that the hills were owned by Northerners. And that some of the best soil in the world was being spoiled because the men who farmed it knew as little about caring for it as the South had known about caring for them. He even believed that he might make some contribution to remedying things like this. And others."

I heard his footsteps as he turned and went back for his glass, and the clink of the bottle against the tumbler.

"If I'm boring you I'll stop," he told me in another voice.

I shook my head.

"Then I'm only boring myself. However, as I said before, our young hero fell in love. And he was lucky again, because he fell in love with a girl who was not only a lover but a friend. His friends were pleased with the girl he'd chosen. It was said that he would 'make his mark.' " He made the cliché scornful. "And then he met, oh casually, another girl. She was very pretty."

He paused, and without looking up I could guess the intent frown that had come between his eyes.

"Did I say she was pretty? She was more than that—beautiful and all shining. And damned cunning. And gay. Everything was an adventure, a last fling. There's a beautiful word we use in the South for a party or an adventure—frolic. She made everything a frolic."

He paused again, and this time there was no movement from him, and no sound, but just a long stillness.

"And then she came to our young hero and told him she was going to have a baby. Not gay now, and not calculating. Oh no! But frantic and appealing and very wistful. And he being a hero," his laugh was ugly as if with it he spewed uncleanliness, "he did what we call the 'decent thing.' He married her, ran off with her on another frolic, an adventurous elopement. And the day after, he sat down and tried to write some sort of explanation to the girl he had—" he gestured impatiently "—tried to write, and found he could put down nothing but his own asininity and stupidity. And within a week our young Lochinvar knew he'd been gulled as easily as any hayseed at a country carnival. There was no baby. The frolic had been planned as carefully as a general plans a battle, and he had been no adventure to the girl who'd gulled him."

He was silent again and I looked up, to find his face still arrogant, his lips quirked in a smile.

"But then why did you—he—go on? Why didn't he break away when he found out?"

He raised the glass as if toasting in mockery a despised companion.

"Oh, but I told you he was an idealist. And very proud. When he found out that he'd been the prize ass of the world his chief concern was to keep it from the world. That—and then the wife had her talents. We mustn't forget that or we make our young man nobler than he was."

"But I don't understand—"

He interrupted, his bitter words coming flat and hard.

"Don't understand how she made him believe he had sufficient reasons for making the best of his bargain? Well that is not suprising. There were times when he couldn't understand it either. When he was bitter and angry at the whole damned world. But mostly at himself. But let's give the devil his due. He tried to break away—"

He put up his hand and touched the scar along his cheek, the first time I had known him to reveal even by so much as a gesture that he was aware of it.

"Well, he bungled that too. And then he found another escape." He went to the bottle and poured again, the whisky brimming at the rim of the tumbler. "This one. And he took it. Because, you see, he'd discovered something about himself that was a much greater shock than anything that had happened to him. He'd discovered that he was a fool and a coward. That he didn't have the intestinal fortitude to kick over the applecart and allow his little world to know how great a fool he was. And finally, there were the children. And then there was no escape—except this."

He held up the glass.

"Not a bad way. A method—referring you again to Lemuel—with divine approval."

He raised the glass to his lips and started to drink; then with a gesture that was not angry but almost casual, tossed it into the corner where the liquor splattered against the bare wall.

"There are times when even that friend gets on my nerves."

He stood, swaying, but with his face sobered and intelligent.

"So that's my explanation," he told me quietly. "Mind you, it explains nothing, not even to me. I've come to know there's no adequate explanation for a man being a fool. That's the part of it I find least comforting."

He was gazing at me with his dark, probing eyes as if waiting for me to speak, to agree or disagree with his estimate of himself. But I didn't speak. And he came to me and reaching took my shoulder in his strong hand and slowly, his eyes on mine, drew me to him. I caught the odor of the sweet, hot whisky on his breath, then his mouth was on mine. And I felt the deliriously sweet hurt of his arms crushing my body, of his lips hard against mine.

Then he stepped back and with his hand still on my shoulder turned me about and pushed me toward the door. I tried to turn back, reaching out toward him, suddenly shameless and caring for nothing but his holding me. He shook his head.

"No, I'll not make you another part of this particular bungling."

"But I don't care—"

His eyes were steady and dark and kind.

"I care," he said. "I'm no saint, my dear, and if I didn't care I'd let you stay and make love to you on that cot. But I care. Too damned much."

Then his hand had shoved me through the door. I heard it close behind me, heard the click as he turned the key, the metallic sound of the bolt sliding into its socket. I went along the hall toward my room feeling as a beggar must feel when he is shoved out into the street with his cup and his pencils—hopeless and cold beyond shame.

It was almost dinnertime and I had just got out of my bath when I heard Phyl enter her former room. A minute later she thrust her head in the bathroom door. "I had an idea this was my room," she said ruefully. "It seems I was mistaken. Don't I live here any more?"

Pulling my bathrobe about me I told her what had been done this day, that she had been moved to the room on Beauty's corridor, that

Trissa and Ted were now next to me. As I told her we went into my room and she sat on my bed as I dressed, her face thoughtful. When I finished she smiled at me. "I see." From her voice I knew she was pleased. "Then you are going to give me the present I wanted."

Wonderingly, I said, "Yes." Then it dawned upon me. She believed that the changing of rooms had been my idea, that thinking it would facilitate the taking over of the children, I had suggested it to Aunt Eva. Of course she was mistaken, but I let her believe it. Why upset her, I thought, for so small a thing? Perhaps she would announce her marriage and leave and need never learn the truth.

As we went downstairs she spoke of it again. "If you only knew, Jen, how I've worried about leaving Trissa and Ted. I knew Eva would get in somebody—*anybody*—" she shivered. "I couldn't bear to think of it. But now," she slipped her hand through my arm, "I know they'll be all right. You're here."

Hearing, I was glad I had let her believe what she believed. But when Aunt Eva came I was less sure I had been wise. She swept into the sitting room where we waited for her and for dinner. Standing at the hearth, still wearing her mink coat and tiny turban, she thrust one slim foot to the blaze. Drawing off the luscious doeskin gloves she smiled at Phyl, her charming smile, her I-am-gracious smile. "Dearest, I do hope you don't mind moving to the other room—"

Phyl, smoking in the big chair, was casual. "Not at all, Eva. On the contrary, I think it an excellent idea."

Aunt Eva tipped her head inquiringly, her eyes shining, her voice humble. "Do you really, darling? I worried so. I know how you are simply *obsessed* with the children. I was afraid you would be upset and wonder why."

Flicking cigarette ashes into a tray Phyl looked at Eva coolly. "I think I know why, Eva. And you were wrong about my being upset. Knowing that Jen is taking over makes it easier for me."

Aunt Eva's eyes turned to me, then back to Phyl, and I saw speculation in them, as if she wondered what had transpired between Phyl and me. "I see." She said the two words softly, lightly. "I see. You and Jen have discussed it. Well," she stretched luxuriously, languidly, beautifully, "that's that. And everybody's happy. But I must go up and take off my things. I'm dead, really dead. A simply terrific day. Lunch and then bridge. Heavens what a game! But," her narrowed eyes gleamed, "I won." The three-noted laugh. "I always win."

Lightly she moved toward the door, but passing Phyl paused, laid her hand on Phyl's shoulder. "Thank you, dearest, for taking the changed room so—so sensibly. I was sure you would be upset."

I saw Phyl's shoulder shrug away from the hand, but she remained casual. "I'm sure you were, Eva."

"And you do understand that it wasn't my idea, don't you, dearest?"

I held my breath. Why didn't she drop it? Why harp on it and harp on it? Was it conceivable that she, so lovely, so gentle in the mink coat and tiny turban, *wished* to hurt Phyl unnecessarily? It was not until Phyl said easily, "I know it wasn't your idea, Eva. I understand. Everything," and Eva after a questioning glance had gone, that I breathed again. Yet all through dinner I was apprehensive, for Aunt Eva came back to the changed rooms with the soup, the roast, and the dessert. She smiled and her face expressed nothing but loving concern, yet I listened with the same feeling of fascinated distaste with which you watch a spider spin a web. But as Tom served the coffee she desisted, went on to talk of other things, told me archly she had seen—guess who?—at the club. Lunching with that simply gorgeous Bronson girl who was visiting the Mabrys. The smile she gave me was roguish. Ty. And so—attentive! And Kitty Bronson? Well you need only to take one look and know that she was simply gaga about Ty.

I put sugar in my coffee, I added a spot of cream, I stirred it calmly. Did she think to make me jealous, I wondered. If so, this time she didn't succeed, just as she had failed with Phyl. Yet the small victory meant nothing. For suddenly it dawned upon me: I *was* jealous. Not of the simply gorgeous Bronson girl but—for the first time I acknowledged it—of Eva. I looked at her as she sat at the head of the table, the small proud head, the leaf-brown hair, the velvety eyes, the exquisite line of throat that ran gently and so beguilingly down to the virginal breasts, and I was jealous—not of what she was, but of what she appeared to be.

She was talking again, this time of Monk Lyons, who, she had heard at the luncheon, was coming back to Atlanta. Oh, not to live —Monk Lyons wouldn't think of *living* in Atlanta. But there was to be a simply tremendous meeting of something-or-other and they had asked him to be the principal speaker. So he was coming back. After all, his life must be simply terrific. Harriet's brother (he lived in Washington too) said there was talk of Monk being the next ambassador to England. Imagine—an ambassador! Monk hobnobbing with royalty. Heaven only knew why anybody would want to hobnob with Queen Elizabeth. She looked as if she never had a thought in her head except just being a good queen. Now the Duchess of Windsor—ah, she was really *something*. Anyway Monk was coming back to Atlanta, right after Christmas.

She turned to me. "Darling, that reminds me. You'll simply have to help me with Christmas shopping, at least with the children's junk. Do you think if I give you a list you could?"

I said that I could and she rewarded me with her most ingratiating smile. "Ah, Jen! You're an angel. And I'm—but frankly, darling, Christmas bores me to tears. After all, it's nothing but a Jewish promotion scheme." The little three-noted laugh. "Those Jews!"

I stared at her, knowing that my eyes revealed the anger which leapt up within me. And I didn't care. For this time I could find no alibi for her and no excuse. I remembered Professor Gottlieb who had come to the flat in New York so many times to drink coffee with Father, the lucid understanding in his eyes, the brilliance of his mind gentled by the goodness of his heart. And I remembered too how he had talked of his family, of what had been done to them in Poland by those others who made the word *Jew* a symbol for scorn.

Suddenly, I could take no more of it. And getting up I left the table without even an "excuse me." As I went I heard her voice startled, wondering, speaking to Phyl, "What on earth is the matter with Jen? Do you think my mentioning Ty and the Bronson girl—"

I heard Phyl's, "You *would* think it was about a man, wouldn't you, Eva?" followed by the little throbbing laugh of admission, "But, dearest, of course! After all—what else? What else is there?"

I went Christmas shopping with Ty. Christmas shopping, which except for the warm muggy weather was no different from shopping in New York. In the stores, tinseled and evergreened, the crowds were as dense and as belligerent. An invisible organ played "Little Town of Bethlehem" with the same maddening repetition. You had to wait as long to be served, and when served had as much difficulty in finding what you wanted. The salespeople were as harassed, your change or your charge slips as long in coming. Which is true of Christmas shopping, I suppose, in Atlanta or New York or Timbuktu.

Ty loved it. He loved the crowds, he loved the tinsel, he even loved the hundredth performance of "Little Town of Bethlehem." In the toy departments where I selected toys for Ted and Trissa he ran trains, rang bicycle bells, danced monkeys on strings, brooded over building sets, erector sets, chemistry sets, with grave concentration. As we left the store at last, I teased him about it. And quite simply he said he loved Christmas. It was the one time in the whole year when people gave their hearts a chance. The rest of the year they were hardboiled and selfish and didn't give a damn. But not at Christmas. It was about the only time that hearts—he laughed down at me—were fashionable.

We walked down Peachtree Street jostled by the crowds as we stopped to look in windows, Ty pausing to drop money in Salvation Army kettles, or to buy a sprig of beribboned mistletoe from the old woman on the corner, pinning it carefully on my coat. And in one window, a tiny hole-in-the-wall sort of window crammed with a hodge-podge of gifts, he spied the clock. A sentimental thing and very rococo, the base flanked by two bisque cupids holding aloft in their dimpled hands a gilt streamer delicately engraved. Vainly Ty pressed his nose against the glass and tried to read it. When we went inside and the old man had brought it from the window and placed it on his tiny counter we found the inscription was in French. It came from France, the old man said and it was very old. It rang "every hour on the hour," he said, and winding it, sounded the three tiny metallic notes.

"It's cute." Ty's hand cupped it lovingly. Peering, he studied the inscription. "I wish I knew what this says."

Looking over his shoulder I read it, translating as I read: "*Today I love you more than yesterday and less than I will tomorrow.*"

He turned and surveyed me surprised. "Say! You're educated, aren't you?"

I laughed. "If you call high school French educated."

He regarded me with mock solemnity. "You'll have to watch out for that sort of thing down here. Our Southern Belles don't hold any truck with this furrin' learning."

"I'm afraid by any standards I don't qualify as a Southern Belle."

"You don't at that. But—well, I'll take you to lunch anyway. As soon as I buy the clock."

In the Mirador Room at the Capital City Club we found a table, and when we'd ordered he took the clock from his pocket and put it on the table. He made it sound its three tiny notes and asked me to read the inscription again. I did.

He said, "You know, it's really extraordinary."

"Extraordinary?" I looked at him amused. The clock wasn't extraordinary, I said. It was adorable, the fat cupids were darlings, but —it was the sort of thing people were always finding in small shops.

"I know that." He nodded gravely. "It isn't the clock that's extraordinary, though it's cute enough. It's the inscription. You see, it says exactly what I've been feeling about you."

"About me?" I made my voice facetious.

His was not facetious. His was serious, and so sincere. "About you. I bought the clock for you so you will remember every time you look at it that I'm saying, '*Today I love you more than yesterday and less than I will tomorrow.*' Will you remember?"

I said sadly, "Oh, Ty! Is it like that with you?"

"It's like that with me."

"Then—I'm sorry."

His hands busy with the clock were suddenly still and he sat without speaking. Then he looked up and shrugged. "Looks like I'm out of the running. Why? Is there somebody else?"

I had a swift impulse to tell him there was somebody else. Somehow I felt he would be kind and generous; that he would understand. Then I knew I couldn't tell him. It wasn't the sort of thing you told anybody—that you loved your uncle, your aunt's husband. Even Ty's understanding, I thought sadly, could not encompass that.

I avoided the direct lie. "Who else could there be?"

He ran his hand through his hair. "I don't know. But something has come between us that wasn't there at the beginning. Maybe you've met someone—"

"No," I said. "No."

He grinned. "Then consider me still in the running."

I sighed, "Oh, Ty!"

"I mean it." He leaned across the table, his eyes earnest. "You may as well know it, Jen. I'm a very persistent cuss."

I put my hand on his and returned his gaze with one as earnest. For he—well, he was nice. And hurt, perhaps as I now knew that love could hurt. I didn't want that. I leaned toward him, "Ty," I said. "You're fine and generous and kind. Ty, I'm so fond of you."

He deftly turned his hand and took mine. His smile was wry. "Fine and generous and kind," he repeated. "The sort of things you say to a friend—or in an obituary. I don't like 'em, Jen. Someday, maybe not tomorrow or next day, but someday you'll tell me 'I love you, Ty.' I guess if you don't mind I'll just wait for that day."

"You can't know—" I began, but he wouldn't let me finish. "Oh, yes, I can," he said equably. "And I do. It will all work out just as I want, because I believe it."

The waiter brought our lunch and we began to eat. I sadly. Because he believed it, he had said. It was only another way of saying what Phyl had said about having faith. She had had faith, and Ty—his also was a sort of faith. I must have faith too, I told myself, must believe with all my heart that someday Beauty and I . . . I would believe and hold on to believing. It would be my talisman against long loveless years.

Ty chuckled. "Say! What's happened to you? All in a minute? You look like a kid that's just discovered there *is* a Santa Claus."

We drove home in the late winter afternoon, escaping at last the tinkle of the Salvation Army bells, the strains of the Christmas carols, the maddening snarl of Christmas traffic. Ty drove sanely, sedately, safely, a wary eye on intersections, and both of us were quiet now and saying but little as if quietness after confusion had new flavor.

He brought the car to a gentle stop at the front steps and laid the little clock in my hands. "It's my 'Shopping-for-Christmas' present for you." He chuckled. "Like the old-time brides who had a first-day dress and a second-day dress."

Smiling, I thanked him. "I love the clock."

"Will you remember what it says?"

Smiling at him I repeated, "*Today I love you better than yesterday and less than tomorrow*. I'll remember."

He was smiling gravely again. "And don't forget you're having dinner with Sue and me a week from Thursday."

I told him I wouldn't forget.

He kissed me gently and opened the car door. I got out, but when I would have gone toward the house he stopped me. "I was just wondering," he said. "Did you ever read the books that I gave you? On bees?"

Apologetically, I told him I hadn't. I had started to one night and something had interfered and since then . . .

He raced his motor, let in his clutch, and patted my hand. "It isn't important. But sometime when you have time—I'm sort of interested in hearing what you think."

He eased the car down the drive.

"About bees?" I called after him, amused.

His nod was dead serious. "About Queen Bees," he called back.

I went into the house and to my room and stood the clock on my bedside table. Nice Ty, I thought, lovable Ty. Sweet to buy the little clock for me. But even as I thought it my eyes fell upon the sprig of dogwood berries. My fingers touched it gently. And I told myself I would have faith, faith that Beauty and I someday—

Ty's little clock was forgotten.

The days between that day and Christmas ran as sand runs in an hourglass, swiftly, relentlessly, bringing with their passing the things that spell Christmas everywhere. Parcels delivered and rushed surreptitiously into closets, the arrival of Christmas cards to be sent out, their adddressing and stamping. Gay paper and seals and cards and ribbons! Aunt Eva's gifts were wrapped and bowed and put in a certain box, Christmas cleaning accomplished with the spicy fragrance of fruitcake mingling with soap and polished furniture, woodwork scrubbed, chandeliers washed, silver cleaned, fresh curtains hung where needed. The big punch bowl was brought out and made ready for eggnog, the whisky for it delivered and at Miss George's orders locked away. Then at last it was Christmas Eve. The tapering tree stood in the foyer waiting to be trimmed, the wreath with its huge red streamers had been hung on the front door, the holly and evergreen sprayed from vases and bowls, and the dressed turkey reposed regally in the frigidaire.

Then came Christmas Eve supper, almost as important an occasion as Christmas dinner, with the children at the table, and Jud and even Aunt Eva. There was pigeon pie, which Aunt Eva explained was an Avery tradition though only Heaven knew why (this to me as Beauty served it) for she simply loathed the stuff. But then it didn't matter about her. She and Beauty were going to a late supper party at the Aherns. Such charming people too, though how Bill Ahern made his money she would never know. After all, he came from the tackiest family. And she'd simply have to rush like mad the minute supper was over. If I (she was speaking to me again) would take over. . . .

I knew of course what she implied. Would I take over the hanging of the stockings, and putting the children's presents out once they were in bed? And trimming the tree, and doing all the things which mothers are supposed to do since Christmas began. But tonight I was willing. It would be fun to watch the children hang their stockings, fun to trim the tree, fun to bring their gifts from the closets and set them up before the fire. I told her I would take over.

"Ah, Jen, you're such a darling. And I'm a wretch, an absolute wretch; to leave home on Christmas Eve." Artlessly, innocently she looked around the table. "I know it. But—it's just one of those things. After all, one doesn't offend the Aherns."

Beauty interposed flatly, "Why this sudden attack of conscience? You're never at home on Christmas Eve."

Her pensive smile bore a touch of the martyr. "I know it, dearest, I really do. It's just that every year stupid people insist on giving a party. Really, I think it is very inconsiderate."

"You don't have to go." Beauty's voice was flat.

"Oh, dearest! But I do, I really do. If it were anybody but the Aherns—but I simply can't offend the Aherns. After all—" Distressed, she looked at him wide-eyed. "But darling, I've just had a thought. You needn't go."

Beauty's laugh was somewhat grim. "Very thoughtful of you, Eva. Particularly in view of the fact that I had no intention of going."

She went on as if she hadn't heard. "I could tell Molly and Dick you have flu, just a touch—" The soft little guilty laugh. "Flu is always convincing."

Irreverently I recalled that flu had prevented her coming to me when Mama and Father . . .

But Beauty was saying coolly, "I don't give a damn what sort of lie you tell, Eva. Knowing you, I'm sure it will be a good one."

She threw the small proud head back and laughed tenderly. "Ah, darling! You're priceless—but priceless! And now I've simply got to run." Came the quick turn of her wrist, the diamonds sparkling as it turned. "Heavens! I had no idea. I'll have to rush like mad—but first a Christmas kiss for everyone." As lightly as a candle flame she darted around the table, dropped brief kisses on Trissa and Ted, on Beauty's scarred cheek (why always the scarred one? I wondered), on mine and on Phyl's. Then she came to Jud. Leaning over him, her lips brushed his cheek briefly yet lingeringly. And though he did not even raise his eyes from his plate I saw the slow red which rose from his neck to his face. Then she was gone, her heels tapping their way up the stairs.

We all of us tried to revive the dinner. Beauty told us why pigeon pie was their traditional Christmas Eve dish. How his great-great-grandfather, a young man returned from the Civil War, had found his house burned, his land barren, his money worthless. And on the first Christmas he had slipped in the night to a neighboring farm and stolen a few of his neighbor's tame pigeons so that his young wife and small son could eat.

He laughed down the table at me. "Ever since," he said, "the Averys eat pigeon pie on Christmas Eve, so that we won't forget the humility of our beginnings."

Trissa said, "Daddy, sing 'When the pie was opened,'" and he began to sing, "Sing a song of sixpence, pocket full of rye," but broke off to exclaim "Rye! Rye! That reminds me. Phyl, you and Jud make eggnog while Trissa and Ted and Jen," he sent me a long deep look, "and I trim the tree."

We trimmed the tree, hung the glistening ornaments upon it, draped the fat gleaming rolls of tinsel about it, sprinkled it with cellophane snow. Then Beauty switched off the room lights and turned on the tree lights and it stood stately and beautiful in the half-dark, lifting its tapering branches toward the roof. Miss George pattered in to exclaim over it. Mellie and Tom peered grinning from the dining room. And Beauty and Trissa and Ted holding hands stood before it reverently singing a little Christmas song which I had never heard before, which I will never hear again.

> "The Christmas tree, the Christmas tree
> Is being decked so merrily
> And far and wide on every side
> We sing the song of the Christmas tree.
> Hail! Hail! to the Christmas tree
> Hail! Hail! to the Christmas tree
> And far and wide on every side
> We sing the song of the Christmas tree."

As they sang their voices, loud at first, became quieter. And the rest of us watching, and at first smiling, turned quiet too. As they sang on, Beauty's deep voice mingling with the thin sweet voices of the children, somewhere far away a horn blew a long silver blast and I felt the tears spring to my eyes. This, I thought, was the spirit of Christmas.

Then the lights were on again, Jud and Phyl were serving cups of creamy eggnog and we left the foyer and the Christmas tree to go to the sitting room by the fire. And Beauty in the big chair, a child cupped in each arm, his eggnog on the table beside him, recited, " 'Twas the night before Christmas," Trissa and Ted, their eyes feverish with excitement, listened almost without moving. Then the hanging of the stockings, accomplished with lengthy discussions as to the exact spot on the mantelpiece. And when they were finally hung, Beauty telling Trissa and Ted it was time for bed.

I made a move to take them but Phyl came swiftly to my side and intercepted me. "Let me take them up tonight, Jen. It's for the last time."

"Why of course, Phyl."

She led them off after repeated good-night kisses. Beauty and Jud and I sat before the fire drinking our eggnog, feeling a little sad, as Christmas always makes you sad. As if defending our inability to be gay we said the usual things: that Christmas was really for children, and how nice it would be if grownups could just sleep through it. But I don't believe any one of us meant it. We were unhappy because Christmas, for us, had lost its magic, as if somehow we had been betrayed.

It was like this that Aunt Eva found us. She came into the room more beautiful and more shining in her white gown than the Christmas angel we had hung in the top of the tree, and swept to Beauty's side. "Beauty," her eyes were for once unsmiling, "I can't find my car keys. You'll have to drive me in."

It was not a request. It was a command, and as arrogantly given as if she were a queen and he her subject. Hearing, I was resentful for him. Across the distance which lay between us I willed that he be resentful too. But he wasn't. He stretched his legs toward the fire and slewed his eyes up at her mockingly.

"I can't," he said imperturbably. "I've got the flu."

No responding to his humor now. No light laughter, no "Darling, you're priceless!" But standing straight and shining in her white gown, her face cold and still, she said, "You'll drive me, Beauty." If she had deliberately set out, I thought, to antagonize him she could not have chosen a better tone of voice.

Slouched in his chair he slowly turned his head and looked up at her, a sidelong glance, half-laughing. "Why should I?" He asked it lightly and uncaring. "You can take my car."

Her reply to that was swift and final. "You know I can't. That heavy thing—"

"You mean you *won't*, don't you?" He was still unresentful.

"That's exactly what I mean. It drags on my arms, it's—it's simply ghastly. I'd be a wreck when I reached the Aherns." Her voice dropped and its imperiousness was edged now with contempt. "You'll drive me." She drew the words out slowly.

He pulled himself up out of the chair and stood beside her, towering over her, and I saw that at last he was resentful. His face was cruel, his eyes a hawk's eyes. Holding his empty glass he looked down at her, his eyes traveling over her—the leaf-brown hair, the bare shoulders rising from the shining gown, the gleaming sum of all her loveliness—then slowly he turned to the table, and putting his empty glass down with a little tap of finality turned and strolled from the room.

She cried out sharply, "Beauty! Where are you going?" and without pausing he answered, "To get a bottle of whisky, by God!"

For a second she stood as before, straight and slim and cold-faced. Then as if she had turned on a tap I saw the yielding warmth flow back into her face, her eyes, even her body. And when turning, slowly, lazily, she faced Jud, her eyes were as velvet, her smile pensive and of a lovely melancholy, "Jud," her voice made his name sound light as silver, "I hate terribly to ask you—I wouldn't ask you," she raised her hands in her small gesture of futility, "But you see, don't you, how it is?" She added, "It won't take you too long. You can be back in less than an hour." A little pause and then, "Oh, it's all so silly! Situations like this—they make me unhappy."

He didn't look at her but continued to sit as he had sat during the entire scene, his hands hanging between his knees, his eyes on the floor. Then, as if pulled by a physical force outside himself, he rose slowly to his feet. "All right, Eva," he spoke doggedly. "I'll drive you."

Smiling her faint illusive smile she walked beside him to the door and stopped as Beauty, a bottle of whisky in his hand, came through it. "Darling," her voice was husky and vibrant and so alive, "where are your keys? Jud—the angel—is going to drive me in."

He thrust his free hand into his pockets, pulled out the keys and saying, "Catch," tossed them. Jud caught them and his bright quick eyes stared across at Beauty, while his hand tossed the keys up twice and caught them again. Then Eva stepped into the corridor and called, "Coming, Jud?" And with his noiseless animal-like tread he followed her from the room.

There was no Christmas spirit after that. Phyl came back and when she learned that Jud had driven Eva in turned so taut and tense that Beauty and I, aware, were tense too and constrained. Rather grimly we filled the children's stockings and brought, with many journeys, the toys from their hiding places to be ranged about the hearth. It was on one of these journeys that I had the chance to verify the little worm of suspicion which, since Eva's departure, had coiled within my mind. Crossing the foyer, my arms bundle-filled, I went to the inlaid chest and thrust my hand into the cloisonné vase upon it—and drew from it Aunt Eva's keys on their little silver chain. And then I knew. She had not "misplaced" them. Too many times I'd seen her drop them there—too many times I'd found them there, at her direction. Tonight she had not wished to find them; neither had she wanted Beauty to drive her in. She had wanted Jud. She had got what she wanted. Even now they were rushing along the dark river of road, Eva all white and shining like a Christmas angel and Jud—almost I could find it in my heart to feel sorry for Jud. I heard Eva's soft laughing voice. Hadn't she said she need only snap her fingers and he'd come running? Then I was sorry for Jud no more. I was only sorry for Phyl.

Heavy-hearted and angry and hating Eva I went back to the sitting room and together Phyl and Beauty and I arranged the toys. We stood Ted's colorful soldiers in what Beauty said was real military formation, ranged the drum, the tool chest, the swooping plane beside them; posed Trissa's elegant lady doll against a chair, placed the trunk with her elaborate wardrobe beside her. We worked quietly, almost without speaking. And I thought of all the grownups throughout the world who tonight with heavy hearts set out toys that the hearts of children might be glad.

Even when Jud returned, the feeling of strain persisted and though Phyl played at being gay it was the gaiety of a wax doll. Almost I could feel sorry for Jud again. He watched her furtively, his quick bright eyes, usually expressionless, for once almost pleading. But hers were so wide and dark and still that I recalled reading how in olden times the Chinese practiced an especially exquisite torture by forcing, with tiny slivers, the eyes of their victims to remain forever open. Too bad, I thought, if Phyl's eyes were forever opened.

When the toys were all arranged and the stockings crammed to bursting Beauty made us a nightcap, and raising his glass with grave ceremony, wished us a Merry Christmas. "I wish it for everyone," he added, "but for you three particularly. Phyl is," he bowed in her direction, "my very dear sister. Jen," he looked at me smiling, "is Jen. And Jud—only my friend now. But soon my brother."

We stood there, our glasses in our hands, knowing he was only half serious, yet somehow feeling serious. Then suddenly Jud moved to Beauty, his hand outstretched. "Hell! You might as well know—Phyl and I were married a week ago."

Phyl cried out, "Jud! You've done it again." And then we were laughing almost hysterically, finding release from strain in our laughing. And after that it was better. We sat around the fire drinking the nightcaps Beauty mixed, asking as he mixed when they had married, and where, and why? Jud spoke of the house, bragging of the job Phyl had made of the kitchen, and Phyl's eyes gradually lost their wide dark pain and became shining again.

And so as the minutes marched past midnight, past one and on toward Christmas morning, we won back to a sort of happiness. And I—I was happy. For now and then Beauty's eyes found mine and told me what I wished to know more than anything in the world. And when Phyl turned on the radio and the Christmas carols came into the room softly, and the fire spluttering gleamed on the toys, I told myself I would forever hold this hour in my heart.

But at last Phyl said she must go to bed. When she had buried her head in Jud's shoulder and he had said, "Good-night, Mrs. Poole," with teasing tenderness, she went. A little later Jud went home. Then only Beauty and I were left. And when he had put out the lights and set the screen around the fire he came and took me in his arms. In the dim room where the toy soldiers stood at attention and the elegant lady doll posed beside the chair and the soft thread of Christmas music chimed, he kissed me long and deep. And I said to myself—and I'll always be glad that I did—that it was the most beautiful Christmas.

I couldn't sleep—I didn't want to sleep. I was afraid sleep would tarnish the splendor of that kiss and I wanted to hold it close and alive and warm in memory as it had really been. I lay in my bed and thought of love and of how countless millions of lovers had known this splendor and yet always it was a new and magic thing, touching ordinary living with glory. How wonderful, I thought, if everyone could have love. In the egotism of my love I pitied those without passion. Then I was thrust by a needle of remorse. It was I who must deprive Ty. I thought of the alligator bag he had sent me for Christmas, of the little clock which ticked at my ear, of the books. I felt guilty because not once had I looked at the clock and thought of its inscription. Neither had I read the books on bees.

As if the action somehow nullified my sense of guilt I reached to the bottom ledge of my bedside table and got out the books. I could at least glance through them, could tomorrow tell him I had started them. A sterile gift, I knew, to make to love. But—he wasn't my love. Beauty was my love. I loved him—I loved him—I loved him.

I opened the books, glanced into them almost rebelliously. Then a sentence caught at my interest, held it, and without volition I was absorbed. Deeper I sank into my pillows, lower my head drooped over my book. Ty, Beauty, everything was forgotten.

The Queen Bee is the perfect or true female . . . wasplike in figure . . . with long tapering abdomen . . . her pollen-gathering apparatus is aborted . . . her spermatheca and ovaries highly developed. . . . She is characterized by some as dumb, by others as beautiful, by all as a clinging vine.

Her bees will circle round, feed her, comb her hair and give her a bath if she performs her feminine function . . . if she fails she becomes an economic hazard and they drive her from the hive.

The workers would welcome another queen—or several queens—for reproduction purposes. But the queen bee is jealous and will not tolerate another queen in the hive. If another emerges, even though it be her own offspring, she stings her to death and when her opponent crumples and dies . . . she promenades over the premises, monarch of all she surveys.

All day that New Year's day it rained. A cold, bone-aching rain that froze on ground and tree and wherever it settled and which by afternoon had transformed the world into a maze of crystal. An impressive world, dazzling as a jeweler's window, but an ominous one. Trees, surrendering to their burden, crashed to the ground; falling electric and telephone wires were deadly menaces. Lights went out, telephones went dead, the frigidaire and oil burner submitted to a greater power and stood powerless. And the house and all within the house were closed in a desolation as complete as if another ice age had moved upon this warm and southern land.

It was an eerie night. Our figures, as we moved about the house with candles supplied by Miss George, cast huge and grotesque shadows on the walls and transformed the house into a dwelling place for monsters. We returned to the leaping fire which Beauty fed and kept high on the sitting-room hearth as gratefully as cave men must have returned to theirs. Here Miss George and I served supper; for Tom and Mellie, fearful of being isolated from their own families, had left early in the day and would, we knew, return no more until the ice was gone. And when supper had been eaten and the dishes had been washed and put away we went to bed. We found a life without lights and heat and radio unbearable. Yet I doubt if any save the children slept much. All night the tree limbs crashed around the house, plunging into and shattering uneasy sleep. All night the sleet fell, tapping against the windows with steely fingers, and when day came at last and we looked out we saw that like a stealthy jailer, the ice had crept up in the night and locked us fast.

For three days it held us captive. But I doubt if any of us measured time by days, or hours or minutes. We knew only that it was a long time, a cold time, a never ending time of makeshift food, and freezing cold, and darkness lightened but little during the day. The house, for all my and Miss George's persistent striving, fell into slovenliness. None could bear the grim cold of unheated rooms long enough to hang up clothes, or change or bathe. We piled sweaters on top of sweaters, we wrapped our feet in blankets when we went to bed and Trissa and Ted, bundled clumsily, might have been young explorers, Arctic bound.

But the limitations of our prison did not irk at first. On the other hand we were stimulated. Beauty popped corn and roasted apples over the fire for the children or with the firelight dancing on his scarred face told them stories: Snow White and the Dwarfs, The Dancing Princesses, The Ice Maiden; and as he told Aunt Eva in a trailing velvet robe, fur-trimmed, paced the floor lightly, going from fire to window and back to fire again, a bright trapped bird beating its fluttering wings against its cage. Now and then she halted her restless pacing and surveyed the disordered room as if it were a shambles; and Phyl or Miss George or I seeing her glance would hasten to bring some semblance of order from the chaos.

But when the afternoon of the second day arrived, as dark, as cold, as comfortless as the first, the stimulation which had made discomfort and confinement bearable began to wane. The children doubly prisoned in extra coats and sweaters turned cross. Miss George's scolding took on a shrewish note. Phyl, feverish from a cold, went up to bed lest she infect the children. And Beauty walked the path between sitting room and pantry tirelessly to refill his glass, returning to drink beside the fire. His eyes as he watched Aunt Eva's pacing figure were as cold as the ice which held us in thrall. He smiled sardonically when, turning from the window, she paused before the mirror and arching her throat, touched her hair with her hands.

Perhaps in the mirror she saw his watching eyes and the contempt they held stung her. Perhaps, I say, because I couldn't know. For suddenly she swung and crossing swiftly to the hearth, looked down at him. "How can you sit there?" Her upflung hands and impassioned voice betrayed the extent of her frustration. "Do something, *do* something!"

He asked, unsmiling, what she would have him do? And she began to pace the room again.

"You could do something—anything. This is unbearable, to be cooped up like animals in a cage." Back to the hearth to face him again. "You and Jud could clear the drive. Perhaps I could at least get to the highway and get to town where there are *people*—"

"I doubt it. And evidently it hasn't occurred to you, Jud isn't here."

She resumed her pacing. But suddenly as if his words had only now penetrated her consciousness she halted and stood with bent head, her small teeth biting at her lip. Then she took up her restless pacing. "So! The gallant Jud hasn't come to ask about his lady." She made the word a sound of scorn, then laughed, not her usual husky laughter but light laughter and tinkling. "I'm afraid he isn't a very devoted lover."

"You'd like it that way, wouldn't you?" Beauty stared at her with weary contempt.

"I?" The laughter was tinkling still. "Darling, it doesn't matter to me one way or the other. Of course," she was pensive now, "I do feel sorry for Phyl. After all she thinks she's going to marry him."

"And just what do you mean to imply?"

"Darling!" Her remonstrance was amused, as if she dealt with an unreasonable child. "I'm not implying anything. Of course I do have my opinions—after all it is my privilege."

He made no effort to conceal his yawn. "And what is your opinion?"

"On Phyl and Jud? Oh, I suppose it's really none of my affair.

But really, I don't believe for a moment that Jud will marry her."

Even across the distance that lay between Beauty's chair and the window seat where I sat, I could see the sly amusement which crept into his eyes. I thought: he is drinking; she will goad him; he will tell her that Phyl and Jud are married.

Hurriedly I got up and said awkwardly that I'd run up and see if Phyl wished for anything. Passing between them on my way to the door, and taking care that she did not see, I laid a swift finger on my lips, hoping he would catch my meaning and keep Phyl's secret safe. I couldn't tell if I succeeded. True, his drink-bright eyes turned toward me as I accomplished my small pantomime. But if he understood, or even cared to understand, I had no way of knowing. Going along the dim cold corridors I told myself that whatever the outcome I had tried.

I sat with Phyl as long as I could stand the cold, talking of inconsequential things, and for the first time I thought her beautiful. She wore for warmth a scarlet jacket over her pajamas and her loosened hair swung like a page boy's round her face. With her chiseled face and dark eyes she had the look of a young knight, gallant and unafraid. And today she wasn't afraid. She was happy again. She talked of the little house, and of Jud, and confessed she'd been a fool to be angry with him on Christmas Eve. But on her oath and by St. Christopher she swore, raising her hand and looking more than ever like a young knight, she would never be jealous again. It was just that Eva—

I said, "I know," then told her how I had fled from the sitting room because Beauty was drinking, and Eva nagging because she thought Beauty and Jud should clear the roads so she could get to town and see people.

Phyl's laugh was caustic. "She needn't expect Jud. He probably stayed at that dinky little hotel near the mill. His house is unbearable in this sort of weather."

When my feet were blocks of ice and the tip of my nose felt permanently frozen I told her I must go. I left her there in her scarlet jacket and went back shivering to the sitting-room fire. Beauty still drank beside it and when I had sent a swift glance about the room to be sure we were alone I asked him guardedly if he had told Aunt Eva that Phyl and Jud were married.

He answered somewhat belligerently. "You're damn right I did."

I said despairingly, "Oh, Beauty! You didn't?"

He looked at me surprised. "But I did. Why not? They are married." His brows lifted. "Why not?"

"They asked you not to tell."

At that he lost some of his cocksureness and was almost humble. "I know it," he admitted, "but I couldn't resist it, Jen. And by God!"—his laugh was savage—"It took the wind out of her sails." His eyes narrowed slyly. "I've watched her play her cat and mouse game with Jud for years. My friend, mind you. Why, he'd cut off his hand before—But by God, I've got to hand her this: until today she never doubted that she'd win. Yet she lost. And she'll lose again. I wouldn't take a million dollars for it."

Smiling he stared into the fire. Then became conscious of me again. "Darling," he whispered the word I loved.

In the almost dark room I knelt before him and lifted my face for his kiss. He kissed me while the fire murmured and sleet hissed at the windows. Then he put his hands beneath my elbows and standing, raised me to stand beside him. Stepping back he widened the space between us. And when I moved as if to go to him, he stepped back again, shaking his head. "No, darling."

I said, "I love you so."

He was grave now. "I know." Then, "I love you too."

"Then why—" I could go no further.

He put his hands behind him and smiled down at me, a smile all loving-kindness. "I'll tell you why, sweet. You're young and good and very dear, and I am old and tired and my faith in everything is worn and soiled. It isn't good enough for you. You need somebody young who can laugh with you and be gay with you—"

"I think you're very gay," I told him desolately.

"And you are—very lovely."

"I—I've never been told before that I am lovely. Ty said I was pretty. But only you have said *lovely*."

He looked at me, his grave eyes denying the small smile that quirked his mouth. "Ty," he said. "Ty would be right for you. He's young and all right." He nodded as if very wise. "Yes, I think I'd like that. You and Ty—"

"But I don't want Ty," I told him steadily.

Now his eyes were smiling too. "Perhaps someday you will. Perhaps at some future time when I am an old man I will hear that you and Ty—and I will be glad about it. And damn well pleased with myself. I will look at myself in the mirror and see how old I am, and how decrepit and probably cantankerous, and I'll think of you and Ty, young and laughing and having fun, and I'll know there was one thing I didn't bungle."

I tilted my chin stubbornly. "I don't want Ty," I said again.

He threw back his head and laughed. It was then that Aunt Eva, a lighted candle in her hand, came through the door. At first she was unaware of Beauty and me, her candle made so small a pool of light against the dark. Then moving to place the candle on a table, she became aware of us. She halted, and standing motionless regarded us through wide eyes lighted by the candlelight to topaz. Then tilting her head she laughed—such a tinkling little sound—an amused sound. "Really," assumed innocence cloaked the malice of her words, "it's simply amazing what you stumble over in dark houses."

Beauty's voice flicked at her like a whip. "And—dark automobiles."

Smiling, she turned to him but not before I saw wariness veil her eyes. But her voice was guileless still and so sweetly gay. "Yes, darling, isn't it? But *whose* dark automobile? There are so many, you know." Laughing softly she put the candle on the table and went toward the door; within it she paused to call back over her shoulder, "Jen!" Peremptory her voice now as if she addressed a servant. "It's time for the children's supper. If you'd only think of the children a little more, and a little less," not trying to cloak the maliciousness of the little laugh, "about my husband. After all, darling," her voice as she went up the corridor came back light and clear and amused, "He is old enough to be your father."

I stood as she had left me, hating her, knowing that Beauty too must hate her. Then impulsively I moved to him, to tell him it wasn't true. It was only her way of putting him—and me—in what she considered our place; as I had seen her, in a thousand small and petty ways, but always sweetly, strip Phyl of human dignity and reduce her to unimportance.

But even as I moved I saw his face. And I remained where I was.

He stood casually, his hands thrust into his pockets, but his eyes gazing into the shadowed space of the candlelit room were dark in his white scarred face, and bleak.

Next morning the world was a giant chandelier hung with millions and millions of prisms. The sun, shining brilliantly, touched them with transient glory before vanquishing them. And all day melted by the sun's radiance, they trickled from trees and roofs and the eaves of houses, but the sun was a kind sun and life again bearable. Lights came on again, telephone linemen reestablished communications with the world, the frigidaire and oil burner again had power. Tom and Mellie reappeared, the house was ordered, the rooms were warm, and at eleven Eva's car—after the search for the keys of course—flashed down the drive like a speeding shadow. And Trissa and Ted and I pulled on galoshes and sloshed with Phyl down the road to Jud's house.

It was a plain little house, the sort that you see by the thousands in the South. "A dog run house," Phyl said. With a wide hall running from front to back and flanked on each side by two rooms, the long low kitchen with its old-fashioned fireplace separated from the main portion of the house by a span of covered porch. Phyl said laughing that she had named this porch The Ghost Walk. Proudly, she and Jud showed me all they had accomplished. The old oak furniture they had rubbed down, the floors they had scraped and stained, the woodwork they had painted. Seeing their pride in it, sensing their love for it, I had a sudden conviction of their ability to build life as wisely. And as women always do, I pretended. Pretended that Beauty and I owned such a little house as this where I in a ruffled housedress covered with a bright apron would cook his food and make his bed and scold him when he tramped his muddy boots across my fresh-scrubbed floor. I did not stop to consider that I knew nothing of cooking or that I had never scrubbed a floor in my life. No matter. In my game of pretense I knew how to do everything; and so wonderfully that Beauty (in the dream of course) told everyone, "My wife is the most wonderful woman in the world." And though I called myself a silly fool and knew it to be true, I recognized my little game for what it was: compensation for the reality which was denied me.

That night Ted had a nightmare. Jerked from sleep by his frantic scream I scurried to his side, and cradling him as I had seen Phyl do, tried to soothe him. I was not as successful with him as Phyl; and of course he wanted Phyl. His little voice said over and over again, "I want Phyl, I want Phyl," until it was not a cry but an inarticulate sound of pain. It was two hours or more before I finally persuaded him to sleep again. Having tucked the covers snugly about him, and Trissa too, I went back to my room as exhausted and drained as if to sustain Ted the blood had been drawn from my veins. No wonder, I thought wearily, that Phyl had so often looked tired.

Yet exhausted as I was I could not sleep and restlessly I wandered to the window and looked out at the winter dawn. It was a dreary dawn and cold, and the band of mauve on the horizon was a scarf laid on the shoulders of the departing night. Yet for all its bleakness—and for some reason this thought gave me comfort—soon the mauve would deepen to rose, the rose to flame and the great sun would majestically thrust its arch over the rim of the universe and spill its warmth over all the world. And people awaking, would stretch and yawn and say "Another day" unmindful of the miracle which each morning brings day to its birth.

Leaning on my windowsill I watched the day advance. I saw the limbs of trees emerging from the night to etch their delicate tracery against the sky. Then the darkness lifting, but slowly, and the blurred outlines taking form. The wing of the house across from me assumed a definite shape. And then so swiftly did day abolish night that there was no darkness but a grayness, the shadows beneath the trees only a deeper gray, with something stealthy and mysterious in its noiseless slipping away.

Leaning there I watched, feeling sleep descending on me again. Then suddenly I sat erect, my staring eyes drawn by some movement—or shadow?—to the little staircase across the way. Then I knew it was no shadow. It was a man, a man stepping through the door which opened from Eva's room. For an instant he paused before he started down the steps. It was in that instant that I saw him clearly and seeing him I was filled with loathing, though he moved as a man moves when he walks from a country he never wished to enter. His face in the light of day, for it was day now, was as blank, as blind as Ted's had been that other day in the woods, but there was no softening in the hard core of my contempt. For I was remembering Phyl: Phyl walking toward a dream, Phyl a young knight in a scarlet jacket, Phyl, her hand raised, saying valiantly, "On my oath and by Saint Christopher I will never be jealous again."

Anxiety blurs remembrance and so it is not easy to be clear about the days that followed. They were, at least for me, anxious days. Often I had the sensation that I was looking on at a struggle, with Phyl and Eva the opponents and Jud the pawn, and that beneath a surface of the commonplace, a foreordained plan marched to its inevitable conclusion.

Yet life was no different. Beauty when he was himself hunted and rode the black hunter with the white fetlock; when not himself he kept to his room with his bottles, stacking them when empty on his window sills in geometric patterns. Eva's days of luncheons and dinners, fitters and hairdressers, coiled ceaselessly giving her the busy air of the woman who is forever on the go yet for all her frantic rushing is devoid of accomplishment or usefulness. Jud came and went with his quiet tread and Phyl sewing curtains at night before the sitting-room fire would hum contentedly, her eyes vague with dreaming. Sometimes, in the commonplace of small daily events, I would be seized by a sense of confusion not, I imagined, unlike the bewilderment which grips the sick mind when it must distinguish between fantasy and what is real. But not for long. A glance, a phrase that expressed more than it said, a small and secret gesture, and the commonplace would be shattered and I would know that the knowledge I carried within me was not fantasy; know too that nothing was finished or resolved. Raising my eyes idly from a book I would see Eva turn toward Jud, see the question her eyes asked of him. And I would know that should I watch (though I never did) I would see him slip down the little staircase at dawn. Then I would sit staring at my book, counting the days which must elapse before Phyl would move into the little house and safety.

Aware as I was of this struggle I was startled and incredulous when at dinner a few nights later Aunt Eva announced serenely that she was going to give a party for Phyl and Jud. "A frolic," she cried gaily, "to let the world in on the deep dark secret in our family."

I was shocked, and I mistrusted it. I knew by now what Aunt Eva's gracious gestures cloaked. I heard the exclamations that went around the table, heard Phyl saying flatly, "I won't have it, Eva!" Heard Beauty's, "By God! we can't afford it. Jud says the canceled orders on burlap will put us in the red—" Heard Aunt Eva's rippling laughter and her, "Darling! But what has burlap to do with my party? After all, nobody wears burlap, simply nobody! And we mustn't seem ashamed of Phyl's marriage—must we?"

It went on, Phyl steadfastly refusing, Beauty backing her up, and Eva listening with the faint luminous smile on her face, her hand worrying at the pearls. In the end it was Jud (and this surprised me) who ended it by stating in his emotionless voice that he considered the party a good idea. Naturally there were old friends, friends of Phyl's parents. Hell!—his eyes met Eva's defiantly—he'd like to tell the whole damned world how lucky he was.

Head tilted, eyes grateful, she thanked him. "Ah, Jud! You are an angel. And of course perfectly right. After all, Phyl's friends *will* be interested to know that *at last* . . ." Pretending abstraction she let her voice trail thoughtfully, then she was all vivacity again. "We'll have such a wonderful frolic! Here—at the house! Dinner first with just old friends, the Randolphs and the Madderns and—oh all the dull important old families. And then afterwards the amusing ones and dancing, and fun—"

Beauty eating said flatly, "It sounds God-awful." She smiled down the table at him. "I know, darling! But," a tiny shrug, "it is—necessary! And after all! We don't want people wondering, thinking maybe that Phyl—" she lifted the word with light laughter, "*had* to marry."

His eyes slewed around at her maliciously. "It has been known to happen," his laugh taunted her, "as *you* well know."

She was amused, she was artless, she was shameless. "Of course, darling! And in the very best families too. But that's what I'm saying, dearest. People! Really, I don't see what makes them so—so clever. They always find out, don't they? When you try to hide it, I mean."

He picked up his fork and began to eat again. "Do they? You know, Eva—I've often wondered." His eyes still mocked.

"Of course, darling! I've heard them talk. There was that horrible

Duncan girl, and the Stacys youngest daughter. Imagine, a debutante! And oh, scads of them. And dozens more if it weren't for that doctor who . . . But it does prove, doesn't it, darling, that you do have to be careful? And not try to hide things. They simply *will* talk."

Her voice broke off. There was a silence, then Jud was speaking again. "I'm sure that Eva is right." He was calm, equable, reasonable. "People will talk. But," deliberately he turned to Eva, his bright quick eyes resolute, "if they should try and splatter Phyl with their filthy gossip I want you to tell them something for me. Will you, Eva?"

Motionless, smiling faintly, she murmured, "Yes, Jud?"

He put his hand palm down on the table and without moving his eyes from her face went on: "Tell them for me, Eva, that Phyl is the only really good woman I've ever known. And you can tell them too," swiftly his hand moved and his fingers touched Phyl's cheek, "that if it wasn't for Phyl I'd go to hell on a greased slide."

He was sincere, so sincere that for a moment we were embarrassed as people are too often embarrassed by truth. Then Eva's laugh came rippling, Eva's voice crying, "But, Jud, darling! Please don't—at least not until I have my party."

Perhaps because there is magic in the word "party" which can never be entirely lost; perhaps because it recalled for me the long-ago days when in white organdy and stiff taffeta sash I had gone to parties, that at the approach of Aunt Eva's with its stir and confusion, its cleaning and arranging, its polishing and shining, I began to feel a little stir of excitement. And when finally the night arrived and I saw the massed flowers, the efficient scurrying of butlers brought in for the occasion, and the arrival of the musicians with their shrouded instruments, I knew again the long-lost childhood eagerness. As I dressed in my room I was aware of the lift roused by the instinct of conflict, a lift which on such occasions even the dowdiest and most hopeless women must know. For parties are to women what battlefields are to men.

When I had taken a last look in the mirror, I went into the children's room to keep the promise I had made them. They waited for me with bathrobes over their flannel pajamas and scuffed slippers, great-eyed and eager. Even Ted, who so often seemed too old and disenchanted, was affected by the gala evening. And Trissa glowed. Perched on the bed they eyed me critically.

"Oh, Jen! You'll be the prettiest one!" This was Trissa offering, I knew, reassurance. But Ted said, "Your dress is pretty like Mama's, but I like you better the other way."

I laughed, pulling them against me for a moment before, like creeping criminals, we scurried down the corridor to the back stairs and the strategic place where, we had decided after involved discussion, they could watch the guests.

"Don't forget refreshments," Trissa whispered when I started to go. I assured her I wouldn't forget.

"Some of everything," she ordered. "And lots of those cakes with pink icing."

I promised, smiling as they crept down another stair or two and leaning, peered around the corner of the wall into the rooms below. I looked down upon the two heads, so different in their blondness and darkness, and yet so alike. Both so like Beauty's, with the same indefinable grace of sculpture, the same cowlick at the top, unruly and somehow precious. Parties belonged to children, I thought, and I—absurdly of course—resented that they, the rightful heirs to gaiety, could only watch while usurping and unworthy masters danced. Then, shaking the thought away, I told them I would come back soon and descended the stairs to the gleaming lower rooms full of bright, swirling women and suave, impeccable men. As I went I heard the first strains of horn and violin.

My eyes found Jud and Phyl the center of an ever-changing circle. Jud's face was impassive as the bosomed matriarchs, pulling bored husbands in their wake, said the things that women say at such a time. But Phyl was proud. She took the hands they held out to her, she smiled, she answered, poised and sure. And I knew whatever Eva's cunning had planned to gain from this party, it was Phyl's triumph. In this she had won. Her victory was not the usual victory of the female who has captured an eligible male, but the winning of a whole new existence and escape from a vicarious one where, as satellite of another's life, she had found her own pointless and ugly.

When the circle thinned about them and broke I went to Phyl

and Jud. "I'm glad Eva had the party for you." I took Phyl's hand. "Or I might never have known how many people love you."

Jud answered me with his bright waiting eyes, but Phyl laughed. "I'm glad too, Jen, much as I hated it. It's the first party I've ever wished would last for always. But," her voice was significant, "I don't flatter myself that *I* am the guest of honor."

I laughed at her. "Of course you are."

"I'm not sure. You haven't seen what I have seen."

"What have you seen that I haven't?"

Thrusting her tongue in her cheek drolly she said quietly, "Look, it's coming now."

Turning, following the direction of her eyes, I saw. Monk Lyons, *the* Monk Lyons, came toward us, a glass of champagne in his hand. Reaching us he bowed before Phyl gallantly.

"I want to be among the first to drink to your happiness," he said. When Phyl quietly but with grace had thanked him, he stood beside us making the small talk reserved for such occasions. As I had the first time I saw him at the club, I realized that extreme ugliness could sometimes acquire the quality of handsomeness. Perhaps you sensed power behind the ugliness, and certainly Monk Lyons, in his faultlessly tailored clothes, with his deep but exquisitely timbred voice, gave an impression of power. Somehow I knew that he had contested with many men in many places and had proved himself, at least in ruthlessness, their equal. And now he was confident, as few men in the world are confident, that somehow he would always have his way.

When he had raised the glass and drunk deeply, his glance found me. He noticed that I was glassless and signaled authoritatively to a waiter to bring his tray. He served each of us himself, emptying the glass from which he had drunk his toast and choosing another. Then his glance found me again and I answered its unspoken question.

"I am Jen," I told him, "Mrs. Avery's niece. We've met before. At the Nine O'Clock."

He was unembarrassed by my discovery that he had forgotten me.

"Of course. Perhaps I should say I remembered. But it wouldn't be true."

"No. There was no reason why you should remember."

He shook his head, his eyes appraising me with complete frankness and yet without offense. I realized that it was thus that he appraised everything. Men and women, cars, houses, furniture, or the many enterprises he controlled.

"You mistake my meaning. It is quite clear why I didn't remember you. You are not the same person."

I pretended surprise.

"I am different?" I held my voice to lightness, but he did not respond lightly.

"You are different. Quite another person, in fact. Something has happened to you since that other time. And changed you." He offered his cigarette case and held a lighter for my cigarette. "I am intrigued by this change—and interested."

"But things are always happening to people," I fenced.

He smiled at me with his heavy lips, and I felt that deliberately crashing through the customary polite preliminaries he had established an intimacy between us. I realized that beneath the suaveness and the perfect clothes there was earthiness and animality and crudeness. And I wondered if this was the actual source of his strength.

"Whatever it is," he told me bluntly, "I hope it makes you happy."

I did not answer, and he drank again from his glass of champagne, looking at me over the rim, a gleam of something, not appraisal now but approval, in his eyes. It was as if when he learned I was valued by someone else I assumed more value in his estimation. For this was how he appraised and judged the worth of women.

"Whether it makes you happy or not," his silken voice added meaning to his words, "it's made you a very attractive young woman."

I recognized this for what it was. The first tentative feeler which a possible purchaser makes toward the owner of coveted merchandise. And though he was ugly and the thought of belonging to him was unthinkable, I was nevertheless female enough to gain satisfaction from the implication of the half offer.

"Thank you. I'm glad of anything that makes me seem more attractive," I said.

"But I didn't mean just that—" he began. His heavy, gross body had bent toward me a fraction of an inch, his huge predatory face was near mine—and then suddenly, laughing gently, her skirt swirling as if it were liquid brightness poured around her slimness, Eva was between us, the leaf-brown head arching, the girl's breasts flaunting their whiteness in the shadows of the subtly indecorous gown.

"Darling!" The word was enchantment as she cried it, gay and eager and yet somehow caressing too, "How sweet of you! To look after my little niece. But," her eyes reproved him, "not too much champagne. After all, she's really just a child."

On the verge of pointing out that my glass was still half full and that I was neither intoxicated nor as young as she would make me out to be, I realized I didn't care and held my words. Amused, I saw her white hand against his dark sleeve, saw too his eyes as they slipped over her body, touching the slender throat, the subtly revealed breasts, as if they savored the white flesh.

"Darling, some perfectly wonderful people are simply dying to meet you. They want to hear that marvelous story of yours—about the governor and the bathing beauty—"

She drew him away, flinging a brief, "You'll excuse us, Jen," in my direction, her hand clinging to his arm. Her yielding body, as they made their way through the maze of guests, was an admission. And watching I knew that Phyl had gauged correctly the reason for this party. Monk Lyons, not Phyl, was the guest of honor. All of it had been planned with cunning calculation in order that he might see her as a hostess and appreciate the beauty and the graciousness which she realized were essential attributes in any bargain Monk Lyons might make. And suddenly I passionately wished she might be victorious again, that this triumph might be hers. I did not doubt that she desired it too. She had evaluated Monk Lyons and his assets with a shrewdness that matched his, weighing his position and his money (and the rumor that he was destined for the Court of St. James's) against his gross ugliness. Having weighed them, she had resolved that she wanted Monk Lyons.

The music, muted and throbbing, started up again. The floor became a whirling, swaying maze of bodies and I stood there alone, caught in the vortex of the dancing for a moment, but hardly aware of it because of the hope that made a tumult in my breast. If Eva won again, I thought. . . .

In the dining-room, from the silver platters and bowls that banked the table, I filled plates for Trissa and Ted—and carried them to their place on the stairs and sat with them while they ate, and with them watched the scene below, inclined to agree with Ted's disgusted, "People look silly when you see them from above." Undoubtedly some of them did look "silly." An Atlanta dowager magnificently regal on arrival appeared somewhat less regal now as with ludicrous dignity and glazed eyes she weaved from group to group, her progress halted repeatedly as she scooped another glass from a hurrying footman's tray. Then the music began to beat its cadence through the house again, the groups stirred and broke into pairs and they were suddenly dancing. I saw Eva clinging to Monk Lyons as she danced, her face lifted to his, and I saw Beauty leaning against a wall, dark and saturnine and obviously bored, a dispossessed prince who had wandered among usurpers. But his eyes followed Eva. And watching I saw him thread across the floor to where they danced, saw Eva raise her arms as if in answer to his, and then they were dancing. Her body against his somehow suggested complete fulfillment, by some trick making it seem that they were intent each on the other. Impossible to believe, I thought, seeing his dark head bent over her small proud one, that they were not lovers, that they were not perfectly matched. I felt a clutch of raw and ugly jealousy at my heart and I knew that Monk Lyons over his glass watched them too. I knew that he felt, as I felt, left out and envious.

We gathered in the sitting room after the party was over, Phyl and Jud and Beauty and I. The laggard guests with numerous assurances of "a marvelous party" had at last bundled into coats and scarves and departed. A rising young attorney had been borne off on the shoulders of friends, his head lolling weakly upon his shirt front. A once impressive dowager had made a weaving exit, her thickened voice calling, "S'nice spotty," as her dignified husband pulled and pushed her toward the door. Monk Lyons was the last to leave. And Eva, as lovely, as shining as if this was the beginning and not the end, had gone with him to the door, her hand light but somehow possessive, upon his arm.

From the hall I heard her soft laughter as they stepped out to the porch, followed by the deeper tones of his voice and then the closing of the front door. Phyl, beside Jud on the couch, glanced toward me, her eyes amused. I knew that she too realized that Eva's lingering "Good-by" to Monk differed vastly from her sweet but swift dispatching of less honored guests. But Beauty, sunk deep in his chair near the hearth, was oblivious not only to Eva's absence but to everything. His hands lay inert on the arms of the chair, his lids drooped over eyes which drink had made dull and lusterless. Unhappily I looked away. And presently he got up, swaying before his chair, and went down the corridor with heavy and uneven steps.

Eva came into the room drooping with childlike weariness and yawning, her white hand tapping her lips.

"Heavens! I thought Monk would never go. I was actually on the point of telling him he must pay board."

None of us, Phyl or Jud or I, had response for this, but she was unmindful.

Jud, standing as if her entrance were a signal, said that he was tired, dead tired. He guessed he'd go. The party had been swell—his eyes met Eva's bright and hard—and good-night everybody. And as he left the room, Phyl moving proudly at his side, Eva, her eyes amused and slightly cynical, looked after them. Then, having no other audience, she turned to me. "Really! It's rather nauseating—Phyl, I mean. About Jud. So," her eyes widening innocently, "so—possessive!"

"Jud *is* her husband," I told her.

"Of course, darling. Oh, I suppose it's because—well, Phyl isn't so young, you know. And like all old maids who finally get a man she believes she owns him body and soul. That he actually belongs to her."

"Doesn't he?" I asked coolly. "Isn't that what marriage means? Belonging to somebody?"

The slim brows lifted above the gleaming eyes, her shoulders moved in the tiniest of shrugs. "That depends, doesn't it? Personally, I think that sort of thing can be overdone. After all, there's a difference in being a husband and being a prisoner."

I did not answer. I was remembering Jud as I had seen him on that gray morning when he came down the little staircase, and how tenuous a thread Phyl's happiness since that day had hung upon. But, I thought, it's soon over. Phyl had won. Only a few days now before she and Jud would be in the house together. And what had happened between Jud and Eva would be nothing but an unpleasant secret. One that they must share and, though they did not know, which I too shared. But Eva's hold over Jud would be broken. He would be free of something which, I knew now, he found hateful and sickening and which, I sensed, had together with his anger at himself been part of his reason for marriage. He believed that Phyl and her tenderness and honesty offered escape from his bondage as he, in another way, provided escape from hers.

I came back to the room, to Eva's voice, Eva saying, "What in Heaven's name are you thinking about, Jen? You look positively *obsessed*." And I, clumsy and inept with guile said, "Was I?" as Phyl, her cheeks glowing, her head lifted, a woman loved and confident in her love, returned. Seeing her like this touched with the glow of love, I realized for the first time how greatly she had been Eva's victim and how through all the years she must have winced in the dual role of dependent kin and unpaid servant, only partly alive, enduring but a half life which must in the long hours of night have seemed less endurable than death.

She paused in the doorway, smiling across at me. "How about bed, Jen? Ready?" and yawning, I pulled myself up out of my chair and through my yawn said, "Ready," and moved toward her.

Eva, standing before a small table, stirred and wheeling faced the room—and us. "But, Phyl dearest!" her smile was bright, her voice amiable, "You haven't said—did you like your party?"

"Oh yes!" Phyl's clear cool voice lilted the words.

Eva, the skirt of her gown swirling—such a gown as only her slenderness could dare—floated to the hearth and from that point she regarded us with a disarming frankness. "Personally, I thought it went off rather well. But," she tipped her head, her eyes puzzled, "I did wonder if you two," she veered her eyes from Phyl to me, then back to Phyl, "had fun. Or if you were bored to tears?"

Obligingly I told her I had enjoyed the party, that it had gone off well, that I hadn't been bored.

"And you, dearest?" She looked at Phyl again.

Phyl said, "Of course, Eva. I loved the party. I told Jen that I wished it would go on—forever."

"I'm so glad, darling." I doubted the genuineness of her soft humility. "I couldn't guess, could I, what you thought? And you haven't thanked me for it, have you?"

Phyl's high sweet laugh was honestly amused and forbearing. "I'll thank you now, Eva. It was a lovely party and," lightly she dropped a childlike curtsy, "I am very, very grateful."

With tilted head, Eva's eyes narrowed now. Speculatively they considered Phyl as if trying to penetrate the façade of this suddenly attained confidence. Then she shrugged, said, "It was nothing, darling," but in a tone of voice that suggested it decidedly was something. "After all," her eyes were soft, wistful and achingly sweet, "I *am* fond of you. And I *do* want you to be happy."

If the gleam which for a second glinted in Phyl's dark eyes was ironic, she concealed it. And again, and with seemingly natural friendliness, she said her thanks. Then, turning to me she said she really must go to bed. Tomorrow—her smile included both Eva and me—she had work to do. Hang her bedroom curtains, stock her pantry, and dozens of other things. Her laugh was shamelessly happy. Hard to realize, she said, that in just a few days now she and Jud would be settled in their house, that she would be cooking for Jud—poor Jud. But then he swore he would help her, teach her.

Sleepily I leaned against the back of the wing chair, hearing the silver-clear voice but not hearing, the thoughts that slipped through my mind, muzzy and not clear. Thinking: Phyl is quite a person managing to be friendly and gay with Eva, all of the unhappiness that lay behind this hour suppressed. A thoroughbred, I thought, a thoroughbred walking proudly and with lifted head, too proud, having won, to wound uselessly, and accuse and blame.

It was then that my aimless, drifting eyes came to Eva. Listening, she stood near a lamp, its glow enfolding and caressing the soft hair, the sweet lifting breasts, the singing line of body. Her hand rested on the back of a nearby chair. And seeing the body not yielding now but tensely held and wary, the tilted head, the raised chin, the lambent eyes which seemed to look at something far off, I was suddenly afraid. In her tense stillness there was the deadly, wary waiting of the reptile, its poisonous fang sheathed but ready to strike, swiftly and with cunning accuracy.

I jerked to wide-awakeness, I moved to Phyl. I said, my ragged voice cutting over hers, "Come on, Phyl! Let's go to bed." She stared at me with the blankness which follows unexpected interruption, then laughed, saying, "Of course, Jen!" She turned back to say good-night to Eva, saying it with her frank and friendly smile and so unhurriedly that I took her arm, my hand, with pressure, urging her toward the door, even as Eva called—so cool her voice, and tinkling and somehow evil—"Good-night, dearest."

We were at the door. I stepped into the corridor, expelled my long-held breath in relief and almost laughed. I was a fool, I told myself, and probably a little mad. Else how explain the unreasoned apprehension? Or the weird fantasy which transformed Eva, Eva so bright and shining always, into a watching, waiting menace? Undoubtedly I needed dosing, my liver needed stirring. . . .

Phyl, her lips shaping a small gay whistle, stepped after me through the door. Laughing foolishly I slipped my arm through hers. Then stopped. Stopped—and listened.

It was Aunt Eva's voice, still cool, still tinkling, calling, "Phyl! Phyl, dearest!" I felt the impulse to hold Phyl, to tell her she mustn't—but I didn't. Instead with Phyl I turned and stepped back into the sitting room, heard Phyl saying matter-of-factly, "Yes, Eva?"

She stood as she had stood before, her body tensed, the arched head and her wide eyes bewitched by lamp glow, her hair gleaming reddishly and her white teeth glinting behind her curved and coral lips.

"Phyl, dearest—"

"Yes, Eva? You want me?"

"Yes, darling. I feel that I must have a talk with you. After all, you have no mother."

Phyl's smile was deprecatory. "So I haven't, Eva."

"Someone *should* talk with you."

"About what, Eva?"

"About marriage."

I broke in again, striving to keep desperation from my voice, "Isn't it terribly late for that—can't it wait?"

Intent upon Phyl, she spoke across my words and I knew she had neither heard my voice, nor remembered my presence.

"I want to talk about you and Jud."

"Me and Jud!"

"Yes, darling."

"But—" Phyl began and stopped, and I saw that she too had sensed some devious and stealthy purpose in this and now her voice was guarded: "What about me and Jud?"

"Darling, you're not—strong. You mustn't forget your father—"

I saw Phyl flinch, her eyes turn hostile. "No danger, Eva. You've seen to that."

Eva went on swiftly, "I want you to be prepared—"

"Prepared for what?"

"For anything—that you find out about Jud."

Their voices clashed like weapons in the quiet room.

"I know all about Jud."

"Oh no."

"I suppose you do—"

"Yes."

"What do you know that I don't know?"

I broke in, my hands gripping the back of the chair, "Eva! Don't!"

But already she was striking, "I know men. And I know Jud."

"You know—*your* men."

"Any man is my man, if I want it that way."

Phyl's head was lifted in disdainful laughter. "Not Jud."

"Jud is like other men."

Phyl's voice was scornful: "Are you trying to tell me, Eva, that Jud has been having some cheap little affair that I don't know about?"

For a second Eva waited and I heard my own voice choked, "Eva, for God's sake!" but she was slashing now and ruthless.

"*Ask Jud!*"

I saw Phyl involuntarily step back. I saw her body brace. "You would like me to go to Jud with something as stupid as this, wouldn't you, Eva?"

"I want you to ask Jud."

Phyl's laugh was less certain now and ragged. "You think I'm a fool."

"Perhaps."

"That I'll run to Jud with this? And make everything we've had together ugly? That I'll let you soil it?"

"You're afraid to ask. Aren't you?"

"What would I ask him? You've told me nothing. You've hinted and suggested, as you always hint and suggest, but you've told me nothing. And if you did, I'd know you were lying."

"Oh no. I'm not lying."

"Then what are you trying to tell me? That Jud is carrying on a cheap liaison? That there's another woman? You see, if you were not lying, you could tell me who it is. But you can't—can you?"

"Ask Jud."

"I shan't ask Jud. Go to him with your poison and your lies? No."

"Of course you won't. You're scared. Scared to death."

"Scared?"

"Because it's true."

"Then if it's true you tell me who it is—"

Again I heard that little three-noted laugh as I had heard it in the sitting room that night when she was with Jud, wanton and conquering.

"Who do you *think* it is?"

Phyl's voice was frantic now, her face ravaged. "You're lying!"

And Eva's, "Am I?" taunting.

Watching Phyl I felt as if I watched someone struggling wildly, desperately against a vast and irresistible current that roared toward certain destruction. "It's not true! You want to destroy this, as you've destroyed everything for me. The way you destroy everyone. Beauty and your children and— This time you won't. I won't let you. It isn't true."

"Ask Jud."

"I will ask him. You said that I'm afraid to ask him. I'm not. If I didn't know you are lying I would be afraid. But I'm not."

"Oh yes, you are. You won't ask him. You will go on worrying about it the rest of your life. And wondering."

"No."

"You'll go on trying to pretend to yourself that he loves you. Wondering where he is. And what he thinks about. And never trusting him for a single minute in your life."

She moved her head, "I can't. I won't—"

"Then ask Jud."

Then I saw Phyl find from somewhere strength and courage. She stood defiantly, her head high and challenging, and again I thought of a young knight facing proudly the forces of darkness. Then Eva's voice came, sensuous, sly and almost a whisper.

"Ask him, darling."

My gasping, "Don't Phyl—wait!" was too late, for she had turned and gone swiftly toward the foyer and though I followed her, it was still too late. The front door closed as I reached the foyer, and flinging it open I saw from the porch her dark figure as she stumbled away, blinded and desperate, against the immensity of night. And I knew I could not stop her, that it was beyond my or any power to help. It was too late. And I turned back into the house where Eva waited, aware suddenly of my clenched hands, of my angry blood roaring in my ears.

But when I reached the sitting room she was gone and there was only the illusive haunting fragrance of her perfume hovering on the still air of the silent echoing house.

I waited for Phyl's return, waiting I do not know how long and praying desperately as I waited that Jud would make her believe that the truth was not true but only wanton viciousness. But, recalling the slashing insistence of Phyl's voice as she had whipped her questions at Eva, I knew that she would force her way to a truth she did not wish to hear, and hearing she would believe that Jud had used her only as refuge from Eva's shameful possession of him. Even in escape Eva had managed to lay in waste the new land she had found.

Waiting there, aching with tiredness and fear, I thought of absurd and useless tricks by which Phyl might be deceived into happiness. Suppose, I thought, that Jud was not at home, that somehow I could manage to see him first and tell him that he must preserve his secret at any cost. I thought of Beauty and half rose as if to go to his room, then remembered his stumbling step along the corridor and told myself that even sober, there was nothing he could do. Or anyone.

I sank back into my chair again and to my cramped waiting, recalling how time and time again I had told myself only a few days and Phyl would be safe. The words mocked me now and made absurd any belief that Eva could be defeated. I asked why fate had to inflict unjust punishment and undeserved reward. What purpose could Eva have in smashing Phyl's chance at life? But at this moment the reasons, abstract and slippery, didn't matter. Only Phyl mattered.

I heard the door opening, and moving went to meet her. She stood with somebody's coat hanging from her shoulders, her drained face revealing clearer than any words the completeness of her destruction.

I went to stand beside her and spoke her name, but when she turned her white and sightless face to mine I could say nothing more. How comfort her, I thought, with words? Or persuade her that any tomorrows would be better? I tried to touch her—for she was so alone—but she slipped with ghostly elusiveness from my hands. Standing in the foyer I watched her climb the stairs, then followed her, going down Beauty's corridor and pausing at her door. And calling.

There was no answer. So then I knocked and tried the door, only to find it locked. From behind it there was only silence and a great quiet more terrible than any noise. At last I went to my room, undressed.

I did not sleep. I found myself at Phyl's door again, though how much later I will never know. Standing there I raised my hand to knock.

Then I thought that if she slept I would disturb her and though I did not believe she slept, indecision sent me to my room again and to my bed. But I could not rest. And so again to her door, and again and again as the night dwindled. How long this night, I thought, and then I went and found her door open and a lamp burning and her bed smooth and untouched. Could she have gone out walking about the place, hoping to escape somehow from thinking? I wondered. Or had she fled to another roof, finding it impossible to remain beneath the one which sheltered Eva? Or—had she perhaps gone back to Jud?

I went back to my room, pulled the first clothes my hand touched from my closet and put them on. I slipped down the stairs and went out into the first faint graying of shadows. I blundered toward Jud's house, the house where she and Jud had meant to live, where, I remembered as if it were an eternity ago, she had painted a kitchen—

a kitchen with a fireplace and big chintz chairs. When I saw the house, its windows blank and unlighted, I was frantic and my fists beating against the door were frantic too. And when Jud opened it and I saw his face in his hall's dim light I knew that neither had he slept this night.

"Phyl—is she here?"

"She isn't here. She was, she left a couple of hours ago."

"She isn't at home. She hasn't been to bed. I'm—I'm worried. Afraid—"

Without waiting for me to complete the sentence he moved past me, leaving his door standing open, and walking swiftly, noiselessly he turned back up the road. I ran after him, my breath laboring as I ran. Could she have taken a car, driven to town? Perhaps—

He swerved and left the road, plunging in oblivious to underbrush and stinging thicket. I ran slipping, falling to my knees, scrambling up and somehow following, hearing the yelping of a dog chained somewhere and the first shrill cries of roosters.

In the garage both cars crouched, their metal coldly glistening, the smell of gas and rubber heavy on the air. She had not gone this way. I turned to Jud, cried out, "But then where?" and he stood there, his bright quick eyes shifting in his face but not answering. I thought: but she must be somewhere. She must—but then how would she go, the cars are here—and then I thought of the little mare, and I remembered how riding had been for her a way of escape.

I said "Mimi!" and then we were going toward the stables, running now.

The day was growing stronger but the stable loomed dark, somehow foreboding against the pallid light. When I saw that the doors stood open I gasped with relief. I followed Jud into the waiting blackness, sensing rather than seeing the bales of hay, the stalls, the bags of feed. I heard the frantic whinny of Beauty's hunter, then as the darkness thinned I saw Mimi, the little mare. And almost before I could grasp the meaning of her being here I heard Jud's cry guttural and animal and saw the bridle rein hung from a rusting hook set in the beam.

Then I saw her. Still wearing the party dress and the silver slippers . . . turning . . . twisting. . . .

Three

I had the flu—Trissa and Ted had had it and I had nursed them—and now I lay in my bed shivering and aching and miserably dull. Then as the fever mounted I lifted to float in a void timeless and shapeless, yet not strange. For Phyl was there like a young knight in her scarlet jacket, and Mama and Father, and Beauty. But when I, like an eager child returning home after a visit with strangers, ran breathlessly toward them their eyes were cold and unseeing. They turned away and left me standing desolate and despairing. Then Ty—why was he there? I wondered—came and stood beside me while I wept brokenhearted, saying over and over, "It's only a dream, it's only a dream, it's only a dream, it's only a dream. . . ."

And suddenly it wasn't Ty. It was Miss George leaning over me, easing me against the pillow again saying "Child, don't cry, 'It's only a dream, only a dream.' Try and sleep again."

I slept again and I was in another place, a huge and vaulted prison honeycombed with tiers of cells, but not of steel as prisons are but of a shining golden transparent material which I couldn't name yet which was somehow familiar. We—it was Ty again—walked through the lanes between the cells while numberless tiny figures scurried tirelessly and a small sound, only a monotonous hum at first, crescendoed into a monstrous, maddening droning. And then I knew. This was a hive, the golden transparency was honey, the tireless scurrying figures, the workers. A voice cried out above the droning, "Make way for the queen." Vast doors, which a moment before had not existed, swept open and Eva with her light and resolute step and proudly lifted head came toward me all gold transparency and shining, her eyes like amber flames fastened upon me. I heard Ty's voice reciting, patly as a guide on a sightseeing tour might recite, "The Queen is a jealous queen . . . if another queen emerges she stings her to death, then promenades the premises, monarch of all—" And suddenly high and sweet above his voice I heard Phyl's. "Be careful, Jen!" it warned. Step by step I backed away from the shining figure that so steadily came toward me. And now the droning filled the place and beat against my brain; then I was a cornered thing seeking escape frantically, dashing from side to side. Wherever I ran, the shining figure stalking, stalking. Then Ty's voice came again, saying, "Only a dream, only a dream, only a dream." And again it wasn't Ty but Miss George, her hands on my shoulders, pressing me back into the pillow, saying, "Child! child! Don't take on so—it's only a dream. . . ."

After that nothing except drifting on a tide which bore me out and turning, brought me back again to half-awareness of the doctor standing above me, his voice low and grave, "Thin! No resistance! Run down." And Miss George's, "Laws, no wonder! A lot of sadness! First her father and mother, and then the dreadful thing of Phyl—and right after nursing the children through the flu. Too much. Too much. And her so young—"

"She must have a nurse." This was the doctor, and as if he had produced her from his bag the nurse was there, square and squat and all crisp white and smugly competent. Saying, "Come now, don't be a baby," or "Now, now! We can't have that," or "Come, come! Drink all of it," and I weakly obeyed, but afterward peering at her from beneath my lids and hating her.

But, as the tide on which I drifted bore me back to awareness oftener and for longer periods, I became aware of other things. Of the flowers, but never the same flowers, which by some alchemy I couldn't fathom appeared on my chest of drawers. Roses, pink one time, the next time glowing red, once cool pure white; another day violets, hundreds of them spilling from a bowl; and still another, daffodils gay in their yellow and green. Then I would forget the flowers, for I sensed somehow that Beauty stood above me. And thought the act of opening my eyes required more will than I could summon, nevertheless I saw the scarred face and dark unsmiling eyes and heard the bright brittleness of the nurse's voice, "Better this morning, Mr. Avery. A splendid night." And I floated away on the timeless tide again.

I awoke in a cold gray dawn as spent as a swimmer who has tirelessly fought an uneasy sea but has at last been swept to shore. But my mind was clear. My eyes took in the dimmed light, the dawn's sick face at the window and Miss George nodding in the chair beside me. I thought, surprised, "Why—I've been really sick." My mind reached, groping for the beginning and coming to a day when I nursed the children blind and dazed. I had stood with the bottle of sulfa drug in my hand, unable to remember if they should have another dose. And after that—nothing, and I had lain here with all the answers I wanted unanswered. When Miss George awoke perhaps she could—would know them.

She was awake. I found her eyes upon me, peering through the lifting gray of the room, and smiled at her. "Hello." I heard the thread of sound that was my voice unbelieving.

She said, "Child," and broke off, but not until her hand dashed at her cheek and I saw the tears. Then she was herself again. "You're better! Thank God for it!"

I asked, "Have I been—so sick?"

"Sick enough. And no wonder! Nursing Trissa and Ted! Child, no rest day or night—I've blamed myself over and over."

"You mustn't. Are the children—all right?"

"They're up and sassy. And missing you."

Already I felt sleep's reaching hands but remembering the questions for which I had no answers, I resisted.

"What day is it?"

"A Tuesday, child."

"But which Tuesday? What date?"

She told me and I figured. "Five weeks since Phyl . . . ?"

She nodded. "Yes, child. But don't think of that. It's no use. And you must get well and strong."

But there was another answer I must have. I said his name. "Beauty?"

With her sad old eyes peering at me through the dawn she gave me my answer. Beauty was all right, she said, though he had worried about me as if I had been his own. And not a drop had he touched since I came down sick. He had taken over the nursing of the children, and nursed them well. He had been wonderful. She paused, then cackled. And that Ty McKinnon! He had near run her crazy. Telephoning three, four times a day and flowers every day. Not one day missed. But now—getting out of her chair stiffly she put out the lamp and smoothed my cover—now, she said, I must go to sleep. She had spelled the nurse to let her snatch a few hours' sleep, but it was time to wake her now. She laid her dry old hand on my forehead. I must go to sleep, she said. Go to sleep. . . .

When I woke again it was night and Beauty was stretched in the chair beside the lamp, his eyes staring into space. I tried to speak, tried to shape my voice to his name but there was no voice and my lips moved soundlessly. Then it wasn't important any more. It was enough that he was there.

Day by day the tempting food, the cool drinks, the periods of rest poured strength back into my body as a transfusion renews the blood. For the first time I was allowed to sit up in bed, then allowed to stagger on uncertain legs to the bathroom, then to sit in a chair for an increasingly longer period each day with Miss Breen, the nurse, ordering and directing as inexorably as an army sergeant, forcing me to sit up when I preferred to sleep or ordering me back to bed when I would have stayed up. Her "Come, come!" and "Come now!" were so briskly said and so patronizing, they rasped me to anger and near rebellion.

Each morning as she sponged me I lay with tight-closed fists and biting my lips, flinched at her "Come now! Other side! Back now! Stomach!" She rolled me as she would a log, the washcloth trailing a dank cold end across my body as she sponged. And talking, talking, talking. She *did* think that Mrs. Avery was the loveliest person! So sweet and so, er—gracious, and a good-looker too! Or Mrs. Avery had said this or that. Mrs. Avery had asked her opinion about this or that. Mrs. Avery, Mrs. Avery, Mrs. Avery—but (this in a dark prophetic voice) it was easy to see that Mrs. Avery's life wasn't all beer and skittles. That sister-in-law now—a terrible business! Nutty as a fruitcake of course, but that didn't make it any easier for Mrs. Avery. And what that sister-in-law had done to the children! It just went to prove, didn't it, that money couldn't buy *everything*.

I, clenching my fists and biting my lips, fought back the things I would have said. I knew that Aunt Eva, probably smiling her faint smile and with her wide eyes pensive, had related so, so sadly what she wished Miss Breen to believe. Even Miss Breen, I thought grimly, Miss Breen, square and squat and somehow ordinary, must perceive her sovereignty, and bow down and worship.

Achingly, I looked forward to the day when Miss Breen would go, when I would no longer have to hear her say "Come, come!"—when I would be a person again and not a robot moving to her smug ordering.

Now I cherished each small sign of my progression toward health. The day when for the first time Trissa and Ted were allowed to visit me and came with their gifts of love. Trissa's half-dozen dog violets —"The very first," she told me proudly; and Ted's gift, his favorite paper ship, handed to me silently, his still eyes upon my face. Then came the afternoon that Ty drove out, coming into my room quietly, sitting beside me, saying, "You've had a bad time, haven't you?"

I said yes, and stopped.

"You must get well. So we can have fun."

"Fun?" I repeated the word dubiously.

"Yes, fun. Winter's nearly over. Atlanta has wonderful springs. And early springs."

I glanced at the warm sun that filled my room. "It's like spring already."

He shook his head. "Not quite. This is false spring."

"False spring?"

"We have it down here. False spring. Warm and with that lift in the air that makes you think spring's here. And then it's cold again. Maybe ice and snow. But," he put his nice hand on mine, "spring *does* come."

Spring, I thought. The sweet winelike air, the fruit trees blossoming, the violets pushing their way up, the trees laced with tender green. Windows opened and curtains blowing. The curtains in Jud's kitchen blowing, billowing—the curtains Phyl had made and hung. All the world renewed and coming alive again, I thought. But not Phyl. Not Phyl, ever again. . . .

I came back to Ty, found his eyes, steady and so kind, upon me. I said, "It's hard to believe sometimes that spring will come."

"Yes," he said, "but it *does* come."

We were at dinner, Aunt Eva and Beauty and Miss Breen and I—I for the first time since my illness. Dressing, I had been irritated almost to anger by Miss Breen who—with her "Come, come!"—had directed me as if I were a retarded child and, her hand on my arm, had descended the stairs beside me. Our steps were punctuated by her "Come now! Not so fast!" or "Easy does it!" It was as if I were a cripple or senile.

When we entered the sitting room Trissa and Ted ran to meet me, their faces bright with welcome. When I had hugged and kissed them, all of us laughing happily, I raised my eyes and looked across their heads at Beauty. He welcomed me too, smiling gravely but with tenderness. Then Miss Breen's clicking orders again, "Come, come! Don't overdo. Come now, you're not strong yet!" She put me in a chair, not, I sensed, because it was necessary but because she must impress Mr. Avery with her competent officiousness. As, despite my protestations, she put a sofa cushion at my back, she said, "Doesn't she look marvelous?" knowing I looked as *marvelous* as a sick cat.

Her inquiry was directed at Beauty. He answered, "She does indeed look," his eyes met mine, "marvelous," and she laughed her abrupt raucous laugh. "It sure is a wonder what powder and paint will do." Her eyes slid from me to Beauty. "Why she's almost pretty, isn't she?"

"Yes, almost pretty." He was quietly courteous and when he added, "But you've given her such splendid care," he was deferential and she preened.

"Well, of course I'm not one to brag," she simpered modestly, "but I do know my job. The trouble with most nurses is they're too soft. But not me. I make 'em walk the chalk line, I can tell you."

"I'm sure of that."

"Keep 'em in line! That's my motto. Why, you'd never believe the trouble some patients give you. I had one case, an old man. And, would you believe it, like a spoiled brat. Wore out two nurses before they called me on the case." With lips pursed and eyes narrowed to shrewdness, she tossed her head. "Well, he didn't give me any trouble. I taught him a thing or two."

"You must be—very clever."

Some intonation in his voice stirred suspicion and she glanced at him swiftly, but reassured by his unsmiling deference, she turned simpering again. "Well," she laughed self-consciously, "I don't know about 'clever' but I do know you have to keep 'em in line."

It was then that Eva came into the room, as soft, as shining and—I had to admit it—as beautiful as I had remembered her. "Darling!" Lightly she swept to me, her arms were about me, her fragrant cheek brushed mine. "So wonderful to have you up! Such a long time since I saw you, dearest. But they did look after you, didn't they? And after all—I simply couldn't risk flu." Stepping back she scrutinized me, then turned to Miss Breen. "She looks simply dreadful. So pale and thin and—but dreadful. Are you sure," she gestured vaguely, "this isn't too much for her?"

Miss Breen's voice dripped sweetness. "Now, don't you worry, Mrs. Avery. I'm watching out for this little lady. You just trust me."

Eva's eyes were wide and wistful, her voice touched with martyrdom. "How nice to feel there is someone I can really trust."

Miss Breen's square hand reaching over patted the slim shoulder and she was as briskly authoritative as a policeman. "And tonight when I've tucked this little lady in I'm just giving you a real massage."

When Aunt Eva had drifted from the room to freshen up a bit, she said, for dinner—and she wouldn't be a minute, she'd simply rush like mad—Miss Breen looked at Beauty sternly. "Easy to see, Mr. Avery," she said it portentously, "that your lovely lady has *too much* on her mind."

Beauty's voice was equally stern, equally portentous. "How right you are, Miss Breen. I think even you would be surprised if you knew how much—too much."

His mocking eyes, amused beneath the quirking brows, met mine across the space which lay between us. And careful that Miss Breen should not see, he thrust his tongue into his cheek and winked.

While Old Tom served and we ate, Aunt Eva, the faint luminous smile on her face, her hand worrying at the pearls at her throat, spun her web of talk. That simply gorgeous Bronson girl had gone back to Charleston (this was for my benefit) simply wild because she'd made no headway, none at all, with Ty. And everyone in Atlanta was talking about Ty and how while you were ill, darling, he turned down absolutely every invitation. And we simply must hear the perfectly priceless story about the Conroys: When their daughter married, of course everybody knew they'd worked their heads off to snare the Winston boy, half-witted as he was, they had staged that simply tremendous wedding for her—but to get back to the story, Mrs. Conroy had gone to a certain jeweler and bought—or pretended to buy—a magnificent silver service—their present for their daughter, you know—and had displayed it *so* prominently among the wedding gifts. And then a few days after the wedding she had *returned* it—imagine—saying it wasn't *exactly* what she wanted. Of course (the little three-noted laugh) everyone knew they were absolutely stony. But imagine, borrowing a wedding gift to give your own daughter!

It went on but I didn't listen. I made some semblance of eating without really eating, was suddenly aware that I was tired. I saw that Miss Breen listened reverently, adoringly—as once, I thought grimly, I had listened. Suddenly it struck me as unbelievable and monstrous that Eva should be unchanged, that the soft little laugh should sound as often, that her eyes should be as velvety, her smile as deliberately charming. And then it dawned upon me that it was I who expected her to change, I who was absurd. Somewhere in the long-ago years she had visioned what she wanted to be, what she wanted to have; and in her struggle to attain and hold, she had sluffed off the softer virtues of tenderness and pity and mercy, even the capacity for loving, as one eliminates surplus hampering baggage, coming at last to the hard, unyielding core of greed, as incapable of change as stone and equally incapable of feeling hurt. This, I realized bleakly, was why she always won. She could wound and tear without fear of retaliation, for you cannot wound or tear stone. So she was invincible.

Gradually as I grew stronger I went about my normal life again, took over with the children, helped Miss George with small tasks, and was at last partly freed of Miss Breen; but not entirely. For Miss Breen, it turned out, wasn't leaving. She was staying, at least (she told me smugly) for awhile. To take care of dear Mrs. Avery who, her sly eyes regarded me accusingly, had so many responsibilities, so many claims upon her, and besides all that had to fulfill the demands of her social life. If she—she meant herself—could make life just a teeny bit easier for dear Mrs. Avery she would consider it a privilege.

I answered with an indifferent, "That's nice." But as I got into my coat and wrapped a scarf about my head for a walk with Trissa and Ted I pulled a wry face at my reflection in the mirror. The queen, I thought scornfully, had acquired another lady-in-waiting to fetch and carry, to flatter and worship. I told my reflection flippantly, "And that's all right with me," and ran down the stairs and out to the yard where the children waited. Running through the woods, racing with the children, hiding behind trees while they circled and searched, Miss Breen ceased for me to exist. When Trissa tired and walked more quietly beside me, her dark eyes lifting to mine, she asked if I "liked Miss Breen," and this question revived her hateful image.

I told her, trying to be objective and tolerant, that I didn't know Miss Breen too well. But she had been quite nice when I was sick. Undoubtedly if you knew her you'd like her.

Ted trudging beside me said flatly, "I don't like her. She called me a brat. Her eyes are like black buttons."

Trissa spoke more slowly. "She told Mellie that Ted and I are spoiled. 'Spoiled brats,' she said. Are we spoiled brats, Jen?"

"You are the very best children in the whole wide world," I said, then realizing the fierceness in my voice I laughed. "But let's forget Miss Breen. I'll race you! To that big tree down the road."

Later, on our way home we passed Jud's little house and I thought of Jud and his lonely life. Driving in his Ford to the mill each morning, each night returning here to face the vacant echoing horror of the rooms which he and Phyl had planned. Some Sunday when he was at home, I told myself, the children and I would come. Perhaps if I brought the children he wouldn't mind. . . .

Ted had murmured and I snapped off my thoughts to ask, "What did you say, darling?"

He said, "Sing 'My Lady,' Jen—"

Laughing I told him I had no more voice than a woodpecker and besides I didn't know the song. He'd have to ask Daddy to sing it for him.

He didn't insist, but as we walked on he said quietly, as if to himself, "My lady for whom I would die." He looked up at me with lost eyes, "Phyl was the lady, wasn't she Jen, who died?"

I said gently, "Darling, Phyl was so tired. She is having a long, long sleep." As I spoke I wondered what he had heard? He had never seen Phyl, after. To answer his "Where's Phyl?" we had invented a trip. We had been careful not to speak of it before the children.

Pretending a casualness I did not feel I asked, "Ted, did somebody tell you that Phyl was the lady who died?"

"No."

"But why do you say that then?"

"Miss Breen said it. To Mellie. Do you know what, Jen? She said that Phyl was nutty as a fruitcake. Was she, Jen? Was she?"

As we neared the house Eva's car flashed round the drive and stopped and getting out she waited for us. "Really, Jen!" she exclaimed as we reached her, "I think it too thoughtless of you. Keeping the children out *this* late. Just over the flu, too."

"It's only just past four, Eva. And it isn't cold."

She turned her wrist, consulted the diamond watch. "A *quarter* after," she said, gently accusing.

I was tempted to laugh, but conscious of Trissa and Ted listening, their small faces concerned, I resisted. I said instead, "I'm sorry, Eva. I won't keep them out past four again."

Her eyes, innocently wide, met mine. "No, darling," she said it softly, "I'm sure you won't." Crossing the porch lightly she opened the door, but paused and looked back, "And oh, Jen! Will you come up to my room for a moment?"

I said "Yes," and when I had helped Trissa and Ted out of coats and leggings and hung them in the closet, I went up the stairs to her room and with a small warning knock entered. She was lifting a dress from a Wendell box which had been delivered earlier in the day and she cried out, "Darling, do you want to see the most heavenly frock?"

I waited, standing near the door. Preening before the mirror she held the dress against her body. "Of course this doesn't begin to give you an idea," tilting her head she surveyed herself, "but when it's on—" Her eyes reflected in the mirror were soft and shining with a sly gaiety. "Really, it's simply the sort of dress that," the little three-noted laugh, half guilt, half victory, "Monk will go out of his mind about. He's so—so vulnerable."

Her eyes met mine in the mirror and whirling abruptly she dropped the dress on a chair and faced me. "Darling, I'm simply terrible. Forgetting the talk with you. Do you mind if I undress while I talk? I've a dinner on—given for Monk! Really you'd think he was Harry Truman the fuss they make."

Unzipping her frock with a swift long gesture she stepped from it, then posed before the mirror. Wheeling she surveyed admiringly the sheath of black that was her figure, her eyes caressing the uplifted breasts voluptuous against the clinging silk. Her voice speaking to me was abstracted, as if what she said or was to say was of no importance. "Darling, I do want to talk to you—" She broke off, called to whoever had knocked on the door, "Come in."

It was Miss Breen, white and stiffly starched. She swept me with her button-black eyes and spoke to Eva. "I thought maybe you'd like for me to run your bath, Mrs. Avery."

"Oh, Miss Breen, how nice of you!" Then as Miss Breen started toward the bath, "Just a minute, Miss Breen. After all, you might as well be in on it. My talk with Jen, I mean."

Stepping out of her slip she looked at me over her shoulder. "It's about the children, Jen. Of course you remember what Dr. Peeples said about Ted—how he should have a firm hand?" Her hand moved vaguely. "And so on and so on?"

She paused as if she expected an answer. But I gave her none. I knew with swift prescience what she was about to say; and I knew too that I could not prevent her saying it. And something cold and hopeless twisted inside of me.

She was talking. "And really, dearest, you're simply not well enough. It isn't that you don't *try*," her voice lifted the word lightly, "but, well," a disarming little laugh, "you're like Phyl, darling. Too easy with them. And really, their manners are too, too dreadful. After all, they will go about with well-bred people—when they grow up, I mean. I simply can't have them perfect little savages. Now, can I?"

Her eyes were upon me. Obviously she waited for some sort of response. I said flatly, "So?"

"Darling." She laughed infectiously. "Don't act as if I'm selling you down the river. Really I am thinking of you. Of your health. So —I've asked Miss Breen to stay on—and take complete charge of the children. And," so warm the smile she sent Miss Breen, "she has said that she will."

I told myself, It's to hurt you. Don't let her know it hurts, or try to change it. Useless to try. But with my next breath I knew that I must try, for Trissa and Ted.

I said, not swiftly but slowly and with my voice level, "Eva, you must not do this to Trissa and Ted. They are such wonderful children. With fine minds, and sensitive and so loving."

Her eyes widened with astonishment. "Well, really, Jen! It isn't necessary to tell me about my *own* children. After all, I *am* their mother. And a mother knows her children better than anybody." Her shrug was a gesture of bored dismissal.

But I would not be dismissed. "Eva." I still spoke slowly. Passionately I wished to convince her. "Eva, do you love your children?"

"Love them?" She looked at me through narrowed eyes. "But—but I adore them! And no one—no one can say that I don't."

"I say it, Eva," I said. "Or you couldn't do what you say you'll do. And I'll tell you why."

"Really, Jen, I don't care to hear it. Heavens, what wild preamble —all of it. I suppose like Phyl you're simply obsessed with my children. Really! Why you old maids don't have children of your own!"

"You know I'm not obsessed, Eva. Any more than Phyl was obsessed. It's just that we, both of us, loved Trissa and Ted."

She threw out her hands. "So! You love them! And Miss Breen wouldn't, I suppose."

"I don't know. Perhaps in time she would." I ignored Miss Breen's, "Well this certainly beats me!" I went on: "But Miss Breen is arrogant and ignorant, and stupid—"

Miss Breen cried out, "Now just a minute, you—" Again I ignored her and went on: "Eva, she has no sympathy or understanding. She wants to impose her will even upon adults. She will impose it upon Trissa and Ted, press them, squeeze them, distort them." The picture of Trissa and Ted abject before Miss Breen was too much to bear. Raggedly I said, "Eva, don't. Don't."

She had pulled on a robe and now, unflurried, she tied it carefully before she even looked my way. "Really, Jen, I think you should apologize to Miss Breen."

"I don't apologize. I've only told the truth." I looked at Miss Breen deliberately, but without malice. And though she returned my look without speaking I knew she would be my enemy to the last day of my life.

"Then, darling," Eva's voice was gentle but her eyes as she looked at me were unsmiling, "really, there is nothing more to be said. Tomorrow," even gentler her voice now, "I'll have you moved to the room on Beauty's corridor, the one Phyl was in, and give Miss Breen yours. Next to the children." She added, but oh so gently, "I'm sorry, darling."

I turned and left the room and closed the door behind me and slowly descended the stairs, frozen and bitter and despairing. And hating Eva Avery as I had never dreamed I could hate. This, I thought, was how Beauty felt. How he had felt in all the years of his defeat. No wonder he drank. No wonder he sought release. How else could he not kill her?

Next day I was moved into Phyl's room down the other corridor and Miss Breen settled herself in mine. Carrying my things to the other room I heard her rasping voice, as she settled in, speaking to Trissa and Ted: "Come now! We aren't going to leave these toys about, are we? We must be little ladies and gentlemen, mustn't we? Come, come! Get this junk piled neatly or Breensy will slap lazy hands."

Miserably I sat on the bed in the new room remembering the glimpse I had caught of Trissa's wondering and half-frightened face. Trissa, I thought, always quiet and eager to please and with an understanding that made her seem older than she was, would be threatened and bullied; Ted with his secret pride, humbled and browbeaten. It was too much to bear, I thought, too much. And if it was too much for me, then what of them?

Ty drove me out the highway, his profile catching the glow from the dashboard of his car, his hands firm on the wheel. He had called me, had asked me to go to dinner. Not to a restaurant or a club, he said, but to a special place he wanted me to see. A fairly long drive, but the food, he guaranteed, would compensate for the distance we must travel.

Eager to get away from the house and all it had come to mean, I had said I would go and now slumped in the seat of his car, watching his sure hands as they drove, I realized that I was more comfortable, more at ease with him than with anyone I had come to know since I had come South. With Ty, and only with Ty, I could forget that there was reason to be afraid of tomorrow. I could be content and quiet and certain that he would allow nothing to harm me.

His sure hands turned the car from the main highway into an unpaved road and I saw that we were in the country. We passed clumps of wood, the loose planks of a wooden bridge rattled beneath our wheels.

I asked the name of the place to which we were going, and he grinned.

"Cabin in the Cotton. Lord knows why! Not much cotton out this way. But we do have to be Southern even when it isn't particularly appropriate."

"But if it's so far out I don't see how anybody can expect—"

He still grinned.

"Oh, this is one of our more famous joints—in a quiet sort of way."

"Famous? Really?"

"Sure. Clandestine and a little risqué. Or supposed to be. I've never understood why. Frankly, I've always found it pretty tame, but maybe I just don't know the password. Anyhow, it's expensive enough to be sinful so you can feel properly naughty. And, incidentally, if we're seen together there, people will think the worst."

"Heavens! Do you mean I'll be compromised?"

He nodded assuringly.

"Absolutely. They're even supposed to have rooms upstairs and for all I know, can-can girls. Our best debutantes get initiated into a life of sin at Cabin in the Cotton."

The road had narrowed and now, curving, led to a rambling low building, its windows glowing warm against the darkness. A Negro held the door of the car, we got out and went up the stone steps and across the rustic porch. Ty opened the door, I saw a long room, low-roofed and dimly lighted with small candlelit tables, arranged, I thought, to invoke at least the feeling of privacy. Ty said, "Welcome to our den of iniquity. Sin provided at a price."

"I think you're kidding me again," I accused. "It looks horribly proper to me."

"Oh, well, if the debauchery isn't up to your Yankee standards that's not my fault. Anyway the food is good."

We were led by the head waiter to a secluded corner table and I glanced around at the other tables. Not many were occupied. Perhaps we were early. The Cabin was a place you went on to after dinner or earlier parties. Ty ordered cocktails, and when we had tasted and nodded approval to each other he leaned toward me over the table.

"Our sin may not be so impressive but our devotion is Grade A," he told me. "If you'll have another drink I'll propose to you again."

"I adore proposals," I answered as lightly as I could. His grin was rueful.

"But you're still not accepting them this season, at least from me."

"From no one."

He leaned back. "Oh well. Nothing tried, nothing gained. I always make my offers before dinner when a girl's hungry, hoping she'll mistake her clawing hunger for a deeper feeling."

I laughed, fond of him, loving him, but not as he wished me to love. I felt regret because I could not love him that way. There was no patronage in my pity. I was sorry, but not for him. For both of us because we loved and had so little hope of fulfillment.

"Do you propose to every girl you bring here?" I asked smiling.

He put his hand upon mine.

"You mean, 'Do I tell this to all the girls?' " He shook his head. "In a dreary but reliable way I'm a one-woman man, Jen, and I'm afraid you're *it*."

"You can't propose to me every time we have dinner," I told him.

"Oh no. Just as soon as we're married I intend to give my best thinking to ways and means of ending the vicious habit of asking for your hand."

I laughed, "Oh, Ty! I think I like being with you more than with anybody."

"You could make it permanent."

I saw then that he was serious, that his eyes were grave above his smile, and I was contrite.

"No," I said, "no. Please, Ty."

He still smiled. "Whatever you say. But there is the classic question I'd like to ask."

"Classic question?"

"I've asked it before and you've told me no, but I'm not completely convinced. So I'll ask it just one more time. Is there someone else?"

I started to tell him no again, but I was aware of his watching, and I knew his goodness deserved better than a lie. "There's someone—" I began, but at his, "Who?" I left the sentence unfinished. I said, "Does it matter, as long as there is someone?"

He nodded. "It matters whether or not he deserves all this luck, Jen."

"No," I said, "it doesn't. I can't have him, you see. There's no chance of my having him. Ever."

He said quietly, "So we're both out of luck," and I nodded.

The waiter brought our dinner and we lifted our forks and tasted the food, but we had no appetite. Ty gave up first and pushed his plate away. He asked gravely, "You're in love with Beauty Avery, aren't you?"

Avoiding his eyes, seeing the pattern of crumbs on the white cloth, I nodded.

"Don't be angry," I said. "There's nothing. There can never be."

He had looked up, his eyes gazed over my shoulder into the dim room.

"I wouldn't be too sure of that," he said. "Mind you, I'm jealous but I wouldn't be surprised if you had a chance."

I was puzzled. "I don't understand. What do you mean?"

"Look behind you, Jen."

"Behind me?"

"Not too obviously," he said. "Drop your napkin."

I dropped my napkin and leaning to retrieve it followed the direction of his eyes.

"Eva and Monk get around," he said quietly. "There's considerable talk about them."

I saw them then, though the table was almost lost in shadow. Eva's slim, proud grace as she curved toward Monk Lyons, the reflection of dim light upon her hair. And I saw that he too leaned, close and absorbed, that an indefinable intimacy quivered between them.

I saw him reach out and touch her hand, saw her fingers curve white into his, saw as he raised it to his heavy lips. Even across the space between us I heard the three husky little notes of her laughter and her, "Oh, Monk, darling! Don't be absurd!"

Ty stood signaling to the waiter.

"I think we've had enough."

I said, taking my coat from my chair, "Thank you, Ty." And then we were in the car again, Ty driving steadily and with sure skill along the dark road which led back toward town. For a long while we rode not talking, passed a field, a tree, a barn, each of them lonely somehow against the night. Then scattered lights began to pepper the darkness.

"You see," Ty said quietly, "perhaps it isn't hopeless. Perhaps there is a chance."

I said nothing, shamed somehow by his kindness. I looked down at my hands folded in my lap as if I expected them to hold the answer to his hoping and to mine.

"Don't give up the ship," he told me steadily. And without looking, I knew from his voice that his smile, gentle and steady, had returned.

"You see, *I'm* not giving up," he said. "Not this easy. Not yet. If you love somebody, you keep believing. You keep believing that sooner or later your luck will turn."

"Ty," I said. "Oh, Ty."

He put his arm round me.

"We're in the same boat, Jen. And a damned uncomfortable little boat, isn't it?"

"A horrible little boat." I said then, "Ty," and he passed his handkerchief to me. I cried against his shoulder while he drove, hiding my face from the lights of the city into which the highway led us. Then finally I was quiet. I blew my nose, gulped.

"I'm a terrible fool, Ty. You ought to find a girl with a sense of humor."

He shrugged, his eyes intent on the street ahead.
"I'm not in the mood for laughing either, Jen."

That night undressing for bed I was, if not happy, at least not hopeless. And I marveled how small events could change a day for you or a life; as tonight, and seeing Eva and Monk Lyons had changed things for me. I told myself there was nothing tangible which justified my sudden lifting hope that the affair of Eva and Monk Lyons could have permanent results, yet still that little hope persisted. Like a child at its prayers asking the gift of a greatly coveted toy, I promised as I went to sleep that if I were granted the thing which I so wanted I would all the days of my life be good.

Ted had a nightmare that night and though his screams came to me but faintly I awoke and lay in the dark, my ears straining to hear, as if by hearing, I could banish fear for him. So well I knew the progression of his fear. The first frantic scream of waking, less frantic as he received assurance from someone. Then the gradual diminishing of his cries, dwindling at last to hiccoughs and, finally, sleep. But tonight there was no such progression; instead his screams increased in volume. And when I could bear it no longer I slid into my slippers, pulled a robe around me and padded down the corridor to his door.

Standing beside it, listening I knew the reason for the passionate and prolonged screaming, now almost hysteria. For Miss Breen's voice, nagging, berating, threatening, lashed against the closed room and his screaming with the persistence of a whip. "Want Breensy to spank your hands again? Breensy will. You're just a great big baby!" Her voice dropped, was vicious, ominous. "And—if—you—don't—hush I'll slap your hands—and good."

I heard Trissa's pleading voice then, frantic, "Please don't slap his hands again," and Miss Breen's, "You keep out of this, Miss Smarty Pants! Or you'll catch it too!"

Boiling, and caring for nothing except that Trissa and Ted should knew they were not wholly abandoned to her, I knocked on the door. Her voice stopped, and her footsteps were angry before she unlocked and opened it warily. The button-black eyes above the salmon pink robe glared out at me. Before I could so much as speak, she slammed the door with venom and turned the key viciously in the lock. I was angry now and my anger swept me on swift padding feet back up the corridor and down the other one and to Beauty's door. Without knocking I opened it, stepped inside the dark and silent room and called his name. His voice, alert and sober, answered. "Jen! Is anything wrong?"

Standing in the dark I began to tell him, the words tumbling pell-mell and incoherently from my mouth but evidently conveying what I wished. Before I had half done he was up, had snapped on the light, had found slippers and was pulling on his robe as we hastened along the corridor again, Ted's screams sweeping to meet us. At the door I gestured Beauty to quiet and for a moment we stood listening, our heads bent. Miss Breen, frustrated now and cold with fury, gibed and sneered and threatened. "I told you I meant business, didn't I? Didn't I? Now cut out that yelping." We heard the flicking slap of flesh on flesh.

Then Beauty's knuckles were demanding against the door. His eyes were hot in his white face as opening the door she peered around it warily. His arm swung against it, sweeping it wide.

"Why, Mr. Avery!" In her salmon pink she simpered up at him.

He strode to Ted's bed and gathered the child up. He said, "You'll sleep with me tonight, Son. And you, Trissa." The smile he bent on her pale and patient face was all tenderness. "You will sleep with Jen," he told her.

Bridling, Miss Breen objected. "I take my orders from Mrs. Avery. I have implicit orders—"

With Ted in his arms he turned and looked back at her contemptuously. "To hell with your orders! And so help me God if ever again you lay the weight of your hand on either of my children, *I'll beat you to death.*"

The button-black eyes flickered and slid from his figure to mine, taking in, I perceived, our robes and slippers, adding them to the lateness of the hour, evolving something dark and noisome in her mind. "You understand, Mr. Avery," her tongue moistened her thick lips, "I will have to report this—episode—to your wife."

"Report and be damned to you." He had started from the room but in the doorway he stopped. "Another thing. This door is not to be locked, ever. And if my niece desires to enter the room at any time, she may do so, understand?"

"Yes, indeedy!" The black eyes met his meaningly. "I *do* understand, Mr. Avery. Very, *very* well."

We went then, and when I had tucked Trissa in my bed and kissed her, hurt by the question in her eyes, I went back to Beauty's room and tucked Ted in too, gave him his glass of water, wiped his tear-swollen face, proud now because he was to sleep with Daddy. As I settled his covers he looked up at me. "Jen," his voice was solemn, "you know what? That old Miss Breen is nutty as a fruitcake." His eyes drooped. "But," he was complacent, "I got even with her—I spit on her sleeve."

Laughing I kissed him and turned to leave the room. Beauty walked beside me to the door and leaned against it. "Did you and Ty have fun tonight?" he asked.

I told him, a very good time. We had gone to the Cabin in the Cotton, and guess who I'd seen there? Without making him guess (though I know now that he could have guessed easily enough) I told him. Of seeing Eva and Monk Lyons. And sensing from some secret and pleasing knowledge in the dark eyes that smiled down at me that I had not surprised him, I said, "Beauty! You know something. What do you know?"

Warningly he laid his finger on his lips, whispered, "Sh—h—h—I don't even dare think about it," he raised his hand, showed me his crossed fingers, "but I'm keeping my fingers crossed."

I stood before him, my world suddenly a bright world and wonderful, and remembered how Ty had said, "Perhaps there is a chance."

I asked, almost fearfully, "Beauty, do you think so? That Eva—"

He nodded, not gleefully or with triumph, but gravely. "I think," his voice was thoughtful, "I think there just might be a chance." He paused and his smile twisted. "She'd give her soul to go to London," his brows lifted, "as wife of the American Ambassador."

I breathed, "Oh, I hope she gets her wish."

He smiled down at me. "And I too, darling. But—" the smile changed, became an urchin's grin—"God save the King."

I could not believe that she might leave him to me. Something within me rejected the possibility that all I wished for so deeply might be true. I dared not hope, would not allow myself to hope, as if by not asking too much of fate I might somehow propitiate malicious gods.

But there were times when, as if resentful of suppression, the tiny thrusting spears of hope would not be denied: I would tell myself that Eva's leaving would be a natural thing and, wanting what she wanted, logical; that Monk Lyons was rich enough and powerful enough to satisfy her most passionate ambition. Remembering the indefinable but unmistakable desire expressed in his grossness as he had leaned toward her the night Ty and I had seen them, I told myself that just as she had snared others she had in the glowing net of her charm snared him. Somehow, their mating was appropriate; the motives which made the bargain alluring to each, understandable. And still I would not let myself believe that it could happen.

There was other more tangible evidence which, had I been more perceptive, might have been revealing. Eva absented herself from home even more than in the past. Messengers dropped huge and costly boxes of flowers at the door; box after box of clothes arrived, dresses and hats and intriguing underwear which, I know now, were weapons of conquest.

And still I would not let myself believe. I went my way, stealing Ted and Trissa from Miss Breen's rigid rule for games or walks with the dogs. Walking alone when there was no other way to spend my overgenerous leisure, I followed a narrow valley between the low-swung hills or a tranquil path paced by a stream. Returning from such a walk one afternoon I saw her car gleaming and powerful, waiting in the driveway, the back piled with her shining luggage. She was on the porch, her mink coat flung over her shoulders, pulling on her soft luxurious gloves. Her eyes were abstracted; falling on me as I ascended the steps, they were vague as if she hardly saw me.

"Oh Jen, there you are! I was wondering if I'd get to say good-by to you."

"Good-by?" I repeated. "You're going somewhere?"

"For a few days," she said casually. "And, darling, would you mind keeping an eye on Ted and Trissa?"

"I don't mind."

"You see," she shook her head wonderingly, "Miss Breen simply refuses to stay without me. Absolutely adamant, darling!" The little self-conscious laugh. "She simply adores me. And she can be—useful."

Before I could speak, even say good-by, she had gone lightly down the steps to the car, and Miss Breen, carrying her serviceable bag, came out of the house and followed her, turning to fling a last venomous look of dislike and disapproval at me. Then the engine came to life, the gravel spurted beneath the tires, the gears clashed and they were gone.

Still I did not let myself believe it. Eva had gone only on a brief vacation. Perhaps on a visit to friends, I reminded myself as I stepped into the foyer, or to Sea Island. And when I saw Beauty descending the stairs I stopped at their foot and waited.

"Where is she going?" I asked.

He halted on the last step and from above me grinned his satisfaction. "Do you mean the charming Mrs. Avery? Possibly to hell. But more likely to join our Mr. Lyons."

"Do you mean that she's left?" I shook my head in disbelief. "Left for good?"

"For *good?*" he answered. "That, my sweet, is a debatable question. However I understand she'll be at the Biltmore, a more strategic position, her lawyer advises, for the future wife of—an ambassador."

"She's gone to Monk Lyons?"

His smile quirked. "Not exactly *to* him. You see, they're both cautious souls and close traders. And there are preliminaries in divorce—as in any other contest. And even ethics. They require that she leave my bed and board and live in a state of unquestionable virtue for a time. I have agreed to pay her expenses. I too have done some bargaining—until Mr. Lyons can with propriety take over. I will also give her my most earnest cooperation in the matter of divorce, provided I can have the children."

I stood below him, looking up, not caring that my hair was tumbled, that my shoes were stained with mud gathered when I had crossed a stream.

"Do you mean—" I began, and I still was unbelieving. "Do you mean it's happened? Surely, not that easily, that simply?"

He laughed and stepped down to stand beside me. He put his

hands on my shoulders. "That easily," he told me, "and that simply, because she wants it that way. If she didn't—" his face darkened, "it wouldn't be so easily or simply, I'm afraid. But we won't even think about that. She's gone. We'll have to get along somehow without that particular Mrs. Avery."

"*That* Mrs. Avery?"

Smiling, he shook my shoulders gently as if he would arouse me to realization of what her going meant. He said lightly, "There will be another, you know. I'll have to pick up a substitute. Someone who will do in a pinch. I wonder," his voice discarded lightness and was grave, "if you'd be interested in taking on the job. Have you references? Or experience?"

I put my face against his rough shoulder. "I have no references," I told him, "and little experience. But I'll try to be good. I'll try so hard to be good."

Awaking the next morning, I found myself preparing automatically to face her, my nerves tensing as they had tensed each morning at the knowledge that I must be on guard. Then I remembered—Eva was gone! The knowledge gave me an easing and gladness, as if I had awakened from the long ordeal of nightmare. Eva was gone!

The details of those first days after she had gone were little changed. Miss George ordered the house, as always, directed the servants, planned meals. The change was not in what happened, but in the sudden sense of freedom. The tyranny she had enforced upon us, all of us, with her charmingly offered suggestions, with her soft "Darling, would you mind terribly?" was abolished. And only then did I realize how relentlessly that tyranny had held us to servile obedience.

Now Trissa and Ted left battered toys behind them in the sitting room when they went off to bed. This room had never before been littered with children's playthings. The arbitrary rules which she had enforced, always for her own comfort and convenience, were abolished too. Now they stayed up a half hour later to listen to *The Lone Ranger*, had their meals at the table with Beauty and me.

And Beauty and I, those days of glorious freedom, talked of matters that held interest for us. A book, a story in the newspaper, even political questions. This made me aware of how completely her vanity had controlled our talk, guiding it invariably to one and only one subject—herself.

On those nights Beauty and I, after the children were in bed and asleep, sat before the fire, he with his newspaper, I with a book, raising our eyes occasionally to smile across at each other before we returned to our reading. Yet it is not because of any special incident that I remember so vividly those quiet times before the fire but because of the meaning we, and our love and trust, gave them.

There was one such evening which does stand out. A long evening, for it was late when Beauty closed his book and got up from his chair, and the house was heavy with sleep. He said, "Time for bed," and I looked up at him. And my face must have told him what he already knew: that I belonged to him, that if he wished me to give my love I would. His eyes were darkly tender in the firelight. He came to me and, raising my face with his hand beneath my chin, bent and kissed me gently.

"I've bungled too many things, darling. I won't bungle this."

So we turned out lights and went up to our separate beds. It did not seem important then because, I believed, we must wait only a little while. Only a few weeks, or a few months, and I would be his wife and we would go up to bed, not lonely—but together. Yet I was human enough and woman enough to wish, lying in my too-wide bed, that it might have been different, to wish that I could be a woman of fatal loveliness, with charm greater than reason or caution or—his respect. But I was no fatal beauty or haunting siren. I was only Jen.

Another incident stands out, not because it was important but because it gave me an understanding of Eva which I had not before. One morning, Beauty having driven to town on the business of changing his will, I explored the house, looking into strange corners, trailing down into the cellar, finally up into the attic, a high dim place beneath the dusty, web-hung vault of roof. It had, I saw, the usual accumulation found in attics: an old phonograph, broken; stacks of books and magazines; decrepit furniture past its usefulness; aged lampshades, their silk tattered and faded; a straw hat; trunks heaped against a wall and one, smaller, thrust back and almost hidden in the narrow peak of roof. Kneeling before it I was as intrigued as if in a cave I had discovered a pirate's rotting chest. Sneezing from the aged dust I raised the lid.

At first, looking through its jumbled contents, I did not realize it was Eva's. When I knew that the contents were from her past, from days she had forgotten, I drew back as if her shining loveliness had risen before me suddenly in the dimness. Then curious, I bent over it again, lifting out the musty silks, the odd shapes of yellowed satin. There was a box of snapshots, old and faded and terribly revealing. One picture was of her as a girl, even then lovely, wearing a dress of stiff organdy. Another was in a cardboard frame—and I searched the triple rows of graduates standing on the steps of a school and found her face, beautiful and a little sulky at the necessity of sharing the attention of the camera with others.

At the very bottom of the trunk I found the scrapbook. I took it out, catching the stale, dry odor of old paper and pressed flowers, and sitting on the dusty floor I looked through its pages, puzzled and at first amused by its contents. Clippings from society columns, smug, flowery newspaper stories of "Socially important weddings," of "Outstanding parties of the season," with their gushing descriptions of decorations and table motifs and the gowns. Pages saved from ancient rotogravure supplements picturing fashionable people trapped by the camera as they watched races or attended operas or strolled in the gardens of country houses.

I leafed through them. There were literally dozens of them, their paper dry and lifeless, crumbling often at my touch. There were celebrated beauties of other years, the Number One debutantes of the season who because of money or family or, more rarely, unusual beauty had attracted the attention of the press. The clippings related their marriages, their divorces, their remarriages, their jewels, their furs, their fabulous wardrobes. They were interspersed, as if their glamor had inspired desire for like glamor in the breast of the young Eva, by articles taken from newspapers or magazines on "Make the Most of Your Beauty," "How to Cultivate Poise," "You Too Can Be Charming," "The Perfect Hostess."

And now the tenor of the clippings and articles changed, as if personal glamor was not enough. Now I found pictures of palatial homes with private swimming pools or magnificent individual rooms, or advice on silver patterns and the choice of fine china and linens. Beside these were lists of the ten best-dressed women and articles on how to decorate your home to suit your personality, all in the artless gushy prose affected by newspaper women who write for women. Yet as I read snatches of them, read their silliness ("Even on a limited budget you can afford afternoon tea,") I was less amused. I pictured the young Eva and numberless girls like Eva, accepting the criterion of success imposed by a feminine world, visioning a similar future for themselves, climbing painfully step by step toward it. The right schools, the right contacts acquired or discarded, the right marriage.

Somewhere along the way the greater number took the misstep that leads to failure and oblivion, but a few like Eva were luckier or shrewder or more ruthless and achieved their goal—and in achieving revealed the emptiness of their success.

I returned the faded silks, the laces, the snapshots and the clippings, replaced the scrapbook in its dark resting place, and closed the lid of the trunk. Rising, I brushed the dust from my skirt and hands and went downstairs with, I thought, a clearer understanding of Eva. But it was not reason enough to forgive the *terribleness* of her vanity and ambition and greed. These were the ugly fruits evolving from the tiny seed planted years ago, nurtured by the shallow soil of her environment and climbing tirelessly toward the world of parasitic frivolity, without knowing that the world to which it aspired was doomed.

I remember sharply too an afternoon a few days later. A deceptive warmth had returned, though it was still March and that month is often bitter in the South. Beauty and I took Trissa and Ted to walk, releasing the dogs that clamored from their run. Frisking they ran ahead, racing almost out of sight, and then one or the other of them returning now and then to sniff at our knees and make sure we still shared the adventure.

Nothing of extraordinary novelty happened during that walk. Ted, charging through a scrap of withered corn flushed up a covey of quail and stood in wide-eyed astonishment as their wings thundered. Trissa, called with delight, "Daddy, Jen, come here," and showed us the heart shaped leaf she had discovered hidden in the soggy mouldering earth between the roots of trees. We knelt and examined it, admiring its loveliness and the temerity of its daring so early out into the weather.

"Does that mean it's almost spring?" Trissa asked.

"Almost," Beauty told her. "It won't be long now."

Later, while Ted and Trissa raced from tree to tree upon a brown hill, Beauty lay sprawled, his head in my lap. There was contentment in the very air, a quietness between the low hills. He reached up and touched my lips with his finger like a blind man tracing a shape he cannot see.

"Have I told you," he asked drowsily, "that I love you very much?"

"You haven't told me like this," I said, "but I've known."

"I'm not a very impassioned lover, am I, my dear? I'm afraid it's what you deserve for taking up with an old man."

"You've said you love me," I told him. "That's all I want you to say. What I waited for you to say for so long."

He was silent, his dark eyes brooding. Then he drew me down to him and kissed me, holding my body close against his.

"Be still," he murmured. "Be still. We might scare it away."

We were quiet, his arms holding me, while a shadow spread slowly beneath a hill and finally reached the place where we sat. Then gently his arms released me. He stood, slapping the pine needles from the tweed of his coat.

"We'll have to start back home."

"Yes."

He drew me to my feet and once more held me, his kiss light and tender upon my lips.

Then the children burst upon us, shrieking, the dogs romping at their heels. We walked back slowly, sharing the last pale quietness of the day. I thought how strange that love should make me feel so humble and so small.

We started back toward the house through the still afternoon, the dogs running ahead to make side excursions of exploration, Ramble pausing occasionally to look back over his shoulder, his long ears drooping dolefully, to see that we followed. Beauty walked ahead of Trissa, Ted and me, holding back the branches of the small pines that overhung the path, pressing down the long, writhing brambles beneath his feet. When Trissa's small legs tired and she stopped, with a weary but contented exclamation, Beauty leaned and swung her to his shoulder where, delighted and triumphant, she rode clutching his dark hair in her little hands.

This, I thought, was what it could be, the way it would be always with us. For the four of us had somehow created another being which was no single one, but the result of our combination. This whole, I told myself while I stooped to slide between the strands of rusting barbwire Beauty parted, was in spite of the geometry books greater than the sum of its parts. I paused, watching as the others went on ahead. Trissa was still riding Beauty's shoulder; Ted, though weary too, with masculine pride disdained assistance. And it struck me that until now each of us had been alone, not literally but in a deeper way, because we belonged to no recognizable pattern shaped of love and respect. Only since Eva's departure had we found a pattern. And though its varying elements had existed before, only in these last few days had we blended and shaped them and created a family.

We came through the woods and I saw the house and it, too, somehow was different, as if it too understood that its walls and floors and beams had gained a significance lacking in the past. The high windows caught the reflection of the setting sun flinging its raw gold against their panes. Before I had been almost afraid to think of this house as more than a place where I would stop for a while, as if I were a traveler between trains, or a guest. But now I thought of it as a place where I belonged, as I belonged to Beauty and the children, a place where Beauty and I might grow old together, and Trissa grow to womanhood, Ted attain his manhood. Dreaming, I saw it as it would come to be, the front rooms less pretentious, not like jewel boxes or rooms seen in museums with little cards on the historic chairs and priceless secretaries as Eva had made them. But comfortable, with tennis rackets in need of restringing in the corner by the front door and the furniture a little worn, the rugs scuffed with use. As we went toward it through the waning light, I thought, "We're going home." And for the first time I knew the deep and satisfying sense of belonging which is so vital a part of home. Then, as we rounded a corner of the wall, I saw Eva's car, Eva's car waiting in the driveway, its sleek, glistening lines confident and assured as if it were the swift and powerful chariot of a returning conqueror.

Beauty saw it too and paused, breaking off the tune he had whistled gently, and I saw his body tense. Then, not speaking, he went on, bearing Trissa up the steps to the porch. With Ted and me close behind he opened the door. Ted's body too, I saw, had braced defiantly, and the silver-gilt head had lifted as Beauty's had. The unchildlike wariness and awareness broke my heart. It was then that I realized that my own hands were clenched, that my nails cut my palms, that my body was taut with quick anger at this return which, whatever its excuse or reason, I felt as an unbearable intrusion.

She stood in the sitting room before the mirror, arms raised, her hands touching the shining hair, her body slim and lithe in the crushed beige wool of her dress, her legs long and glowing in sheer stockings.

She heard us and turned, the movement beginning at the neck beneath the soft hair and flowing with uninterrupted grace to the tips of her fingers and to the small feet in the arrogant slippers. And I was suddenly conscious of my rumpled tweed skirt, of the beggar's-lice caught in its hem, and that my cheek was smeared where Trissa and Ted in affection had brushed it with grimy hands.

Feeling disheveled and powerless, and as if her perfection assured my defeat, I saw her charming smile, her swooping movement toward the children, the embrace which managed to avoid too-close contact with their griminess. Her voice was warm and throbbing and assured. If aware that her welcome was other than it should be, that Trissa stood mute, her face bleak, that Ted's eyes were cool with distaste, she did not betray it.

"Darlings! Where on earth have you been? Really, you look as if you've been playing in a pigpen."

They faced her unanswering, their small faces blank. Stepping back she looked down at them.

"Heavens! Can't you even speak? To your own mother?"

Ted, his face still set and cold, eyed her with dislike.

"Why did you come back?"

She dropped her head, her chin nestling against her shoulder, her lashes dark against her cheek.

"But, darling! It is my home, you know."

"No. It's ours. Mine and Daddy's and Trissa's and Jen's."

Laughing in delight, she arched her throat, her hands lifted in helpless wonder.

"Really, Ted! You simply defeat me! And," a new tartness in her voice betrayed at last that she was not unaware, "you get more like your father every day."

Hearing the tartness, I intervened and sent Ted and Trissa to Miss George. This, I knew, was not their struggle. Whatever fight there was to be must be between Eva and Beauty and me. The responsibility was ours.

From the door she watched them go along the corridor then turned back into the sitting room, her soft laugh deprecatory. "Really, Jen, I can't imagine the wild stories you must have been telling the children about me! Why, they behave as if I had the plague or were disreputable."

I told her quietly, "I've told no stories, Eva, nor mentioned you to them." But Beauty broke in, moving casually to stand between us, his hands in his pockets.

"No one had to tell them anything, Eva." His voice was flat and without emotion and his manner as he pulled a cigarette from his pocket was easy. "Children are not fools, you know."

She was at the mirror again, a jeweled compact in her hand, touching her face, her eyes intent with the puff.

"Really, do you think so, dearest? That they are bright? I've never been quite sure. About Trissa. If she isn't just a wee bit retarded, I mean. I even talked to Doctor Peeples about it."

Beauty said evenly, "Did you, Eva?"

"Of course. And he told me of a school—" Over her shoulder she regarded him reprovingly. "Dearest, if I say I asked him, I did. You know I never claim to have done something when I didn't. Though it doesn't always work the other way round. After all! I can't tell everything I do, can I, darling? But getting back to Trissa, Dr. Peeples told me of a school where they don't try and make geniuses of children, if they're not geniuses, I mean. It would be too terrible if Trissa were expected to behave as if she were Einstein, wouldn't it?"

Beauty, still casual, cut her off. "We won't discuss Trissa's intellect, Eva."

She faced him, shrugging. "But you were the one who brought it up, darling. I never discuss anybody's intellect. Really, I'd as soon discuss the state of their intestines!"

"Why did you come back, Eva?" His voice was blunt, and matter-of-fact but not quarrelsome. Turning, she faced him, her hands flung out, palm upwards.

"But where in the world would I go? You forget I live here."

His eyes were sardonic. From her slim feet in the gleaming slippers they traveled with mocking appraisal over all her body to her face. His mouth was faintly quirked.

"Am I to understand that Monk Lyons wasn't as easy as you expected, after all? I suppose your return home is merely a falling back to an old line of defense."

Her lashes fluttered darkly. "Really, darling, I never know what you're talking about when you say things like that. It's so simple to say things clearly. Monk is simply mad about me, if that's what you want to know. Simply mad!"

"But not mad enough to assume you as a public liability."

She laughed, a sound delightfully and ever so subtly bawdy, which acknowledged the unpleasant facts of life.

"Men!" She dismissed them. "They're so horribly intimidated by what people think—as if people who are worth bothering about ever think anything at all. Darling, you'll love this! Poor Monk is simply dying to be an ambassador. You'd think from the way he goes on, you know, that if he could have dinner with the Queen he'd be absolutely ready to try and change the guards at Buckingham Palace, and single-handed. He doesn't even seem to realize that the Queen has perfectly terrible taste in clothes."

"I assume that he didn't feel you'd be much of an asset as an ambassador's wife," Beauty said drily. "Let's put the cards on the table, Eva. Monk Lyons sent you packing."

Her face wore an expression of assumed innocence.

"Don't be insulting, please, Beauty. Poor Monk! I actually thought he would weep when I left. I warned him that he simply mustn't. He has those perfectly terrible ulcers you know, and they simply go insane if he gets emotional."

"Will you tell me why you decided to come back—here?"

"But, of course, darling. It's my home. You seem to forget that. Actually—oh I suppose I'm just a sentimental fool but I realized that I belong—here." Her smile was a confession of unimportant guilt. "Really, Beauty, I do expect you to be a little more understanding. After all, Monk is important and money does matter a little—and it's terribly hard to just ignore so many million dollars even if they do belong to a man with a big stomach. But you see, darling, I *do* retain my senses, even if my head—oh, I'll admit it—was the tiniest bit turned. And of course I knew I would never spend another comfortable night if I left you and the children without somebody to manage things for you. You know, darling, you aren't very good at managing things."

At the absurdity of her pretense, the calculation behind her artlessness, I was seized by a wild impulse to laugh aloud, but Beauty, I saw, was not amused. His face was grim, the muscles at the corners of his lean jaw knotted and hard.

"You're wasting your breath, Eva. It won't work."

"Work? Really, darling—!"

"You're not coming back, Eva. You made your decision. By God, this time it's going to stick. You left me for Monk Lyons and you can't come running back like a whipped dog because Lyons threw you over."

Her brows were raised in amusement. "But, darling, I never run. Women are so terribly awkward when they try."

"I'm not joking, Eva." His voice was level, slicing through her lightness. Her lips twitched in the beginning of a smile, then she made her face grave as a child's seeking pity from an elder.

"But, darling! I do have to go somewhere. Where else would I go. Surely you wouldn't throw me out into the streets?"

"I would. At any rate you'd be at home there."

She gazed up at him, her shining head lifted and her velvet eyes calm and confident.

"Oh no, darling! Oh no. I wouldn't be at home in the streets and," walking to the mantel, she shifted the position of a small ivory figurine, "and I'm not going there." She spoke abstractedly, as if the position of the figurine were of much more importance than her discussion with Beauty. "No, Beauty, I'm not going anywhere. Anywhere at all. I'm staying here. In fact, I've already unpacked my bags." She turned, her body arching, the beautiful head lifted with disdain. "You see, darling! You can't get rid of me. Don't dare try to get rid of me."

"I'm through, Eva. All washed up."

She smiled serenely. "Oh, I think not, darling. For a very good reason. After all—I am your wife."

"A divorce can correct that."

"Yes, it could, couldn't it? But I'm afraid, darling, divorce would be very, very difficult—for you. And for Jen."

I saw Beauty's face, not angry as it had been angry before, but closed and tight now and sneering. "There's nothing you wouldn't do, is there?"

"I don't think so, darling. But, of course, I haven't met all the temptations yet. At least," the little laugh of admission, "I hope not."

"I want you to get out, Eva. Today. Now."

"Darling, relax! You'll have those terrible ulcers like Monk. And you may as well. Relax, I mean. After all, darling, we must consider Jen, mustn't we? For I'm not going."

"Jen has nothing to do with this. This is between us. You and me."

She shook her head, smiling patiently as if someone obtuse and clumsy of mind was failing to comprehend a simple fact.

"Jen has a great deal to do with this, darling. I'd have to go into court, you know, and tell the truth. Dearest, can you imagine what the papers would make out of it!"

"Would make out of what?" His voice was a swift whiplash but she did not flinch.

"Why, my testimony, darling. How you've had this affair, and with my niece right under my very nose. And that, of course, is why I simply had to leave the house. The way you were carrying on! Why, people would laugh themselves to death at poor Jen."

I saw his face, white and thin with his anger. And I too was angry on my own account.

I told her, "You're lying! You know you're lying."

"Am I?" She turned toward me lazily, her lids drooping. "Do you deny that you love Beauty? And that he isn't absolutely *calf-eyed* over you?"

"I deny that there's been—anything like the things you said."

Her topaz eyes were amused and I was suddenly conscious that I was stuttering and stammering like a guilty schoolgirl.

"It isn't true," I said. "You know it isn't true."

She laughed gently as she would at a schoolgirl. "Darling, the truth is what the world believes, and if Beauty should divorce me and—marry you, I'm afraid—"

Beauty's voice was almost a snarl. "I ought to break your God-damned neck," he said slowly, and she shrugged.

"That would hardly solve matters, would it, darling? For you or Jen either. And I think you're forgetting that I'm not in the least intimidated by threats. I never have been, you know. And I never will be as long as I live with you. And," her eyes looked at him, steady and unwavering, "I mean to live with you for quite a while yet, darling. Unless, of course," she added sweetly, "someone perfectly fascinating turns up and I'm simply unable to resist him."

She strolled toward the doorway, her hand deftly touching the soft hair at the back of her neck.

"It might be wise, Beauty, if you thought things over before you do anything rash. You don't want to ruin Jen's good name, do you? Or give up the children?"

She turned and I saw again the Eva who had destroyed Phyl. The body tensely held, the arching throat, the wary, waiting stillness of her, and suddenly her voice, cold and ruthless and certain.

"Don't be stupid enough to think I won't fight you, Beauty, if I have to, and with any weapon I can find. Because I will. And I have a weapon or two. After all, you *are* an alcoholic, you know, and Miss Breen can testify to a thing or two. And don't think I won't do it, Beauty. I'll take the children and you'll never see them again and I'll drag Jen through the mud. I won't hesitate to do whatever I must do to get my way. Because I like having my way. I've always had it." Her voice was supremely confident. "I always will."

She smiled again then, her face softening back to loveliness, her expression indicating that she considered the whole situation absurd and ridiculous. Her small gasp of laughter was deprecatory.

"And, darling! I forgot to mention it. I brought Miss Breen back with me and she's to have *complete* charge of the children. And no interference, please, dearest, from you or anyone. And one more thing. I'm afraid I'll have to insist that you and Jen stop carrying on so *openly* before Miss Breen and the children. After all," the music of her laughter welled in her throat, "After all! This is my home."

Then she was gone and we stood there, Beauty and I, avoiding each other's eyes as if, indeed, we were as guilty and soiled as she had made us. I remembered the happiness and contentment of the long afternoon with the children, the sweet aching goodness of our being together, our quiet talks before the fire and our gaiety, and I was wrenched by an anger so violent it was akin to sickness. I looked at Beauty, at his face so still, so gray, so cold, and my anger and hatred burst out in furious words. She could not do this, I told him incoherently because of my anger. Do this to us, to him, to the children. Clutching his arms I shook him as you shake a clock you wish to start again.

"She shan't! I won't let her. I'll do something. I will! I will!"

His eyes as I shook him looked down at me, but they were dark and meaningless, telling me nothing.

"She can't be allowed." Under his dark gaze my anger lost its passion. "She mustn't be allowed. She mustn't—she mustn't—"

And then I was sobbing against his chest, my hands still clutching his coat, and his arms were holding me gently, as he would hold Trissa. I knew without looking that his face was gray and hopeless and defeated.

Stretched on my bed I lay staring at the wall, unwilling to admit any alternative to its blankness. I wanted a world of blankness in which nothing could hurt or wound. I desired a world of pale vacancy and unshaped time, so I tried to make my mind blank as that wall, tried to avoid the pointless goading of my thoughts.

I did not want to remember that Eva had returned. I wanted to forget that each morning she was there having her coffee in bed, taking her bath. I did not want to admit that again she spent hours dressing for luncheon or for cocktails and dinner. I did not wish to know that she walked with light grace and exquisite laughter through the house.

Neither did I wish to remember Trissa and Ted marching with Miss Breen, as prisoners march under guard, to breakfast, to lunch, to supper, bewildered and unhappy. Or that Beauty had retreated to his room and to his drinking. I recognized that for what it was, an admission of another defeat at her hands. And though I told myself he accepted this defeat because of his concern for Ted and Trissa and for me, because of his fear of the harm she might inflict upon us, I knew that he was not excused by his concern. He could not accept her victory in our behalf.

But even this knowledge I rejected, avoiding the burden of an ugly truth. It was only when I realized I was lying crouched as embryos curl in a mother's womb that I knew I must find will to escape back to life. Then I forced myself to get up and dress and struggle into a coat. Leaving the house I walked in the woods beyond the house, plunged through the brush of overgrown fields, climbed stony hills, pushed through tangled thorn-guarded gullies, heedless of their sharp whips across my face. It was like this, though whether by subconscious will or accident I will never know, that I found myself moving through the knee-high broom sedge toward Jud's house.

Though the windows were blank and staring, I saw a bluish feather of smoke rising from the chimney and turning in the gate I went up the steps to the door. I knocked and waited and after a little Jud's voice said, "Come in" and opening the door I entered the kitchen.

He sat beside the stove, the gun which he was cleaning across his knees, his bright, quick eyes looking up at me. He needed a shave, and the stubble of beard and the soiled woolen shirt and his hands with their broken nails increased my feeling—which I had known before—of an animality in him such as you feel in a creature of night and of secret lairs.

I closed the door behind me and stood there, not knowing what to say or even why I had come. Then moving his head he indicated a chair, and when I sat upon it he began to run the ramrod with its scrap of flannel through the barrel of the gun again.

I said, "I've wondered how you were," and added stupidly, "I've wondered—"

He raised his head and looked at me briefly through the bright quick eyes.

"I'm okay," he told me and then his eyes dropped to the gun again and his hand continued its work. Then suddenly I leaned toward him and laid my hand on his shoulder, trying with the gesture to gain comfort, but whether for him or for myself I cannot say, and he glanced up again.

"Jud," I said, "I've got to talk to—someone. I need somebody, Jud. You're the only one who could understand, or know. . . ."

He sat unmoving, his bright eyes steady as I told him, told him of Eva, of her going away, of her returning. And of Beauty and me —and the children. And somehow the telling of the things I had had to carry comforted yet left me weak and tired.

He stood up and taking the gun to a corner placed it against the wall, then turned back.

"You mean he's going to let her do this to you?"

I explained again, wearily told him how Beauty because of me and the children had no way out, that she had won again as she would always win, I said, because through others she could hurt him; and she could never be hurt.

As I talked his eyes were fastened upon my face which I knew reflected the defeat and hopelessness I felt. My eyes were red rimmed, my cheeks drawn by the flu and by the greater sickness of knowing that Beauty too accepted defeat. Perhaps Jud's eyes, bright and still as they seemed, gauged my despair. For suddenly he stood and found a leather jacket, stained and scratched, and put it on. Without speaking he went toward the door.

"Let's go."

I asked, "Go where?" and he moved his head impatiently.

"To talk to Beauty."

I shook my head. "It's no use, Jud. I've tried. He's drinking, you see, and—"

He stood waiting, offering no argument, but waiting. Finally I rose and together we left his house and went up the hill and across the grounds and up the stairs to Beauty's door. Without knocking he opened it and entering faced Beauty who sprawled in a chair, a glass of whisky in his hand. And waiting by the door, I saw Beauty's lids raise a fraction over the lusterless, bloodshot eyes. When he saw Jud he raised the glass, sloshing the whisky with drunken gravity.

"Hava drink." It was said with careless disinterest, the words slurred.

"No."

Not moving, Jud continued to stand before him and slowly Beauty's eyes were raised again.

"Don't wanta drink? Something wrong with anybody doesn't wanta drink."

He rose, and lurching went to the table where the bottle stood, and poured another drink unsteadily.

"Have a drink m'self since nobody'll join me. Always have another drink. S'good for you, good for everybody."

I spoke to Jud. "I told you. It's no use." My voice was hardly more than a whisper but Beauty heard and his eyes swung toward me, seeing me for the first time. He nodded owlishly.

"No use," he agreed with vast gravity. "Lady's right. Intelligent young woman, always right. Drink to Jen. Jen understands. It's no use. Very perceptive. Drink to Jen always being perceptive."

He raised the glass to his lips, but before he could drink Jud with a single catlike pace came forward, slashed with swift, animal violence and the glass shattered against the wall, the dark stain of the liquor streaking downward. Braced against the door I waited, expecting Beauty's anger turning on Jud. But he wasn't angry. His face was expressionless. The hand which had held the glass was still raised, and then he laughed.

"S'all right. Plenty more liquor. Lotsa liquor."

He turned again toward the bottle but Jud swiftly moved to stand between him and the table and when Beauty, laughing foolishly, tried to shove Jud from his path, I saw the muscles ripple beneath Jud's jacket, saw Beauty flung back, his body sprawling against the chair.

Moving toward Jud I cried out, "It's no use! Let him alone."

His bright, unblinking eyes swept me briefly. Then Beauty laughed again. "Jen protects me, Jud. See? Jen doesn't want me hurt."

Although the words were slurred, I thought there was a measure of returning sanity in his eyes and watching I saw the effort of will by which he pulled himself erect.

Jud said flatly, "You've had enough to drink, Beauty."

"Enough?" His grin was mocking. "Never have enough." Holding the arms of the chair, he pushed himself erect. "Still able to stand up. Means I haven't had enough. Long as I can stand up—haven't had enough."

"You've had enough. I've got to talk to you."

"Talk?" Beauty gazed first at Jud, then at me and back again to Jud. "No use—talk. Nothing to talk about. All finished."

Jud said, "It's not finished."

Beauty's eyes were amused, tolerant.

"No good." He shrugged. "If you want to talk, no objections. Listen to lecture from old Jud." His smile had the patient tolerance of the adult toward an adolescent. "Listen. Very patiently, to old Jud. If—excuse me . . . something attend to."

He went into the bathroom and closed the door. I said to Jud, "You see? It won't help. He can't—it's too late."

He did not answer or even move and I went and sat on the couch, my hands in my lap, feeling the bitter, empty hopelessness, and understanding why Beauty sought escape for now neither courage nor strength remained to me. I no longer desired to goad Beauty back into reality to meet shameful defeat again in an impossible contest. And he would meet defeat, I knew. She was too strong, too skillful and too cunning.

I looked up as he came out of the bathroom, his face, flushed before from the liquor, ash gray, the dark hawk's eyes shrunken and sick. But his voice was steady when he spoke, and aware, and his speech no longer blurred.

He said, "Thanks, Jud," and going to the table poured two fingers of whisky into a glass. "This," he explained smiling, "is purely medicinal," and drank it in a gulp. Then he faced us, his eyes sane and serious. "I assume," he spoke to Jud, "that you want to discuss Eva."

Jud with a barely perceptible motion denied it.

"No, I want to talk about you."

"About me?" He shrugged. "It's not a subject worth your time or concern."

"This time—it is. It has to be."

Beauty, in his chair again, had slumped wearily and now he raised his hand, resting his forehead against his lean, strong fingers, "Why waste talk on me, Jud?" He paused and then went on, his voice flat, as if he discussed a merely casual matter. "What do you think you can say to me that I haven't said to myself? Do you think I make excuses or by any chance persuade myself there's something dramatic in standing helpless while those I care for are sold down the river? Do you or anyone think you can feel more contempt for me than I feel for myself?"

"That's just another way of saying you're licked." Jud's brief laugh spewed contempt. "That's the easy way."

Beauty raised his head, his brows quirked.

"Easy, you said?"

"Too damned easy," Jud repeated doggedly and suddenly he stood at Beauty's chair, was dragging him by his robe to his feet.

"Damn you, Beauty! You won't sit back and whine you're whipped."

They faced each other, then Jud swung away, his shoulders hunched, swung back and faced him again.

"It's your job, Beauty, because you let it happen."

"Do you think I'm not aware of that?"

Jud faced him, his voice quiet and lifeless now. "I saw my wife hanging by the neck. That was Eva's murder—and mine. And yours." Bitter contempt for himself tore through his voice. "You didn't know that, did you? That I was a weakling and a fool? Sneaking like a damned schoolboy behind your back to your wife. Taken in first by her lies and because she's more beautiful than any woman I've ever seen. Afterward, because I couldn't get away. Even when I had married Phyl, I couldn't get away—"

Beauty, motionless, stared into space. Then his hand brushed his face. "I didn't know," he said dully. "I didn't want to know."

Jud swung to face him again, his body poised like a stalking animal's. "I knew you didn't know. You," he laughed roughly, "you thought I saw through her. I didn't. I was blind and drunk with the way she smelled and the sound of her voice and the tricks she could play with her body. With the knowledge she had which no woman should have." His voice sagged. "That was years ago. And ever since I've gone when she wanted me. I hated my own guts—afterwards I wanted to put a shotgun into my mouth and pull the trigger—but when she smiled I went sneaking back."

Beauty, still motionless, still staring into space, said again, "I didn't know."

"You think I didn't know that too?" Jud's emotionless voice was suddenly weary. "I tried to talk to you that morning after Phyl—" He stopped then as if he lacked words for the thing his mind saw.

"You ran away from it as you've always run away. You couldn't face the weakness that had let you stand by while she hounded Phyl to her death."

Beauty said evenly, "I tell you I didn't know."

Jud's laugh was not unlike the bark of an animal. "You knew," his voice was ugly with contempt, "but you wouldn't face it. You would have had to do something about it."

Beauty said quietly, "Oh I saw her—" His smile twisted. "But I thought you despised her."

"Despised her?" Jud's voice was a snarl. "Hell yes! But what has that to do with—letting her alone? She won't let go of anything that belongs to her—ever." He lifted his head, his eyes bright and vacant. "You know that."

"I know it," Beauty said.

Jud paced the floor, a panther measuring its cage.

"So I cheated. You and Phyl. And I should have blown my brains out. Instead Phyl—" He broke off then and his eyes met Beauty's squarely. "She told Phyl, Beauty. To see someone you love—dead—because of Eva Avery—God help you if you live so long as that."

Beauty, unable, I thought, to endure the self-hatred and the shame he saw in Jud's face, wheeled suddenly and went to stand at the window, his hands thrust into the pockets of his robe.

"You think," he was thoughtful, "that I'm stronger than you, Jud?"

"You've got to be." Jud poised as if he were ready to spring, his shoulders hunched. And I thought again of some solitary beast, lurking in rocky clefts and along barren ridges. "You must be stronger, Beauty. Because," his voice slowed and deepened, "you are to blame for everything she is and everything she's done."

Beauty, staring out upon the lawn with its black, leafless trees, did not answer.

"You are to blame," Jud repeated. "You could have stopped her, once. You were the first one to know what she is. But—you were a gentleman." He made the word one of infinite contempt. "And a damn fool. You let her get away with it, all of it, and when you couldn't face the knowledge of what she was and what she did to the people around her you ran away from it—to drink."

Beauty said quietly, "I know this better than you or anyone, Jud."

"You know," Jud's tone was freighted with hatred, "you know. So what? I'll tell you what. You sit, your head muddled with whisky while she—hell, I know you've realized what she is. Too damn long ago. Think I don't remember you drinking yourself blind drunk three months after you married her? Smashing your car against a tree."

Beauty's fingers lifted to touch the scar on his cheek.

"You didn't make a good job of it, did you, killing yourself? So you tried another way, didn't you, Beauty? By way of liquor. But it's no good. It won't keep you from knowing when she puts the knife into your children or Jen. You saw her stick it into Phyl. And you didn't stop her. God damn you, Beauty, you didn't stop her—"

"I couldn't stop her," Beauty said harshly.

"Once you could have. If you hadn't been afraid—afraid that people would laugh at you."

"I don't pretend that I haven't been a fool," Beauty told him shortly.

"But you go on being a fool."

"Do you think I give a damn now if people laugh?" He swung around slowly, his face white and haggard. "It's too late, Jud."

"Why is it too late?"

Beauty flung out his hand as if reaching for something impossibly distant.

"How can I stop her? Tell me that."

Jud's head dropped between his shoulders, his arms swung curved at his side, and I felt a sudden dull horror at the violence implicit in every muscle of his body. Yet his voice was almost gentle, as if he soothed distress.

"There must be a way, Beauty."

He made the statement as if he merely suggested another route to a distant destination. He was reasoning and patient and for a moment I did not realize the absurdity of his suggestion.

Beauty's eyes turned to him, searching, speculative. "Have you thought of a way?"

Jud's body tensed, the muscles knotted behind his shoulders. Then suddenly his shoulders went slack, his arms hung limp at his sides. He ran his hand through his close-cropped hair, shaking his head.

"No, no. You're right, Beauty. It's too late. Far too late."

But Beauty continued to gaze at him intently, a deep line of thought between his dark brows.

Jud said quietly, "Forget it. Forget everything I've said."

Unspeaking, Beauty watched him. Jud glanced up, his bright animal's eyes meeting Beauty's dark glance. Then he said humbly, "Forget it, Beauty."

He turned and went out with his quiet, always rhythmic tread. And I sat on the couch, my hands clenched now in my lap, and I saw Beauty's face.

I said, "I'm sorry. I didn't mean—"

His eyes were dark and deep and I could not fathom the thoughts that stirred beneath their surface.

"It's all right," he told me gently.

"No." I shook my head, aware only of my love and of my love's hopelessness. "It's not anything you can help."

My offer of comfort rang shallow and I broke off.

"You think I can't help?" He picked up my words. "Maybe not."

He turned to the window again, gazing out upon the bleak mottled earth of winter and stood there—such a long while it seemed—as I watched the dark shape of his head and shoulders against the cold light. I knew somehow that a tumult of thought surged against his brain, that all of the past was there, all of the minutes which had mounted to the sum of this one moment. And I thought his must be dark thoughts and despairing. But when he turned and faced me again I found the dark, mocking laughter in his eyes.

"Perhaps," he told me, "I may be able to help things after all."

I was puzzled and he saw my frown.

"But don't worry about it. I'll have to find a way—"

"A way?" I repeated.

"For helping," he explained, his voice completely matter-of-fact. "Jud's right of course. It is my job."

"But what can you do? You said—"

Smiling he came and cupping his hands about my cheeks, raised my face.

"It doesn't matter," he told me. "You mustn't worry about it. There's just one thing."

I gazed up at him and I'm sure my eyes were as adoring and as trusting as those of the dogs he had hunted over.

"There's one thing," he repeated. "No matter what I do or what you think of me, try to remember that I have a reason."

"I will," I told him. "I will, I will."

"Try to remember," he said again, his voice infinitely gentle. Then he moved away, loosening the cords of his robe, matter-of-fact again.

"You get out now and let me put on some clothes. By the way, do you know if my wife will be home this evening?"

I nodded. "I think I heard Miss George say so."

"Good." I went toward the door and would have opened it but his voice stopped me, and looking back, I waited.

"And, Jen, you might tell Miss George to lay a place for me at table. I'll join the ladies this evening."

He came down to the table that night later than Eva and I. We dined on leftovers: some ham sliced cold on a platter with the remains of a leg of lamb; the peas from two nights ago, a green salad. Eva, at the foot of the table, was frankly bored with the food and my company, eating but little, then putting down her fork. She said, "Really, why Miss George bothers to set a place for Beauty! When he's drinking, I mean. He's simply a ghastly husband. One would think he didn't find us attractive, Jen." The artless little laugh implied she knew better.

I could have told her why she was restless for company, even the company of a man who was only her husband. Monk Lyons had failed her and defeat demanded another victory if only over Beauty. And when we heard Beauty's step on the stair the quick lift of her shining head confirmed my guess.

He came in debonairly, bowed to her gallantly. "The charming Mrs. Avery, I believe," he said, and watching I saw Eva's face light with the surprised pleasure which flattery invariably gave her.

"Why, darling!" Her exclamation was lightly amused. "You've actually dressed. What on earth?"

I looked at him then and saw that he had shaved and wore one of the tweed jackets which seemed somehow to fit themselves with casual perfection to his body.

Going to his chair he bowed toward her again, his eyes laughing.

"I've decided, my dear, there is little profit in sulking in my room. Particularly when there are more attractive alternatives offered."

Her eyes widened. "Alternatives, dearest?"

"You." He glanced toward me then a courtesy glance of recognition. "And of course—Jen." His tone when he spoke my name was careless and Eva's tiny smug smile betrayed her satisfaction because I had received no more than the crumbs of his compliment.

With a tart suggestion of wariness and distrust she laughed.

"Really, darling! Aren't you overdoing it a bit? After all you haven't been too devoted lately.

Serving himself from the platter he said, "You're right. I haven't." He glanced at her briefly. "But you didn't really expect it, did you Eva, while you and Monk Lyons—"

The corner of her mouth quirked. "Now, darling, you're just pretending. That you're jealous, I mean."

He asked quietly, "Wouldn't most husbands be? Jealous?"

It was, I thought, too blatant. It was play-acting so sardonic, so mocking and so obvious that she would suspect despite his pretense of gravity.

Eyeing him somewhat cautiously, she did.

"You've never been like other husbands," her voice was dry, "so don't pretend."

"But I'm not *that* exceptional, Eva."

Her eyes, regarding him, were questioning, calculating, but he met them with ardor and summoning the maid told her to bring glasses and a bottle of champagne.

"Champagne!" Eva was genuinely startled. "Heavens, darling! For just us three? When you're always complaining about expenses?"

"To hell with expenses!" Leaning back in his chair he watched Mellie pour and then taking his glass he raised it, his eyes on Eva's lovely guarded face again. He said, smiling, "To the dead past, Mrs. Avery. May it rest in peace."

He continued to look at her with meaning tenderness, and the doubt in her eyes was replaced by an amused gleam of assurance. I knew she believed that jealousy had won him back to her, that he still considered her beautiful and desirable. The small three-noted laugh, as she raised her glass, was deprecatory and delicious.

"But *darling!*" Laughter rippled over her face. "This is so—so sudden! Really, I'm simply overwhelmed!"

His hawk's eyes watching her, he said, "I've been something of a damn fool, haven't I?"

She was all wide-eyed innocence. "Really, dearest, I haven't the least idea what you are talking about. And I do wish you wouldn't talk in riddles. Really, it's so easy to say things simply—"

"I'll say it simply then." He was grave now. "I've realized, rather suddenly and thanks to Mr. Lyons, that all these years I've been, shall I say, a trifle difficult? Refusing to go out with you, refusing to like your friends, sticking at home—and drinking, like a sulky schoolboy. Well," his eyes met hers dead serious, "that's the past. The future will be different. I'll go to your parties and dinners. I'll even"—his brows quirked—"like your friends." His smile was tender. "It's suddenly very important to me that Mr. and Mrs. Avery be known as Atlanta's most devoted couple." He raised his glass again: "To our second honeymoon. May it go on forever."

Dutifully she raised her glass but the almost indiscernible movement of her shoulders was cynical. And when he insisted, "You're not drinking with me Eva," her answer verged on tartness. "Really, Beauty! One would think you were leading up to a seduction."

"Let us say," he was teasing but intimate, "that one would be correct."

She laughed then, a lilting sound of pure delight, her chin nestling at her shoulder, her lashes fluttering. "As if you've ever found *that* difficult to arrange, darling." Then her eyes lifting, and as if fleeing the gravity she found in his, fell upon me, observed my untouched glass and, in the instant before she cloaked them, sparkled with malice.

"Jen, you aren't drinking to—our second honeymoon. Beauty, see. She isn't drinking."

He turned toward me casually. "She will, of course." He nodded toward my glass. "Won't you, Jen? To our second honeymoon and —the dead dead past?"

Even though I knew it for a game he played I was resentful. I told myself I would not drink, would not touch my glass though I should die for it. He could not use me in this way, as a pawn sacrificed to his game. I heard him, reasonable, casual, saying, "Jen knows how important the dead past is"; and knew the meaning in the words was for me alone. Still I was resentful. And when Eva, sweetly spiteful, said, "You will drink with us, won't you, Jen? To our second honeymoon?" I found my glass in my hand, I was raising it to my lips, I was saying, my voice as resentful as I knew my heart to be, "To your second honeymoon. May it last forever."

Later, lying on my bed I told myself that Beauty only played a game, trying with his game to win safety for Ted and Trissa and me. Or perhaps he still groped for "a way," hoped to hold Eva to friend liness until that way was clear. Only this morning he had said, "Try and remember—there is a reason." I said to myself over and over like a child holding fast to a lesson that it must not forget lest punishment descend, "There is a reason, there is a reason, there is a reason—"

Often I said that lesson in the next few days. Said it when watching I saw his grave but tender wooing of her; said it when polished and glowing they departed for this or that dinner; said it on that late afternoon when going into the sitting room and finding him (I thought) alone, I went to him swiftly, saying his name: "Beauty—"

His "Yes, Jen" was so detached, so uncaring that I stopped before I reached him and only then perceived Miss Breen on the window seat, her button-black eyes flickering in the firelight. When I had invented some inane ending to my sentence and left the room, I told myself, "There is a reason."

But then there was the night—I think the next night though I cannot be sure—when the words were stripped of their meaning and their solace. We were in the sitting room after dinner, just the three of us, they murmuring and laughing before the fire, I, stiff and awkward as an uninvited guest, pretending to read on the window seat. I heard her soft "Oh Beauty!" (more a sigh of ecstasy than words) and looking up I saw that he dangled a bracelet before him.

She cried, "The star sapphire bracelet! You—you got it for me?" Almost she was unbelieving.

With lazy tenderness he drawled, "You wanted it?"

"Dearest, I was mad for it." Her white hand reached.

Imprisoning her wrist in one hand he clasped the bracelet with the other. "It's yours. Now you can die happy."

"Die?" Her eyes questioned wonderingly.

"Remember," he was testing the clasp, his eyes upon it, "you said if you could just have it you'd—"

Remembering she nestled against his shoulder, one hand against his cheek, the other outstretched, displaying the bracelet. "Ah yes! I remember. I said that I would die happy."

His lips touched her hair gently. His voice was gentle too. "Now you can. Now you can."

I left them there before the fire and went to my room, telling myself again, "There is a reason." But as I went I heard his voice, heard her laughter warm and sweet and husky. And I could not banish the picture that rose in my mind. Another man before her at that same fire. And she moving toward him, the fragile robe revealing the white uplifted breasts. I remembered too that other laughter. Even when I reached the protecting solitude of my room the laughter was there. And as I lay face downward on my bed I heard it, still ripe and warm around me, its lovely echo throbbing against my walls, wanton and conquering.

I told myself again, now desperately, "There is a reason," but the words were like dust in my mouth. Whatever the reason for his first pretending, in the end she had got him back. That was all too clear. I tried to revive my faith in the old arguments. "He only played a game, he thought to win something or other, perhaps this was the way he had found—" All this I told myself anew, but without conviction. For I was a woman, and jealous; madly, furiously jealous, my heart storming its contempt for reasons and excuses.

So in the dark I lay turning and twisting and at some time later —when, I do not know, for I had no thought or care for time—I cried into my pillow with a sodden hopeless crying. But out of the fury of hurt pride and pain I resolved that *now* I would go back North— I would show him I didn't care. He'd gone back to her ("Remember there is a reason," he had said) but I didn't know the reason; perhaps because even now he would keep the world from knowing, perhaps because she'd snapped her fingers. But whatever the reason,

I didn't care, I didn't care. Knowing even as I whispered the words with which we bolster hurt pride and humiliation, that I lied.

And then the afternoon . . .

Because Miss Breen had a heaven-sent toothache the children and I had walked in the woods that afternoon and just before dusk were making our way back toward the house. It had been such a lovely afternoon. Gentle and warm and with the lilting air of real spring, the trees dotted with buds, the bushes of bridal wreath white and cascading. And in the violet dusk of sky the face of the first small star peered out timidly.

Trissa and Ted, discovering it, stopped to chant "Star light . . . star bright . . . first star I've seen tonight." With serious upturned faces they made their silent wishes. Waiting beside them I looked up at the lonely star and thought how once I too would have wished. I didn't wish now. I only waited. And it was like this that Beauty, riding the black hunter, found us.

He reined Beau in, surveying the motionless unspeaking children quizzically, then as they continued to stand motionless and silent, asked "Am I intruding?"

Ted said sharply, "Daddy, be quiet! We're wishing," and returned to his stargazing. Beauty swung from the saddle to stand beside the hunter and asked gravely if he might wish too.

"Yes, Daddy. But be quiet." This was Ted again.

Beauty looked at the star and for another moment we were silent. Then it was over. Trissa and Ted, crying, "Daddy! Daddy!" rushed over to him. Ted unable, as usual, to contain his wish. "Daddy, do you know what I wished? I wished Miss Breen's tooth would explode and blow her ole head off." Laughter gurgled from his throat. "Then ole Miss Breen wouldn't have no head."

Trissa joined in his laughter but Beauty's face was grave. "You mustn't speak discourteously of Miss Breen, Son." He laid his hand on the silver-gilt head. "And you could have saved your wish. Miss Breen is going away."

"Away?" Both children lifted hopeful faces to his.

"Yes. Mama has consented to send her away. Tomorrow. You will not need to make foolish wishes about Miss Breen, ever again."

I thought: he has persuaded Eva to this, persuaded her perhaps to other things, and a tiny stir of life moved in my heart. Then Ted was asking, "What did you wish, Daddy? Tell us, Daddy, tell us your wish." And Trissa, always gentle, begged, "Please, Daddy."

He smiled down into their eager faces. "I wished," he told them quietly, "that Ted and Trissa and Jen will be safe—and together always as they are today."

Ted said disgustedly, "Gee! What a crazy wish." Then, his attention attracted by something he saw in the distance, he scampered off and Trissa followed.

Beauty asked quietly, "Do you think my wish crazy too?"

For a moment I didn't answer. I wanted to cry out that I cared nothing for his wish, that I only wanted to know why he had gone back to Eva. Was it because he still cared if people should laugh? Was it because Eva had snapped her fingers? But I didn't cry out. I reminded myself that I didn't care; and though I knew it wasn't true it helped me to answer.

"No." I marveled that I spoke as quietly as he. "But it has no chance of coming true. You see, I am going away."

"Going away?"

"Yes." I even managed to meet his eyes.

He asked, his voice low, "Will you tell me why?"

"You know why." Then when he didn't speak, "I must make some sort of life for myself. You would want that for me, wouldn't you?"

His eyes, his dear dark eyes, met mine steadily. "Yes," he said, "yes."

I continued to look toward him, but I could not see him for the blur of pain between us. Still I managed my voice. "I don't want you to think that it doesn't hurt. It hurts, terribly. I cry at night." Then realizing the maudlin childishness of that, I added quickly, "But I will get over it."

"Yes," he said again, "yes."

He stood there tall, his hands in his pockets, looking at me it seemed as from a great distance, solitary and proud. Then pulling a crumpled pack from his pocket he found a cigarette and lit it, his hand cupping the flame. As he smoked he looked over my head at the tall reaching pines.

"Better to cry now," he said, "than later. You'll get over it."

I had no answer for that.

He laughed shortly, dropped the cigarette and ground it with his scuffed boot. "Don't, my dear, romanticize the facts of life. Women have done too much idealizing of cowards and drunkards. The truth is—they're not to be trusted."

I looked across at him, wanting to cut through the barrier he held between us to that which was more important to me than all the rest of life.

"I thought once," I told him evenly, "that trusting was important. I don't any more. It's love that is important." I could not hold the tremor from my mouth or voice. "And I want to say it: I love you and I will love you to the day I die."

He was silent, his eyes looking down at the cigarette he had ground with his heel. Then he raised them and unsmiling looked across at me. "I know," he said quietly. "God save us both."

I waited, my body aching for his hands, my mouth for his. But he did not say he loved me or come closer. And his eyes meeting mine across the space between us told me nothing of what I wanted to know. Then he stirred, turning toward the children who straggled back to us.

"We had better go in," he said. "It is later than we think."

Somewhere in that night I fell asleep and awoke stiff and cold to a dawn streaked with rain. From the window I saw a world drowned and dispirited, of dripping eaves and widening, sallow puddles. An early robin fluttered down from somewhere to move with unenthusiastic hops about the yard in search of food, then discouraged flew away, a poor little devil of a bird, hapless and out of season.

So now I was beaten.

I knew now that Eva's victory was complete. Whatever motives had sent Beauty back to her, he had gone back. Could it have been, I wondered, as she had intimated? That I had been only a young girl in the house of a man older and wiser and more cynical? Someone with whom he, no more alluring person being available, could make love. Or had I been merely the excuse by which he convinced himself that he was young again, and in love?

For I didn't doubt and I must never doubt that Beauty had believed in his love for me, that even if he had lied to me he had believed it too. He had been deceived, as I had been, by some kind of desire, however unimportant. If I had given his love more importance than it deserved that surely was my own fault. If I had loved with everything I had to give I was to blame again. And I was not sorry I had loved in that way because any other way would, I knew, have been a betrayal of myself. I still would not love less than all I could.

If he had deceived me, he had been equally deceived, by propinquity and by my eager, schoolgirl passion which made me fling myself at his head. Since I still loved, I found excuses, made explanations and, as other women in love, forgave everything in my beloved, even the loving of another love.

And I did not doubt now that there was another love. For a man in love is the dupe of the world and always transparent. He was always, it seemed, at Eva's side, his eyes dark and laughing at her adorableness, his voice depreciating fondly her most extravagant follies.

So I was beaten.

I had no place here, and I was settled in my decision that I would leave. I told them at dinner, making my voice as casual as I could.

"I'm going back North," I told them. "I've decided I was meant to be a career woman after all."

Aunt Eva's, "But, darling! What on earth?" was exclamatory and convincing. But Beauty looked over his glass, his brows raised.

"Back North, eh?"

I explained that I had a few hundred dollars of Father's insurance which, I said, would carry me until—and then I laughed, "If I'm to make something of myself, I might as well start now."

"But, darling!"—this was Eva wide-eyed—"What about Ty? You can't mean that you're simply going to let him slip out of your hands for some stupid little girl to catch on the bounce? Beauty!" Her calling of his name was possessive and imperative. "Beauty, you simply must talk to her. After all, you did have influence with her once. You'll explain that you simply don't throw somebody with Ty's money over in order to sell panties in Macy's basement."

His smile was gentle. "I've told her often enough Ty would make her a good husband."

"A good husband? Really, Beauty. What does it matter the kind of husband he'd be? He simply has more money than anyone I know, even if he does act as if he can't afford a pair of shoes."

I told them, "I'm not planning to marry. Ty or anybody. At least, not yet."

"But, Jen." Eva's voice was protesting again and edged with irritation. "You're simply being foolish, Jen. Oh, I know it sounds noble—young girl alone in big city and all that—but really you can't keep him dangling forever. He'll get away."

"Then he'll have to get away," I said.

She turned to Beauty, her hands spread in a helpless gesture of childlike appeal. But for once he did not, as he had consistently in the past days, respond to her plea for support. Instead he asked me carelessly:

"When are you leaving?"

"Wednesday night," I told him. "The eleven twenty-two. I made my reservation today."

He repeated after me, "Wednesday night! Eleven twenty-two," abstractedly, as if he were thinking of something else. Then he asked, his eyes turned to mine thoughtfully, "As soon as that?"

Eva's answer came more quickly than mine.

"But, darling, we can't see you off—Wednesday night I mean. I've already accepted a dinner invitation for us. It's for that terribly fascinating new man—you know the one I mean. Hazel says he's simply terrific and with more money than is really decent."

"You mustn't bother," I assured them. "Ty will see me to the station."

"But, darling," Aunt Eva's voice was plaintive, "if you had only let us know in time—"

I spent my last day saying farewell to so many things and people who, in so short a time, had come to mean so much. To Miss George, who having seen that my slips and blouses were laundered brought them up so I might pack them in my bags, producing tissue paper to lay between them so they would not crease. And I saw as she came into my room that the tip of her thin nose was reddened.

"Child," she said, "take care of yourself. If you ever need help, I've a little money saved. If you need it—"

I sat on the side of my bed then among the open bags and the clothes I had spread out and sobbed bitterly and unashamed. My bad example gave her fortitude. Immediately she began to put my garments briskly into the bags, shaking her head as if she would brush off a gnat which buzzed too familiarly at her ears.

"You're doing the right thing, Jen," she told me positively. "Go back and make a place for yourself. No use pining away because of some fool man."

Then I saw that she wept with me, and folding a skirt to fit the narrow bag she said, "I was in love once myself. Didn't work out to anything. Useless sort of devil. Still, he made me laugh."

I said good-by to Trissa and Ted. Not telling them, of course, that it was for always. I was going away for a little while, I explained, my face stiff with the lie. I would be back. Trissa, pretending to accept my lie, sensed—I knew—the truth. But Ted looked at me so gravely that my heart shrunk like a scrap of paper burning inward toward the center.

"You *will* come back, Jen? You will come back?"

And lying, hating myself for lying, despising my desertion, I said, "I will come back. I will come back."

But he stood looking at me with his still eyes that were so like Beauty's, eyes that would forever look into whatever room I shared, and watch every street where I walked.

"I will," I promised. "I will come back."

That night I stayed beside them until they slept, and before I turned out their light I stood for a long, long while watching their faces against their pillows. Only children sleep in such quiet loveliness.

I called Ty. He would, he said, come out for me. He would see me on my train. Unless, of course, I would change my mind, unless I would stay. I told him I could not stay.

"Then come back." His voice was kind and steady in my ear. "Come back, Jen, some day—"

I answered something, told him I could not promise.

"Then I'll come out for you," he said. "I'll even guarantee to smile when I wave good-by. But if you decide to stay—"

"I won't decide to stay."

"Who knows?" he told me. "A lot can happen in a couple of days."

"A lot can happen," I agreed, "but usually it doesn't."

The receiver was silent a moment, then his voice sounded again in it.

"Something happens every day."

I thought he joked and asked, "Every day?"

"Sure."

Then he quoted: "*I love you more today than I did yesterday and less than I will tomorrow.*"

I said, "Oh, Ty," my voice breaking, and he went on, "So, you see, something important does happen every day. Who can tell? Your train may pull out without you yet."

But nothing happened before that afternoon, and I waited alone in the sitting room before the dying fire for him to call for me, waiting for it all to be over.

I sat in the big chair in the sitting room and watched the log Miss George had earlier put on the hearth break through and fall, smoking and charred, upon the gray wood ashes. A few flames flickered palely, a brief shower of crimson sparks rose against the sooty chimney. Then they too died.

I did not put on another log. In so short a time none of us would remain to feel the warmth. Even now Aunt Eva was dressing for the dinner party and Beauty, who had a cold, kept to his room. The dinner was to honor a distinguished visitor, a man of importance and wealth. I remembered Eva's description of his importance: "Darling, he has just scads of money!" And when Beauty had turned up with his cold and cough she had insisted he must not risk going out, crying, "But, darling! You simply can't trifle with flu." And I knew that beneath her solicitude there was satisfaction that flu again provided her with an excuse for leaving a guardian husband at home. But if Beauty saw or understood he had given no sign of it. He was, I realized, still under the power she somehow had regained over him; her boast that she "need only snap her fingers" had been proved. In spite of everything, in spite of all that had happened between Beauty and Eva, and Beauty and me, he had again accepted his bondage and I could only understand by telling myself that he loved her. Love was not logical, nor just, nor reasonable. That much I knew. Because I too loved, and the thought dawned upon me that I too, despite all that had happened, would turn back to Beauty if he, like Eva, beckoned.

But he wouldn't beckon now and I knew it, for I was leaving. My bags were packed and waiting beside the door, my railroad ticket tucked safely in my purse. And later Ty would come and drive me to the station. The fire would die and not be missed unless Beauty, restless later and seeking warmth, might seek it here. And at that thought I got up from my chair and put on another log. The flames licked up. I told myself it had been a foolish, pointless last gesture; yet I gained some sort of satisfaction in the knowledge that if he came here for comfort he would find it waiting. So I stood watching until I heard Eva's swift, firm steps upon the stair.

She came in, pausing at the door, her silver gown swirling around her slim ankles, her hands searching in her evening bag for her car keys which, as always, were mislaid. She looked across at me, her lovely face bewildered, her eyes helpless and appealing.

"I know I put them in—I even remember. I wanted to be sure—"

Once, I would have scurried to search, to look in drawers and vases, in the purse she had carried earlier in the day. But now I did not move from my place before the hearth. And she went back up the corridor to call to Miss George to look on her dressing table again or in the black suede bag; then she returned, her hands lifted in the appealing gesture of a guilty child.

"But I know I put them in this bag. Of course, I'm always losing them but this time—" she broke the sentence midway with a laugh. "At least I meant to. You see, I *do* have good intentions, Jen."

I answered nothing, watching her, my face incapable of smiling back, of masking what I felt, as her face always concealed what she really thought or felt. I could not, as she could, smile and laugh as if all that had happened between her and me had never happened and did not exist.

She became aware of my silence and her smile softened to gentle understanding. She came toward me, friendly and contrite.

"Darling," she spoke persuasively, as if she remonstrated with an erring child—or a servant. "Darling, it really is a little foolish to be bitter."

I could not answer her. Perhaps, if I had been less concerned, or had been another person able to watch objectively and hear her speak like this, I might have laughed. But to me there was a sort of monstrousness in her pretense that nothing of importance had transpired or that having transpired it could be forgotten now and abolished. For a second I almost wondered if the past months had held no problems of more than trivial stature. Was I the insane, and she the sane, clear-sighted one?

Standing before me she reached her white hands toward me, but I did not take them and they darted up to deftly touch and pat the leaf-brown hair, as if from the first that had been the purpose of her gesture.

"It's simply too horrible, darling, that you have to leave us. I mean, on a night like this. All this dreadful rain! Really, you'd think in all this time they'd have learned to do things about weather. Atoms or something! Actually I think sometimes whoever is responsible *arranges* rain when I'm going out, just to annoy me!"

She went to the window and drew back the draperies which Miss George had drawn and I saw the glisten of fire and lamps reflected in the droplets clustered against the dark pane. She had meant to be humorous, I knew, and yet I thought behind her facetiousness there was a key of seriousness. Deeply, in the place where her being had its center, was the belief that everything that happened resulted from some attitude toward her. Rain or sleet or sunlight, winter or summer were, I guessed, secretly ascribed to some pagan god made jealous or seduced to kindliness by her beauty.

She turned from the window, moved a silver box a fraction of an inch nearer the center of a table and stepping back gauged the improvement.

"And it slows up driving horribly, and I'm already late. Really, I can't understand why Miss George can't find my keys. If she'd only use her eyes—" She swept into the hall, and calling to Miss George asked if she'd found the keys. And when Miss George called back that she hadn't Eva suggested vaguely that she keep looking.

After all, she said, she must have left them somewhere. She had used them when she drove this morning. . . .

She was frowning as she came back to the hearth. Then she saw my face. Perhaps what she saw displeased her, for her voice changed.

"Darling, I've been chattering like mad—and I'm in a terrible rush and so annoyed. The rain, you know, and everything." She paused then. "But there's something I want to say to you. It's—that you mustn't hate me, Jen." Her voice was gentle again, and consoling. "You see, darling, you are so young. And there's so much you don't understand."

My voice was level, I could not match her lightness or her pretended kindliness. "I'm not that young, Eva."

Her smile was tolerant.

"I don't mean that you are not intelligent, Jen. Really, you are—quite bright. I wouldn't be at all surprised if you were rather good at some sort of job. But after all, intelligence isn't everything, darling. Experience *does* count, you see. And I've had a great deal of experience."

When I said, "So I've learned, Eva," my tone was dry. But she failed to notice. Crossing to the couch, she sat upon it, her silver skirt billowing.

"I've learned a great many things, darling. That's why I feel that I know what is best for you, and what isn't. After all, Jen, I do have your good at heart."

"Good!" I ejaculated the word, startled.

"Of course, darling." She smiled faintly. "Oh, I know you think I've been cruel. But in time—when you've thought things over, I mean—you will realize that I haven't, and you'll understand the reasons for what I've done."

"Do not deceive yourself, Eva. I understand your reasons for everything."

She shook her head wistfully, a little sadly.

"No, Jen, you don't. Oh, I know that everything *seems* clear. It's just that you aren't able to look at things objectively."

"You're hardly the person to accuse me of not being objective," I told her.

Her eyes widened.

"But why not? After all, I am objective. Really! I claim so few virtues of that sort, Jen, that I don't feel that I'm boasting. I'm one of the most objective people I know."

I did not argue. There was no point in arguing, and her soft, silver voice went on.

"And when you are older, Jen, you'll see that after all, I've acted for the best. I know you think you are in love with Beauty—"

I said flatly, "I do love Beauty."

She shrugged slightly and rising went to the mirror to gaze with critical, examining eyes at her reflected face.

"Perhaps. And I suppose Beauty—well—did things that made you think he loved you."

"He did love me."

She still gazed into the mirror.

"Sex isn't always love, darling."

"There was nothing like that between us," I told her. "You lied when you said there was and you knew it."

"What difference does it make, dearest? People would believe me, not you."

There was reason at least in that, so I said nothing.

"And they wouldn't call it love, Jen. As you do. And as I do *not*. For it isn't love, darling. You must stop telling yourself it is. You mustn't dedicate your life to something that wasn't even true."

"Perhaps since you say it isn't love," I said, "you can tell me what it is."

She chuckled, a sound I had never heard from her before. A chuckle, not light or gay but deep and gloating and evil.

"Really, Jen! Beauty isn't young, you know. And you are very young. And middle-aged men do lose their heads over young things. You see, Jen, Beauty is very close to the dangerous age."

I hated her then, hated her as never before, because with a few words she had tried to make my love for Beauty, and his love for me, however transient, sordid and senile and snickering.

"It wasn't like that," I told her.

She tossed her small, shining head.

"No? Well—perhaps not." She went to the couch, picked up her fur. "But the evidence does seem to prove it, doesn't it? Middle-aged men, after they've had their fling with a bit of fluff, come back to their wives."

And again I could not answer, though I knew that it wasn't true, that it had not been as she tried to make me believe.

She came to me, reached out and touched my cheek.

"You'll understand someday, Jen, when you find a younger man.

You will, you know. Really! You are quite pretty and could be attractive." She leaned back and regarded me, her eyes calculating. "If you'd just do something about your hair—"

Then she glanced at her watch and with an exclamation she went into the hall and called. Miss George called back that the keys hadn't turned up. She swept back into the room, her anger obvious. "But this is too absurd," she began—then halted. Without turning or seeing him, I knew that Beauty had come to stand in the doorway, his hand thrust casually into his pocket, his dark, hawk's eyes watching and catching up the threads of the situation. When he spoke to Eva his voice was concerned.

"You can't find your keys?"

She too had been unaware that he watched from the door and now she turned startled, and laughed in confession of her irresponsibility.

"I simply can't imagine what I did with them! I've looked everywhere."

He moved a hand in a casual gesture that made her carelessness unimportant.

"It isn't as if it was the first time this particular calamity has ever happened."

"Darling, I know. But I'm afraid you'll have to drive me in. I hate to ask it of you, but I'm already late."

I glanced toward him, remembering his cold, remembering too how she had used it as an excuse to leave him at home, half expecting that he would revert to his old mocking self again, tell her she could go to the devil and that if she'd mislaid the damned keys it was her grief.

But he said none of this. Instead he nodded, smiling tolerantly as if her demanding was endearing. "I'll get my coat."

Her face was smoothed of its anger now, her smile gay and rippling.

"I feel like an absolute brute, darling, to pull you out—but after all, you can wrap up! And I'm so terribly late."

Going to him, she brushed her lips lightly across his cheek.

"If you really don't mind, dearest."

"I don't mind."

He went for his coat and she flung her mink about her white

shoulders, gave her face and hair a last appraising glance in the mirror as if for a final assurance of her beauty, and as he reentered the room, turned to meet him. I waited, aware that I had been forgotten, that his whole attention was for her alone and that I was no more than the furniture or the pictures which watched from the wall. And when I heard his voice, I knew that it too was for her alone.

"We'll have to make this a fast trip. This is *one* party, Eva, I don't want you to miss."

I expected, I hoped, that he would look toward me. Perhaps come over and wish me luck, but he remained oblivious of my presence. He adjusted the mink coat on her shoulders almost gallantly, and with his hand on her arm guided her toward the foyer. I heard the opening of the door and her small, three-noted laugh. Then I heard the door close.

And I was alone. I stood before the hearth and the fire I had made bright and warm for him. He would not need it now. I heard the rain against the windows, the pop of the wood as the fire reached its heart. I felt nothing. I remembered I had read somewhere (or heard perhaps) that when a man is shot by a rifle of high power he feels no pain, at least not at first. The shock provides its own anesthesia. And I told myself that so it was with me. Yet the hurt was there, and I knew it must be paid out for a long, long while, that perhaps it would never be paid out. And I was alone.

Then—and I will never forget—he had come back. He stood in the doorway, a hand in his pocket, his eyes darker and the scar more livid in the dancing firelight. He came toward me, smiling a little, his eyes more tender than any memory I had of them. I only knew that he had returned, that for a moment, at least, he was my love again. And I, his. And that whatever happened, the thing we had made of our love superseded the measuring of time.

He spoke gently, as I had heard him speak only a few times before, as it had been when he spoke to me in the woods, as it was when he spoke to his children.

"You did not think I would leave without saying good-by." It was a statement rather than a question, an assertion of faith.

"I did not think you would go—without saying good-by."

I managed to shape the words somehow though my throat was

choked with gratitude. If there was nothing else, if this were all, as I knew it to be all and the end, for the moment it was enough. I felt as if I were a prisoner condemned to execution but suddenly reprieved to live again.

"I knew," I said. "I knew you would come back. Even if you have to go away again. I knew—"

He seemed to think that over. And then he nodded slightly.

"I'll have to go. There are—reasons."

He went to the mantel, and taking his hand from his pocket held it up. I saw that he held a bunch of keys on a silver chain, the keys of Eva's car that I would know anywhere, which I had searched for frantically time and time again, lest dear Eva be late to her party.

With his eyes—how steady they were—on me, he put them on the mantel and I watched wondering, not understanding.

Then he came swiftly to me once more. He put his hand on my arm and drew me toward him, and I raised my lips. But he did not touch them. Instead he kissed my forehead, as he might have kissed Ted, or Trissa.

I said inanely, "You'll have a long drive. I'll be gone before you get back. Won't I?"

The old, sardonic, mocking light came back into his eyes.

"Probably."

"Then—good-by."

Somehow, God knows how, I held my voice steady against the fullness in my throat and the pounding in my breast and through my blood.

"Good-by," he said, and turning went toward the door. And paused and turned, brushing his hand across his face impatiently as if he would brush something shoddy and cheap into oblivion.

"To hell with good-bys," he said steadily. "There are no good-bys for you and me—even now." And then the smile was back, the smile of a friend who holds your welfare dear, and his hand was raised in a gesture that might have been a farewell, or a benediction. His voice was laughing and tender.

"Good night, my darling," he said and turned away. I heard the sound of the front door closing again and, presently, the roar of the motor of his car, muffled by the rain and by the walls. So now it was over.

I went to the chair and sat down again. He had come back. No matter now where he went, or with whom, he had come back, and now there would never be any going away again. Now, we were together, for he had his reasons that I did not question. I knew that when he had come back to leave the keys and say good-by, his coming had meant more than that. He had, I knew, promised everything that he could not fulfill, assured me that his faithfulness transcended the necessary expediencies of living.

He had meant much, much more than just good-by.

I remembered again, as I would remember many times, seeing him as he stood in the doorway; I remembered his voice as he spoke, the gesture as he dropped the silver chain of Eva's car keys to the mantel. I remembered the keys.

I went to the mantel and picked them up and watched them dangle at the end of their chain. I thought, but then they had not been lost, really. For some reason, for some purpose, he had taken them, had let Aunt Eva believe—

"Good night, my darling," he had said.

The keys glinted brightly as they swung on their chain. He had taken the keys for a reason. A purpose. A plan. As if, for some reason, he had *wished* to drive Eva in, as if he had contrived it so that he would drive her, speeding over the wet, glistening roads, flashing around the tortured curves.

For some purpose—I'll have to find some way!

Even before my mind shaped the thought, I was in the hall. I had pulled a coat from the closet; whose, I did not know nor care. I was running around the drive, clutching the keys. Eva's car stood shining and streaked in the rain. I told myself I was absurd and foolish, that I was, of course, mistaken.

But I wasn't mistaken. I'll have to find a way, he had said. I remembered his voice, weighing, seeking. A way. Now I knew—this was the way he had found.

I put the key into the ignition, pressed the button on the dashboard, heard the whirr of the starter. The engine roared with sudden power. Stupidly, cursing my clumsiness, I stalled the car, started it again.

It was clear now, as if jagged lightning had spanned the darkness of my stupidity.

"I'll have to find a way."

And seeing the silhouetted outline of trees, as the car lurched forward, seeing the shoulder of a bank caught in the slashing beams of the headlamps I prayed: "Not this way. Dear God, not this way."

But I knew.

Another car's blinding lights met me at the gateway. I thought for a second of groaning relief that Beauty had returned. Then I recognized the car, glimpsed Ty's face, pale and startled in the glare. I saw his puzzled recognition, his up-flung hand. Then I was past him, catching in the mirror above the windshield the whipping beams of his headlamps as he swung his car and followed. My wheels skidded sickeningly as the car lurched into a curve. I fought them back into the clear, my foot against the floorboard. I heard the shriek of tortured rubber, the moan of the engine, the shock of springs.

But Beauty drove faster.

The stretch of tar roadway was black and limitless in the funneling glare of my lights. I heard the even clicking of windshield wipers like stolid metronomes. I peered along the road, my eyes seeking, searching the darkness. And at last, far ahead, I caught the pin-prick scarlet of a light, swerving, dancing, sliding against the darkness.

His car was too powerful. I could not overtake him.

I remembered that first afternoon when I had come to stay with Aunt Eva—an unknown Eva then. I remembered driving out from the city with him, the curve with a car smashed and twisted against the tree. Now he drove back toward that tree. *That* tree! He too had remembered, remembered the treachery of the wet curve and the crushed car.

Now I understood the reason for his attentions to Eva. I understood why he had courted her and flattered her, why he had danced attendance upon her like any moonstruck lover. I knew now why he had been at pains to make people believe that he was the fondest and most ardent of husbands. He had seen that it was not enough merely to make his decision, the decision he must have made after that scene with Jud in his room. He had known he must carry it out so that afterwards people would call what happened a tragic accident, nothing more.

An accident—a crumpled car against a tree.

And he had even used me to help prepare the way for the accident, allowed me to doubt so that my behavior would add credence to his pretense. But I understood now that his pretending had been for my sake and for Ted and Trissa. They would not grow up in the shadow that had been cast upon him and upon Phyl by his father's death. I would not be "the other woman" that gossip blamed for his desperation. This would be an accident, silencing gossip by its shattering finality.

An accident! Ascribed to wet streets and twisting curves taken too fast, just as Mr. and Mrs. John Oglesby had taken a curve too fast on their way home from Palm Beach that day when I arrived in Atlanta. And somehow I must prevent it, somehow I must stop him. Somehow.

But he drove too fast.

Again, I glimpsed ahead that dot of scarlet, farther away now. No matter how madly I drove, caring nothing for caution, he drove more madly. In a swift flash I wondered what was happening between those two in the roaring car ahead. Had she guessed by now? Had he told her where they drove? How would her face look now as they thundered through the night toward that tree? I imagined his arm pressing her back against the seat. I saw his face, intent and ready.

Perhaps I cried out, but I cannot recall.

I know only that I drove wildly, losing the glint of his lamp in the rain and darkness. I remember my realization that the race was lost. Forever lost. But still, I held the car to the road, held to the rain-greased curves that twisted, turned, straightened and twisted again.

But finally I slowed, knowing there was no chance of overtaking him, that by now he had reached his destination. He had found his way. I did not need the leaping flames or the sickening glisten of smashed wreckage at the base of the tree to tell me what had happened. I had known far back along the road that this was the way he had found. This was the way.

Already a crowd of curious people surged around the crushed car. I saw the glisten of the rain capes worn by the policemen who pushed the crowd back from the danger and the fascination of the flames. When I came to a stop nearby I could see their expressions of dumb horror, and I knew they were unaware of the snarls and threats of the patrolman who herded them back from the burning hopelessness of Beauty's car.

Unable to turn my own eyes away, I watched too. I watched with terrible fascination the wracked steel and shattered glass. And once before the flames leapt up I saw a flash of silver gown, the white gleam of naked shoulders against the rougher, darker shoulder. And a white arm wound about him in a final assertion of possession. I saw the small head with the shining hair, arched and proud.

Then the glimpse was lost in the final burst of flame. And still I sat there, seeing, but not seeing the faces of strangers in the crowd, hearing, but not hearing the orders of the policemen and the whining sirens that grew against the night. Somehow, out of the terror of flame and blackness I heard him again, imperious and arrogant: "To hell with good-bys. There are no good-bys for you and me even now."

So I would not say good-by, even now as the sirens screamed their terror in the dark. I sat still and stricken, aware at last of Ty standing at the open window of the car, of his hand on my shoulder.

Even now I would not say good-by.

Ty drove me back along the twisting highway. It was much later. All that must be done was finished. It was finished now. But I would not say good-by.

Ty's hands were steady on the wheel as we turned into the road to Eva's house—for so I must always think of it. He drove carefully, back toward the rooms where her husky, three-noted laughter had sounded, where her quick firm steps had clicked across the polished floors. I knew that when we were there I would find the fragrance of her slim, girl's body still haunting the shadowed rooms.

We drove back toward the house where Beauty had sung to Trissa and Ted. To the house where the sills of windows in his bare room were lined with precise rows of empty bottles. It would always be *her* house. But it was also ours—Beauty's and mine. It was the house where we had loved, where he had found, finally, a way of escape for Trissa and Ted and for me; where he had found the way by which he might free us forever from her lovely tyranny.

Sedately Ty and I drove back, as settled folk return home. Glancing up I saw his face, steady and kind and patient, the corners of his mouth creased with the memory of many smiles. Then I looked back into the darkness of the road. We would be there soon now.

And I remembered that Beauty's children slept there, flushed in tousled beds, in need of covering in the long nights. Now, by Beauty's decision, they were my children. And I was grateful. I was proud that he had trusted me so greatly. In the knowledge that he had trusted me I would somehow find whatever strength I would need for tomorrow.

"To hell with good-bys," he had told me. "There are no good-bys for us even now."

"*Even now*," he had said, knowing what he must do.

So even now I would not say good-by.

Instead I whispered to him in the darkness, my lips barely moving as if leaving him for a little while they brushed his cheek . . .

"Good night. Good night, my darling."